The Photograph

Wings
Press, Inc.

Diane Clarke

The Photograph

Gwen reluctantly passed the bear to me. Looking for a label, I turned him this way and that, then laid him on his stomach. Brushing a hand over the waistcoat, I noticed a change in texture. The tweed skated over something smooth. Prying apart a space at the back of his little neck, I stuck my finger inside and touched paper.

'Something's rammed under his waistcoat. If these buttons come undone, we might be onto something.'

As the buttons popped and the material gaped open, a small black and white photograph slipped out.

What They Are Saying About The Photograph

'I enjoyed this sad, heart-warming story and loved the satisfying and unexpected ending. I had tears! I loved the dual timelines, especially as one was at a time of a massive world event. A clever and entertaining read.'

—Lisa Darcy, author of *The Pact.*

'A gripping read that explores the lifelong impact of family secrets on a wartime evacuee. Emotive and thought-provoking, this is a perfect book club choice.'

—Andrea Barton, author of *The Godfather of Dance.*

'I was drawn into this book by the unusual premise of a World War II evacuee looking for a brother whose existence had always been denied, but whose absence she felt throughout her life. Told from the perspectives of a mother and her daughter, I enjoyed the beautifully crafted characters in the family and the unfolding of the story through the nuanced relationships and their pithy dialogue. I gulped this book down in one sitting.'

—Sarah Bourne, author of *Exile.*

'A meticulously researched tale of the long-term impacts for WW2 evacuees separated from their families. Diane Clarke's debut novel explores the heart-rending difficulties of a displaced child postwar spending a lifetime trying to reunite with family and discover their personal history. Plenty of twists and frustrating dead ends keep the drama moving in a story that reverberates down multi-generations, and which is thoughtfully told against a backdrop of the recent pandemic.'

—Sarah Hawthorn, author of *The Dilemma* and *A Voice in the Night.*

The Photograph

Diane Clarke

A Wings ePress, Inc.
Women's Fiction Novel

Wings ePress, Inc.

Edited by: Jeanne Smith
Copy Edited by: Bev Haynes
Executive Editor: Jeanne Smith
Cover Artist: Avison Book Cover Design
For Wings: Trisha Fitzgerald-Jung

Wings ePress Books
www.wingsepress.com

Copyright © 2024 by: Diane Clarke
ISBN 979-8-89197-994-9

Published In the United States Of America

Wings ePress, Inc.
3000 N. Rock Road
Newton, KS 67114

Dedication

To Nick, Tom and Doug

Part One

One

The teddy bear stared at me with embroidered eyes and a big smile. I'd pulled him from a shoebox in the chaos of my mother's ramshackle garage. Standing wedged between two piles of boxes, I examined him more closely, a flutter of recognition nipping at my memory. Only Gwen and I had ever lived in Bryn Cottage, and visitors with children were rare. Yet the bear looked both vintage and unused, nothing like the soft toys owned by my granddaughter. Its torso, arms and legs were long. Hard stuffing jarred with his otherwise sunny disposition, set off by a jaunty tweed waistcoat. Had he been bought as a present for me, hidden away and forgotten? Was it a gift from my birth mother, given to me before we'd travelled as evacuees from London to Wales? I was fifty-nine, had been adopted and cared for by Gwen Roberts for fifty-six of those years, yet references to my past were always met with impatience. I glanced back towards the house as I considered showing her this little gem.

Chilled, I scooted back across the gravel driveway, dodging puddles. A band of early morning rain had cleared, revealing a sky shimmering with watery light, a view that gave an impressionistic spectacle of the surrounding Snowdonian farmland. A carpet of wood anemones spiked with a few clumps of yellow colt's foot complemented the lush hedgerows. The sweet scent of wet grass filled the air.

Wiping my feet on the kitchen door mat, I heard the creaking of springs from Gwen's room upstairs, where she'd been confined for several weeks. Her recently broken hip and the reality of a cluttered, poorly maintained home, sat uneasily in my mind. I didn't know how she'd manage when only my weekends were free. After a beat of hesitation, I placed the teddy bear, face down, on the edge of the prepared tea tray along with the latest edition of her favourite women's magazine.

I climbed the stairs and pushed open the door. Cold drafts seeped through ill-fitting windows. Crossing to a heavy wooden dresser, I studied Gwen's thin grey hair and softly pleated wrinkles.

'You must have read my mind. I'm dying for a cuppa.' Gwen glanced at her bedside clock. 'Are you sure you've time for these visits? You're always so busy with work. How are things going?'

'You'll remember what second term's like. It takes ages to fire them up again after the holiday. I'll probably have to offer some extra lunchtime sessions soon.'

'Yes, I do. I called it the post-Christmas slump. And Stephen?'

'Busy but fine. He's making dinner tonight, so that's one less thing to worry about. I'll bring the leftovers next time I come over.'

'What's over there?'

I glanced around to see her pointing at the tray. 'Your magazine. Charles and Di are on the front, looking gloomy.'

I didn't mention the main headline publicising the forthcoming VE Day celebrations, declaring, "Yes to Vera. No to Spam Fritters!" Our prime minister's throwaway comment had been roundly trounced by the voice of the great British public. They refused to mark the anniversary of the end of six dreadful years of war by battering and deep-frying canned meat. They wanted the comfort of Vera Lynn, the Forces' Sweetheart.

'No, the other thing. What is it? I can't see from here.'

'One moment, and I'll show you.' Balancing two cups and saucers and with the toy stuffed under my arm, I took a seat next to her and handed over the tea. 'I found it in the garage behind a box of broken earthenware.'

'I hope you weren't snooping. Next thing you'll be telling me it's a mess. And don't throw those pots away. They're for drainage when I plant up my summer containers.'

I suppressed a sigh, doubting she'd be gardening this summer.

'The garage needs work. Come on, you know it does. Anyway'—I pushed the creature towards her—'cute little thing, isn't he? I wondered if it was mine.'

She put her cup on the bedside table and reached for the bear. Her mouth slackened.

'Do you recognise it? He looks new, as if he was never played with.'

Her head shook, firm. 'No, I don't.'

'It was in a shoebox. Probably been there for ages. Can't think of any other child who owned it, can you?'

'It's a mystery. Probably best given to the charity shop. Why don't you take it tomorrow?'

I tensed. 'Could I have brought it with me? When Mum and I first came to stay?'

'It's too new. Besides, I'd remember something like that.'

'Is it? It looks vintage. Here, hand him over. Maybe there's a maker's mark. Wouldn't it be great if he turns out to be one of those famous German brands? They can fetch a fortune at auction.'

She sniffed. 'It won't be.'

'What makes you so sure? Come on, let me see.' I swivelled to put my cup on the dresser and held out my hand.

Gwen reluctantly passed the bear to me.

Looking for a label, I turned him this way and that, then laid him on his stomach. Brushing a hand over the waistcoat, I noticed a change in texture. The tweed skated over something smooth. Prying apart a space at the back of his little neck, I stuck my finger inside and touched paper.

'Something's rammed under his waistcoat. If these buttons come undone, we might be onto something.'

As the buttons unfastened and the material gaped open, a small black and white photograph slipped out. I turned towards Gwen. She beckoned me to hand it over. Instinctively, I clung on.

'Give it to me.'

'One second.' I shifted sideways, turning away from the bed.

The image focused on a small group of people in an impromptu pose. Behind them, a vast crowd of adults and children stood on a station platform, carriages idling in the background. The lens captured a young woman crouched on her haunches, clinging onto a child. The girl, young, possibly three or four, was pulling away from a kiss the woman was trying to plant on the toddler's head. An older boy was by her side, body at an angle, his face obscured. A large cotton bag hung from his shoulder filled with objects that bulged through the thin fabric. They carried gas masks in cardboard boxes. The woman grinned, presumably entertained by the girl's antics, though there was something else, something contradictory.

Who were these people?

Gwen stuck out a flat palm. 'I said I wanted to see. Please.'

Handing it over, I watched her closely. She swallowed hard, setting off a gravelly cough. After several grating hacks, she lay back on the pillow, the photo lowered onto the eiderdown.

I leaned forward, drawn to the figures, my vision slipping back to the girl. She was holding a teddy bear with a checked waistcoat, most probably made of tweed. The same bear! My breath caught in my throat. Was this toddler me? More importantly, could this be my real mother? Too young to remember her before she died, and with no other visual record, I'd been forced to imagine her appearance my entire life. Tears brimmed as I examined her features for the first time. She looked young. Not beautiful, but pretty, with her hair curled into a wartime quiff. No doubt, this was a scene from our evacuation from London and I had brought the bear with me.

'It's my mum, isn't it? Look, she's trying to keep hold of me. It's the same bear. This bear.' I picked him up, quelling an urge to shake him under her nose. 'After all this time, I have a picture of her.'

She turned towards me, her expression hard. 'Assuming it's her, mind.'

I recoiled, as if slapped. 'But …it must be.'

'I'm only thinking of you. Getting your hopes up.'

'For what? She died so long ago. It's not as if I can ever meet her. There's no need to spoil it.'

Her chin dropped. 'No, of course not. Sorry.'

'Anyway, don't you recognise her? She was here in Bryn-y-Maen for a little while at least.'

'It's a long time ago. A lot of water under the bridge since 1939.'

'Yes, but even so. It is her, isn't it?'

A speck of pink rose on her cheek as I held up the image. 'Yes, it could be. You're right, I'm shocked. It's ridiculous, but I've always considered myself second best compared to her.

Adopting you because you had no one else. It felt as if I didn't deserve you.'

Her insecurity, the need for validation, almost hijacked my moment of joy. A flash of sympathy returned my manners. 'You gave me a very good home. You, me, this cottage, Wales. It's been great, Gwen. I appreciate everything you've done. What would have happened to me as an orphan in London? I could've been given to anyone.'

Her words came out hard-edged. 'Thank you. I did what I believed best with you losing your mum.'

I'd upset her. She hated me using her first name, a decision made in my early twenties. 'Sorry. I wouldn't have deliberately sprung this on you. Especially when you're not well.'

'Put it somewhere safe. I'm glad you have it, really I am.'

The lull in conversation allowed me to turn all my attention to the boy. Now the identity of my mother had been confirmed, a persistent, lifelong question burned on my lips. Who was he? Was he my missing sibling? A quivering sensation rose up my body. For as long as I could remember, I'd sensed an absence, a physical emptiness at my side. Answers to my enquiries had been gentle in my early years, becoming curt as I grew older. Mum and I had arrived alone, Gwen said. There was no brother.

I studied Gwen's expression. Had she seen him, too? Could I ask her when previous enquiries had caused such friction between us? The words sputtered and died, leaving me scooped out, empty.

I fought to keep the conversation alive, seeking another angle, another way back to my obsession. 'Are you sure you don't recall why the bear was hidden away? It can't have been done in a hurry, otherwise he'd have been shoved in with other things, instead of having his own box.'

She frowned, appearing deep in thought. 'Scarlet fever! I burnt everything belonging to you both, except this. Clothes, shoes, your other toys. Doctor's orders! Get rid of anything that might hold germs, he'd said. Probably an old wives' tale, but we believed it then.'

'Yes, I suppose so.'

'She was awfully sick, mind. Which is a silly thing to say when she died. The fever was terrible. Had to nurse her and make sure you didn't catch it.'

'Or you.'

'Yes, me too.' She plucked at her bed jacket. 'It wasn't an easy time, with losing Paul as well.'

I looked down. Her husband, Paul, a novice pilot, had died in 1939, returning from a training mission to the airbase at Aston Down. Two deaths, so close together, gave her ample reason to shut down discussions about my past. I had many happy memories of my life with Gwen, especially the early years before the preoccupation about my family took hold, but her silence always hurt. It was the reason I withdrew her title as 'Mum.'

We sat quietly for a few moments. Gwen's eyelids closed.

'You're exhausted,' I said. 'I've worn you out, haven't I?'

'A little, yes. I need another rest.'

'Here, let me take the tea things, and I'll leave you in peace.'

She looked up and summoned a smile. 'It's been a good thing. I'm glad.'

I took another risk. 'Megan will be thrilled, having a picture of her other grandma.' In contrast, I held little hope for Stephen or my son, James. James had no interest in the past. And my husband was as unaccommodating as Gwen, but for different reasons. Without hard evidence of my brother's existence, he worried for my mental health. On a good day, I could forgive him, when every search had ended in tears and distress.

Gwen nodded, resigned. 'Yes, I'm quite sure Megan will appreciate it.'

'So, I'll give you forty-winks till lunchtime. Then I'll have to go, sorry.'

'Sounds wonderful.'

In the quiet of the kitchen, I studied the photo again. My mother, my real mother, Kathleen Baker. Each time those words flashed through my mind, my insides flipped over. I wanted to hug myself and shout my delight to the valleys below. After all these years, I could linger over her appearance and recognise our similarities: hair curly and probably the same mid-brown, had the image been coloured and not black and white. Her face was oval, like mine, but pinched, her cheekbones prominent. She had no hat and there was another large sack on the ground behind her, much like the one held by the little boy. Most of the other adults and some of the children lugged suitcases or large carpet-style bags. My heart sank at the prospect of our probable poverty. Based on my birth certificate, which listed my father as 'unknown'. I had long accepted our status as a single-parent family.

I examined the child's profile again, excitement bubbling, but his stance made it impossible to discern a likeness. Surrounded by other people, it was plausible he'd been caught in the wrong group. A cameraman would be forgiven for not knowing who was who in the melee. And yet ...the sense of a missing older brother never left me. I searched for other clues to explain our separation. The boy had a label pinned to his jumper, whereas I did not, but I had no idea if that held significance. He looked to be about seven or eight. I imagined him alone, in a new house and town, cared for by complete strangers, instantly severed from the people he loved. Even if he wasn't part of my family, I wanted to weep for what lay ahead of him.

I carried our teacups to the sink, shaking off my gloom, bringing to mind the picnic lunch with Megan's family. I couldn't wait to show them my new treasures, reminding myself these family possessions were more than I'd ever had. Whether or not they produced further revelations, I should celebrate. I'd start by buying an elegant frame and displaying it on the mantlepiece with the rest of the family portraits. And I wasn't going to worry about where or how to place it alongside those of Gwen.

Two

With my duties to Gwen completed, I drove straight to Conwy under clear skies. Meeting the family at Bodlondeb Park, Chloe's favourite, I predicted my granddaughter's wishes—a visit to Quay House, Britain's smallest home according to the record books, and to continue along the waterfront to inspect the mussel-fishing boats owned by her father's family. A cool box with sandwiches, cake and a flask of coffee sat beside me on the passenger seat. The teddy bear lay on top. I'd tucked the photograph in my handbag, anxious to keep it safe from loss or damage.

The journey from Bryn Cottage took me along narrow lanes and across the hillside. The lush farmland, its livestock, mud and machinery, eased the stiffness in my shoulders until, minutes later, I joined the busy roads and dual carriageways heading west towards the river and the town's thirteenth century castle. Once inside the park perimeter, I caught sight of my favourite people: my daughter spreading a tablecloth across a picnic table, my husband and son-in-law in discussion and a fourth pink ball of energy attempting to keep a hula hoop in motion. As I unloaded my contributions, I put bets on the reactions I'd receive from the adults when the topic of my London family was discussed.

The hoop took a downward dive. 'Grandma! Grandma!' Chloe shouted as she ran towards me. 'We've been waiting and waiting!'

'Sorry, love. I was busy this morning. Are you hungry? There're sandwiches.' Before I had chance to kiss her, she seized a handful of my coat and dragged me towards the others. 'She's here!'

I did the round of greetings. A kiss for Stephen, a pat on the back for Rick and a hug for Megan as I passed her the box. I could see my son-in-law was tired—he'd already brought in an early morning catch of mussels.

'What's that? Is it for me?' Chloe stepped up on the seat, reaching for the teddy.

I grabbed it. 'No! I mean, no, darling. It's mine. From when I was a little girl. I found it at Great -grandma's, today. You can look at him, but he's very special. I'd rather he stayed here with us.'

Stephen broke off his conversation with Rick.

Megan came to my side, pulling her daughter into a sitting position. 'And we don't stand on seats, remember?'

'Let's sit him on the table, and he can join in with lunch, like a teddy bear's tea party,' I said.

Chloe pouted.

'What's all this about?' my husband asked, as he folded his legs across the bench and reached for the sandwiches in the middle. The rest of us followed suit.

'It was in Gwen's garage, in a shoebox. And inside his waistcoat...' I pulled the photo from my bag, holding it level so everyone could see.

Rick pointed. 'Is that you?'

'Yes,' I whispered, noticing my husband's shock and my daughter's curiosity.

'Can I see it?' she asked.

'Careful, it's my only copy.' Out of the corner of my eye, I watched my granddaughter squashing bread up against the bear's embroidered mouth.

Megan peeked at her father, then concentrated hard, appearing to scour the image for every detail.

I couldn't contain my nerves. 'Well?'

'Can he have some juice?' Chloe asked.

'No, darling, just water. Teddies drink water.'

'But it's a tea party!'

'Chloe!' Her dad's severe tone caught her off-guard.

Recoiling, she said, 'Anyway, he isn't clever enough to suck through a straw.'

'So, this was inside his clothing?' Megan asked.

'Yes, tucked into the back of his waistcoat.'

'It could be the same bear, looks like the right size compared to the girl.'

'Of course it's the same, because that's me. Can't you tell?' I paused, patting the air in conciliation. 'Sorry, sorry. Nerves! You've seen those shots Grandma had taken of me when I was little? I was older, four or five, but the likeness is there, isn't it?'

Megan hesitated. 'I think so. But ...the woman? You're assuming she's your mum, aren't you? Can we be sure?'

'Oh, Megan, do you always have to be so ...analytical. It's one thing trying to protect me, but surely it's clear? She's holding on to the little girl—me I mean—trying to kiss me.'

I gestured for its return, suddenly unwilling to share my prize.

'Can I see?' Stephen asked.

I slapped it onto his palm, immediately wishing I hadn't.

'What's wrong, Grandma? You're all cross. Can I see, too? Pleeaase.'

While my husband concentrated, I pulled Chloe in a for a hug, reassuring her nothing was amiss. She smelt of shampoo and lollipops.

After several seconds, Stephen flipped it over, scanned the reverse side and turned it back. 'It's you and similar to the ones at home. And the way the woman's behaving, it'd be strange if she weren't your mum.'

'Thank you,' I murmured.

With her boots banging the underside of the table, Chloe continued her appeal.

Rick stirred. 'Hey, want a push on the swings?'

'But I haven't seen Grandma and her mummy.'

Exchanging looks, we silently agreed to lie. This wasn't the moment to explain my history. In Chloe's mind, Gwen was my birth mother, and it would stay that way until she was old enough to understand.

My husband beckoned her to his side of the table, pointing to and explaining the two figures, allowing Chloe to presume the woman was Gwen. She appeared satisfied, followed by instant disinterest.

'Race you to the fence,' Rick said, and the two of them bolted towards the play area.

'Thank him for me, will you?' I asked.

Megan pressed up against me. 'I'm sorry. It's the statistician in me, always checking my facts. To be honest, after all this time ...I didn't want it to be a colossal delusion.'

'Assumed I'd gone off into fantasy land? If it helps, Gwen agrees. She recognised her as the person who came with me to Wales.'

My daughter's frown melted. 'Why didn't you say? Makes all the difference, doesn't it, Dad? Of course, Gwen knew Grandma Baker ...for a short while at least.' She took the photo again. 'Actually, when you look closely, you do resemble her.'

I blinked. My word alone hadn't been enough.

'And gosh, this is the only one you've ever had, isn't it?'

'And ...the other keepsake from my past.' I pulled the bear towards me, brushing breadcrumbs from his face. Vindicated, I turned to my husband for support.

'This is quite the surprise,' he offered, the words not matching his tone. 'Especially the picture of your mum.'

I tensed. 'Neither of you has mentioned the boy, my brother. You can't ignore him, pretend he isn't there.'

'I see him, a few years older than you, as you've always believed,' Megan said.

'Believed?'

'I'm trying to keep a level head.' She glanced across the table at Stephen. 'And, damn it, the boy's not facing the camera, so...'

'Is he with us? I mean, look at all those people.'

Stephen butted in. 'So, you do have doubts?'

'No. It's him. I'm certain. So why didn't he come with us? What happened to him? In some ways, seeing him makes it so much worse. I was given a new mother when mine, ours, died. What about him? Where'd he end up?'

'Caryl love, please keep your feet on the ground.' Stephen twisted a paper napkin into a tight braid. It was like hearing him speak to James and Megan when they were children and wanted something truly unattainable, like taps running with milkshake.

'Dad, don't ruin it.'

He planted both palms on the table. 'Your mum means everything to me and watching her chasing a ...a ghost? It kills me. We've searched and searched for evidence of a brother, but it's not there.' He raked a hand through his hair. 'Gwen's mystified, always has been. I mean, if a child went missing along the way, someone would've raised the alarm. This woman here, Kathleen'—he stabbed a finger towards my mum—'she'd have raised merry hell, wouldn't she? Insisted on a search. And Gwen would've pitched in, too. Once the authorities became involved, they'd have come back with the boy or an answer of some kind.'

'Would they? At the beginning of the war?' Megan asked.

I mutely congratulated her. Such a challenge would normally come from me.

'I'm damn sure they would. Children disappearing? If word had leaked out, no parent would've let their kiddies go. There was more than one evacuation.'

Stephen's exasperation, Megan's support despite her logical mind and Rick's quiet diplomacy, absenting himself from the Baker family drama, precisely met my earlier expectations.

I inhaled, spurred on by annoyance and my daughter's fearlessness. 'So, I'm to ignore it, am I? Take joy from this picture of my family and behave as if he's not there?'

Stephen leant forward, his expression pained. 'We understand it's there for you, love, this belief, this memory, but we don't want to see you hurt. I've been through all the ups and downs. I've seen what it does to you.'

I took back the precious image. 'I'm sorry, but it can't be helped. I can't not act on this, I simply can't. This is the first piece of evidence I've ever found suggesting, and I agree suggesting, I had a brother. I can see there's a huge crowd, and he might not have been with us, but why have I always had this feeling if he didn't exist? Unless you suffer some serious mental issue, people don't usually make stuff up, do they?'

Stephen's eyes slid away.

I couldn't fail to recognise his doubt and hopelessness, resulting from a lifetime of dutiful, fruitless support. He was there on my first visit to London in 1954, when we were newly dating. On a summer day, when he should have been swotting for his pharmacy finals, we travelled to London together. When my enquiries failed, Stephen had taken me for a soothing cup of tea and lent me his handkerchief, no doubt expecting the search to end. He was wrong. The first of many dead ends, it began his anxious oversight of me, monitoring my reaction to news stories about missing family members as well as anything relating to the evacuations in World War II. It came from a place of love, but it exhausted him and infuriated me.

Unable to bear the tension, I said, 'I'm going to have it enlarged and framed. So, could Rick recommend someone who'd do a good job, spruce it up?'

'I'm sure he can,' Megan replied.

Stephen nodded towards his granddaughter in the playground. 'I might join them. Won't be long. Rick needs company.'

With arms hanging by his side, he trudged towards the play area.

Three

Megan placed a hand over mine. 'Sorry Dad's the way he is. He sounds so awful, sometimes. But his heart's in the right place.'

'It's fine. Nothing I'm not used to. Would've been nice to enjoy seeing a photo of my family for the first time without all this upset.'

'If there'd ever been any progress...'

'I know. Birth certificate no help. Not on the 1939 Register either, though it was never a proper census and couldn't keep up with people moving about at the start of the war. Only for issuing ration cards, really. I'll never forget the woman at the archives at Kew. Polite enough, but she said it wasn't unusual. Lots of people were left off the list.'

Megan stared towards the playground, her hand back in her lap. I tutted, conscious of her boredom, knowing I'd told these stories time and time again. Rehashing the past was conjuring the rabbit hole that had previously swallowed me.

'Sorry, love. Prattling on.'

She tilted her face. 'Come on. Show me again.'

I placed the photo between us. Heads almost touching, we exchanged opinions about likenesses, the clothes and hairstyles of the time, the chaos of the scene.

'What would James say?' Megan asked, picking up the bear.

'He's never been interested. Prone to take Dad's side.'

'But this boy could be his uncle, too.'

'True. I'll show him when we go to London. If he can spare the time. And keep your fingers crossed what's happened today doesn't put your dad off going.'

Footsteps and chatter alerted us to Rick, Stephen and Chloe's approach. They retook their seats.

I straightened my back and turned the image face down. 'Good, I'm glad you're back because we were talking about VE Day.' I leant towards my husband. 'We're still going, aren't we?' A statement, not a plea, challenging his previous announcement he was 'giving it careful consideration,' code for his unwillingness to attend.

He rubbed the back of his neck. 'Can we talk about this later? I'm up to my eyeballs with the new drug trial.'

'On a bank holiday? No, it's up to us to support these celebrations. We're the ones who lived through it. We won't be here forever, and it's about thanking the ordinary people of Britain. Even us evacuees.'

Stephen turned his empty coffee cup back and forth.

I rushed on. 'And I've never been to any major public event, like the recent weddings. I watched Charles and Di on the tele and regretted not making the effort to go. It looked marvellous.'

'As if they've been a stunning success,' Rick said.

'True, but they started off with hope and happiness,' Megan replied.

Stephen bristled. 'I can't understand how anyone believed they were a good match. It defied logic.'

'That's not the point. The day itself was magical, and I'd like to experience something similar, for once.' I caught my daughter's eye, seeking her encouragement.

'Um, yes, go for it. It'll be a great day.' Her pitch wavered.

'Good, it's decided.' Turning to my son-in-law, I drove onwards. 'And, Rick, can you suggest somewhere to have this restored?' Although I'd grown up in the area and currently lived in nearby Colwyn Bay, I valued his local knowledge. Fisherman, amateur photographer, former lifeguard and long-time resident of Conwy, he knew the people and businesses intimately.

'There's a good studio in town. I'll find the number for you.'

'Thank you.'

'Can we go to the little house? The one with the shiny, red door?' Chloe asked.

'Great plan,' I replied. 'Give us a moment to pack up, sweetheart.'

'Come on, Grandad,' Chloe said. 'Your turn to do the hula hoop.'

I couldn't contain a grin at Stephen's look of horror, or Chloe's inability to comprehend his reluctance.

Rick stepped in to save the day. 'No, my turn first. Bamps can watch.' The three of them moved onto the grass.

Megan and I began packing up, folding the tablecloth. 'Before we go, is there any news?'

She shoved her hands into her pockets.

'Careful, you'll make a hole,' I said. 'Sorry. I assumed you'd want to talk.'

She looked down. 'I went to the doctor, like you suggested. No explanation. Keep trying, ha-ha. She dropped in the words, "secondary infertility".'

My brow furrowed.

'It's when a couple conceive easily first time around, then nothing happens when they want another baby. Like Rick and me.'

'Oh, I've never heard of it.'

'Me neither. And it could be either of us. If I knew it was me, I'd be happy to do whatever it takes—hormones, diet, anything. But he won't hear of it. Shuts me down every time I raise it.'

'Pride. Male pride.'

'Don't say a word, please. There must be some medical solution to this.'

'Absolutely. Positive thoughts.'

'If you say, "the sun shines on the brave," I'll hit you.'

'No, love. Too important for flippancy.'

'Oh, God! Look at Rick.' Her tight posture relaxed. 'You can't not love a man who'd make a fool of himself with a rainbow-coloured hoop.'

'And saving Dad's back. I don't want any excuses not to go to London.' A tickle of excitement rose up my spine.

Four

On the morning of the VE Day celebrations, a chilly bank holiday Monday, Stephen drove us from Colwyn Bay to the station at Llandudno Junction where we took the first available service to the city. Weak sunshine did little to raise the temperature, but by the time we arrived at the mainline in Chester, the day looked clear and warm. My excitement was more than being part of the crowd and experiencing the camaraderie of a big national event, seeing the Royal Family. I fidgeted with my handbag, aware the contents fuelled my anticipation.

With tickets purchased, we climbed the stairs to the platform. Several passengers wore Union Jack T-shirts or waistcoats, and carried flags, apparently destined for the same festivities.

'Look at those outfits!' I said. 'Where do people buy them?'

'Don't ask me. Wouldn't catch me dead in clothes like that.'

'Too bad, because I've brought these.' I presented him with two flags. 'Here, take one.'

'Not now, Caryl. Put them away until we get to London.'

I looked sideways into the face of a John Bull look-a-like.

'Off to the big smoke?' he enquired.

'Yes, and you're from London, aren't you?' I replied, recognising the accent.

'Docklands, me. Wife dragged me kicking and screaming up north. No offence.'

'None taken. I came from there, too. Evacuated during the war and ended up in Wales.'

Stephen tugged on my arm. 'Caryl? There are fewer people down this way.'

I managed a quick apology before being propelled away. When the crowd thinned, I pulled up. 'He was being friendly.'

'And I want a seat. It's a long way.'

When the train arrived, Stephen ploughed ahead, securing spots for us both in a booth-style arrangement with a table between us and two future passengers.

'Forwards or backwards?' he asked.

'Forwards and can I take the window?'

He took the space next to the aisle and pulled a paperback from his jacket pocket.

'Before you start ...are you sure we don't have time to go to the East End? Especially now we're not meeting up with James.' Our son had fled London for Brighton, preferring crowded roads to crowded streets.

He sighed deeply. 'I'm not being difficult, but I really don't think so. Besides, where would we go? We've traipsed around before and not found anything you remember.'

Since discovering the photograph, I'd been reconnected once again to my roots, reenergised, craving a return to my place of birth. 'Might be different now I've seen the picture. It's absolute proof we were there in London.'

'Or you'll be disappointed. It doesn't tell you anything about where you lived.'

I readjusted my jacket, pulling on the cuff. 'I suppose not.' Despite his objections to a side trip to Bethnal Green or Whitechapel, he couldn't take away the thrill of disembarking at Euston Station, knowing for certain it was a waypoint in my life story.

'Come on, there's lots to see and do without going out of our way.'

'Next time?'

He held up his novel. 'Can I get on?'

'D'you think we'll get to the palace gates? Imagine swinging off the fountain like they did in 1945. D'you think it'll be the same party atmosphere there was then?'

'You sitting on my shoulders? Like in the old newsreels?'

I blinked. 'You're being sarcastic, aren't you?' I dug an elbow into his ribs. 'You're such a spoil sport.'

I turned to the window, far more content with my own company. In spite of Stephen's dark humour, the miles of weed-infested embankments and graffitied walls, the day held enormous promise, the world appearing bright, shimmering. Catching my reflection in the carriage window, I tried to summon a vision of what my brother might look like today—a late fifties, early sixties man who resembled me. Repeating the process I'd mastered using the hall mirror at home, I allowed my eyes to lose focus, superimposing a firm jawline and male haircut. When a masculine face emerged, a wave of goosebumps crawled up my arm. I wanted to reach out and stroke his cheek, longing to be connected to him by today's momentous event, in the city of our childhood.

A couple got on at Crewe and took the seats opposite. When the men offered to buy us all hot drinks, I pounced on the opportunity to speak to the woman.

'Was your family involved in the evacuation program?'

'My parents took in a lad for a little while. I was young, so I don't remember much. Harry, he was called.'

'From London?'

'Oh, no. He was from Leeds and we lived in Skipton. Far enough away from the city for the little ones to be safe.'

'Leeds was a target?'

'Yes. Huge RAF base and munitions factory, plus it was a centre for the rail network. Bloody big target, actually. What about you?'

I launched in, nothing spared.

When the men returned, I swiped my handbag onto my lap. As I reached for my coffee cup, a sharp judder tipped my hand, sending a wave of coffee over the edge of the table.

'Oh, God!' I yelled, jumping upright, grabbing the items I'd hidden from Stephen, wiping them both against my chest.

'Don't do that. You'll stain your jacket,' he said.

'They're not your prized possessions,' I replied.

'Are you burnt?' The woman dived in her handbag for tissues as her husband slammed a newspaper onto the hot puddle, sending more liquid over the edge.

'No!' I screamed.

'Oh, Chris! You've made it worse,' the woman spat.

Stephen took charge, carefully unfolding the paper to create a bigger, more absorbent sponge, circling and mopping until the liquid was contained in a huge brown clump. 'There, no harm done.'

I glared at him before returning my attention to my mascot and talisman. The bear was soiled, like my jacket, but the photo had survived. I sank back in my seat, massaging my forehead.

'We might take our coffees to the buffet car,' the man said, before they collected their backpacks and sidestepped their way down the aisle.

'We won't see them again,' Stephen said. 'And, why on earth did you bring those?'

I leant back and shook my head. 'Give me a minute, will you? I'm very shaken. Go back to your book.'

In the hour before arriving at our destination, my pulse slowed, the crisis less intense. Once freed from the horror of what might have happened to my family belongings, a new opportunity came to mind.

I nudged Stephen, who folded down the corner of a page and turned towards me.

'Feeling better?' he asked.

'Yes. Sorry. Especially the swearing.'

He snorted. 'Never expect to hear those words from you.'

'I thought I'd lost them both.'

He patted my arm. 'Yes, I know. But if you hadn't...' He stopped.

'I'm not sorry. And now you know I've brought them, there's something we can do together.'

His eyebrows pulled together. 'I said before, we don't have time for...'

I barrelled on, picking up the photo which had been drying on my leg. 'I mean, finding where this was taken. The exact spot.'

Stephen's frown deepened. 'At Euston?'

'Why not? Won't take a minute.'

'But ...you've seen it. Remember? It was rebuilt years ago, but most definitely after the war. In the sixties, I think.'

'All of it?'

'I'm pretty sure.'

'Oh.' I folded into myself.

'We could check, I suppose.'

'Could we?' I sat upright and squeezed his arm. 'Let's hope we're wrong.'

~ * ~

When we pulled into the terminal, Euston was abuzz. The patriotic garb we'd seen earlier in the day was replicated a hundred times as people spilled out of crammed mainline trains onto platforms and concourses, swarming towards escalators leading to the underground network. Moving sideways, we found a quieter space and observed the modern architecture, undoubtedly a product of the sixties, with its minimalist style.

'Sorry, love. Doesn't mean you weren't here.'

'Maybe a staff member will know.'

'It's over fifty years ago. They'll be retired.'

'Or they'll be like Bevan.' Our neighbour was a railway buff. He closed his eyes, ribcage rising.

'Alright. I know. Come on.' It was a small defeat. I mentally tossed it on a gargantuan pile.

Re-joining the throngs heading towards the bowels of the city, renditions of 'Britannia Rules the Waves' and 'The White Cliffs of Dover' lifted my spirits as they echoed off the tiles and tunnel roofs. Bodies squashed into every available space, sweaty, jovial faces maintaining the upbeat mood. St James's Park was the nearest station to Buckingham Palace, but we exited Charing Cross, determined to walk the length of The Mall. Though glad to escape the crush and claustrophobia of the tube carriage, we remained trapped in crowds as busy as any workday rush hour. But, unlike business and office workers, tourists like Stephen and me dithered in front of wall maps and fiddled with tickets and barriers. British-themed souvenirs set out to tempt passersby caused the last pinch point before we launched up the final staircase seeking sunlight and fresh air.

Our plan to walk to the palace was folly, the famous roadway packed, the Queen's residence a blip in the distance.

'Where's the map?' Stephen took it from me and snapped it open. 'If we go into the park here, we might do better by going up the side. Worth a try?'

I agreed, and filled with purpose and determination, plunged into the park between two smart policemen standing on either side of wrought iron gates. After the coffee incident, the renovations at Euston, the lack of time to visit the East End when I knew—knew—I'd belong this time, something had to go my way. The path took us beside a lake, ducks quacking and skittering across water glistening in the sunshine.

'Caryl! Caryl! Please, I can't keep up.' Stephen pulled me to a stop and turned me around. 'Are you okay? You look ...over-excited.'

I grinned and laughed, waving my flag. 'Am I? Aren't you? Surely it's the day for it.'

'I'm serious, Caryl. We'll lose each other if we don't stay together.'

'I'm fine, honestly. Enjoying myself, for once.' I strode towards a gate which brought us onto the roadway. 'No, further,' I shouted, ducking back into the park.

Stephen followed, muttering.

We were close now. Soon I'd be standing on the apron in front of the palace gates, exactly like in the newsreels, the movies. And, if it were a movie, with the teddy bear in one hand, my Union Jack in the other, my lost sibling would be there. I, the star of the film, would take out the photo to confirm our shared history. My brother, the leading man, would recognise it because he had one too. Did he? Why not? He'd pull his copy from inside his jacket, and we'd cling to each other, as fifty-six years of separation melted away. I exhaled and shook my head.

At the western end of the park, we again moved sideways towards The Mall, drawn by thousands of voices. The press of people was suffocating, but the building was in view, heat gleaming off the white stone exterior, the central balcony a focal point. Stephen took a handkerchief from his pocket and wiped his brow.

The woman next to me beamed. 'It's going to be a super day, isn't it? I'm so glad I'm here.'

'Me too. Have you come far?'

'Not really. I live in the East End. My whole family was here during the Blitz.'

'Was anyone evacuated? I was evacuated.'

'No, Mum wouldn't let us go. Sent the officials off with a flea in their ear. My husband was, though. Here, Bill, another evacuee for you.'

A man appeared at her side and said, 'Hi, so where'd you end up?'

Flags flickered at the edge of my vision. 'I'm hoping someone will recognise this?' I pushed the bear forward. 'Or this man?' I brandished the photograph.

He pulled back.

My husband stepped forward. 'Caryl, what are you doing?'

'No, love, sorry,' Bill said, clutching his wife's arm.

'What about the people next to you? Are they with you? Can you ask them?'

'No, I don't think so.'

'No, they're not with you or no, you can't ask?'

Bill moved strangely. The woman froze. Stephen swiped at the picture, but I snatched it back, pushing onwards, past the couple towards the next group of spectators.

'Sorry to disturb you. This might seem a little odd, but I wondered if you recognised this boy?'

Despite the noise of a thousand conversations, their silence stung.

'I'm not asking for much. Please look, can't you?'

The next man in line turned towards me.

'I'm only trying to find this boy.'

I held up the photo. Faces turned waxy. Blobby heads swayed like pendulums. I pushed in front of him.

'Steady on, love. You can't come crashing through. We all want a good view.'

'No, no. I'm looking for my brother. He might be here ...somewhere.'

Stephen wiggled sideways to stand beside me. 'I'm so sorry. My wife's having a funny turn. The crowds, I think. Sorry, again.'

He firmly lowered and removed the image I held mere centimetres from the man's nose.

The words, 'funny turn', filtered into my brain. I bit my lip and took in my surroundings. A line of people peered towards me, transformed, sharpened. Fear and bewilderment leeched into the surroundings. Flags hung limp. Mouths gaped.

I held the bear to my chest.

'Come on, love. Let's go.'

Forced to make our way back the way we'd come, I heard my husband offer apologies as I fixated on the ground. The tight spaces prevented us walking side by side. I gripped his hand, not daring to peep upwards until there were fewer pairs of feet, and we were back on grass.

'Oh, Stephen. I'm—'

He cut me off, hand raised. 'It's all my fault. We shouldn't have come, end of story. Let's look for a café, then go home.'

He gently prised the bear out of my hand, took the photograph out of his pocket, and put them both in my bag, the flags on top.

'I've made a fool of myself, haven't I?'

'No, love. But I am worried about you.'

'If only I could find him. Please, will you help me?'

He placed a finger under my chin, gently lifting my gaze to meet his. 'Look what's happening to you. See what it's done? You need to let this go, love. Put it to bed and enjoy your real family: us, the kids, Chloe. And another grandchild, one day, if Megan and Rick get a move on.'

A waterfall of ice slid down my spine, as nausea rose in its place. 'I need to sit.'

'Oh God! You've lost all colour. You're in shock.' He put an arm around my waist, swivelling to locate a seat. 'Over there. Can you walk? I'll help you. Come on.'

'I'm cold. So cold.'

As soon as we reached the bench, he whipped off his jacket and wrapped it around me.

A police officer approached. 'Is everything okay? Do you need assistance?'

Stephen looked up. 'Overwhelmed by the crowds. She'll be fine in a minute. But thank you. It was very kind.'

'Are you sure? She looks peaky. The St John's volunteers are over there if you change your mind.' The young constable pointed to a nearby tent and strode away.

'How's that? Better? You could do with something sweet.' He rummaged in his pocket and produced a packet of fruit pastilles.

'Don't tell Megan about this, please?'

He hesitated. 'Alright. Agreed. On one condition ...will you stop, love? Please? I can't bear to see you like this again.'

'I need to lie down.'

'What? Here?'

He helped me curl up, the discoloured bear doubling as a temporary pillow. With a strong, warm arm draped across my shoulder, we listened as a distant roar drifted across the park from the palace.

Five

The photographic studio in Conwy phoned to say my picture was ready. When I told Megan, she insisted on coming with me. Initially hesitant, I was glad I changed my mind. I could sit back and let her navigate the traffic and parking. Besides, as my biggest supporter, she deserved to share the moment.

The back door swung open, and Megan stepped through to find me in the garden. 'Runner beans, I'm guessing. Dad said you were out here ...again.'

I moved back to admire the bamboo tepee-style supports I'd constructed, a skill Gwen had passed on many years ago.

'Hello, love. Thought I heard your car. Sorry, I won't take a minute to get ready.' I wiped my grimy hands on my trousers and pushed strands of sweaty hair behind my ears. I loved my garden. From this vantage point, on our terraced vegetable plot, I could see over our bungalow all the way to the coast. 'Come back inside and talk to Dad while I change.' I descended the stone steps to stand beside her. 'And the raffle tickets are on the dining table. Thanks for offering to sell some.'

'No problem. How much are you hoping to raise this year?'

'A few thousand, if we can. Are you sure you and Rick can't come? It's always a good evening and my charity gets the benefit this year. Your neighbour would babysit Chloe, wouldn't she?'

'We'll only cramp your style. You and Dad, sashaying across the dance floor. Besides Rick doesn't have anything suitable for a fancy ball.'

'As if the Bosnian orphans care. Sometimes I think there's something very wrong with people needing to enjoy themselves in order to show their generosity.' I clicked my tongue. 'Two minutes and I'll be with you.'

On the journey to Conwy, I sat rigid, arms tightly crossed.

'Excited?'

'Feel sick, to tell the truth. What if they've made a mess of it?'

'What if it's amazing?'

'Or it's been destroyed in their equipment. They've already said they can't decipher the name label on the boy's jumper.'

She glanced sideways. 'You seem down. Dad, too. Ever since your trip to London, actually.'

'I told you. It wasn't quite the day we expected. Too crowded, couldn't get a view,' I snapped. 'Sorry. I'm tired.'

I didn't want to think about London or my husband. Memories of VE Day, my behaviour and the promise he tried to extract, continued to haunt me. Mention of the Hospital Summer Ball and Megan's quip about our love of the quickstep, had been unintentionally ironic. We'd been doing exactly that—dancing around each other. I sidestepped his company and tiptoed through unavoidable chitchat. Stephen followed suit. We were gradually descending a mountain of trepidation but continued to scour the ground for conversational trip hazards.

'Is Dad worried your charity work with war orphans will bring back memories? Though, I suppose the photo trumps that, doesn't it?'

'No, he's fine with the charity stuff, but the photo's put him on high alert. And I'm just nervous. I want something to go right, for once,' I said.

'Rick's on tenterhooks, too. Luckily, he has a lot of respect for the people who work there.'

'You'd never know from the shop frontage, would you?' I giggled, popping the bubble of tension inside the car. 'How old is that bridal portrait? I expect it'll change now the son's in charge. Got very excited about a new computer program. Says it can work magic. I hope it's true.'

We parked in a nearby street and walked the rest of the way, noting the brand-new window display, clean and contemporary, the ancient wedding photo presumably relegated to the store cupboard. A bell tinkled in the background as we entered. Inside, the walls had been freshly decorated, the paint smell wrinkling my nostrils. When the young man recognised me, he bounded into the workroom returning a few seconds later with a flat parcel wrapped in tissue paper.

'I know how precious this is. Wanted to keep it safe, mind. He placed it reverentially on the counter.

I hesitated.

'Go on, Mum. Open it. Crickey, it's like Christmas!'

Heart hammering, I peeled back the wrapping. My tiny, creased black and white was glorious, flawless. Restored. I gasped, my fingers hovering over Mum and my brother.

An arm encircled my shoulders, a tissue pressed into my hand. I hadn't noticed my tears.

'It's amazing,' Megan said.

'We enlarged it as much as we could. It's the pixels, see. If you stretch it too much, you lose the sharpness,' the photographer said.

I coughed and dabbed my eyes. 'No, it's perfect, exactly as it is. Thank you, so much. What I need now is a frame to finish it off.'

'There're two more copies here. And the image is on our computer, so if you want more, we can run them off for you.'

'That's good to know.'

'Your family, isn't it? Will you want one for him?' He pointed at the boy.

Megan's embrace tightened. 'Frames. Mum wants a frame. What size would you recommend?'

While my daughter discussed the merits of a compact frame or one with a surrounding mat, my eyes drilled into the portrait of my family. Nothing bad had happened. The three of us hadn't faded into oblivion. Though I knew the process wouldn't involve chemical tanks or rooms with special lights, my imagination had led me to dark places where paper scorched, mushed or reversed into a negative. Instead, the boy had grown in stature, become more solid and real. Enhanced, enriched, improved, it was magic.

Although I'd known not to get my hopes up, I couldn't hide one crucial disappointment. The photographer had been correct: whatever wizardry and new-fangled whatnots had been applied in the workroom, the name label pinned to the boy's jumper remained resolutely obscured. And nothing had turned my brother towards the camera.

~ * ~

During the evening, struggling over a dry, fact-filled policy report, I slapped the documents onto my lap, pinching the skin on the bridge of my nose.

'What's up?' Stephen asked.

'Not in the mood for this, tonight.'

'You shouldn't be bringing work stuff home, especially when you're not stopping for a proper lunch break. At least I get to read in worktime. Did I mention the paper in the British Medical Journal about stem cell research? Astonishing!'

'Yes, you did, and those extra classes are working wonders, by the way.'

'I do hope those kids appreciate your thoughtfulness.'

'So long as they pass their exams, I don't care.'

'Did you ask Megan about the ball?'

'Yes, and the answer's "no." Apparently, Rick's business is a bit slow. First I've heard of it.'

'Me, too. That's a shame.' He looked up and caught my eye. 'Do you need a new dress? Why don't you go to Chester, treat yourself to something nice?'

'Thanks. I'll think about it.' I chose not to argue but knew the war orphans would benefit far more from the cost of a fancy gown.

'Cuppa?' he asked.

When Stephen left the room, the photograph of my family on the mantlepiece caught my attention. Megan had made an excellent choice of frame. I took it down and retook my seat.

'Who are you, little boy?' I whispered.

Eyes closed, my fingers gripped the frame. His name. I could never recall his bloody name! Rubbing my thumb over his outline, I willed myself to fire up long-forgotten neural connections. In desperation, I opened them and stared.

Come on, come on, speak to me. What happened to you?

The void reminded me of past embarrassments with all the records administrators I'd ever met. Few knew what to say when I couldn't offer the most basic of details. My ridiculous hope the restoration process would reveal the words on his jumper had come to nothing. For all its sentimental value, in terms of finding my brother, the picture made little difference.

Staring again, different letters jumped out at me. Painted on the side of the carriage, they spelt, SOUTHERN, a word I'd not noticed in the smaller, original version. Gwen had always told me I'd travelled with Mum directly from London to North Wales. Yet North Wales was north, not south.

I gazed towards the kitchen, conscious of the ceasefire Stephen and I had so carefully cultivated. Even if I could obtain information without him guessing my intent, I doubted he could help me. The person I needed was Bevan, my shy, bachelor neighbour, who owned shelves of books on every aspect of the rail network and had constructed an intricate replica of the local line in his garden shed.

Slipping past Stephen in the hallway, with an excuse to phone Megan, I eased the study door closed and picked up the phone. Bevan's gruff tone answered after two rings.

I cupped my hand around the handset. 'Bevan, it's Caryl. Sorry for the late call. A question for you. Where in London do Southern Railway trains run from and where do they go?'

'It's not called Southern Railway these days, mind. In 1948, it changed to the Southern Region.'

'Good, yes, but I'm thinking of war time. So, the first question? Did they leave from Euston?'

'Good Lord, no. It's a different line altogether. No, the Southern trains left mainly from Waterloo, Charing Cross, Victoria.'

'And where would they have gone?'

'All over. The ports down south, Kent, the southwest. Why the interest?'

'I'm looking at an old evacuation photo. Curious, you know? So, to be clear, they wouldn't have come up here to North Wales?'

'Definitely not. No, you'd have left from Euston.'

'I thought so. Thank you, Bevan. You've been a great help.'

'Have I?'

'Yes, yes. Thank you. Come round for tea sometime. In fact, are you free tomorrow, when I get home from school? About four?'

'Right-o.'

'Super. See you soon.'

I put down the phone, exhilarated. Finally, a new, valid lead and the tantalising possibility that if we'd gone somewhere else before arriving in Wales it might explain the boy's disappearance. Bevan's words proved there was more to uncover, whatever I'd promised Stephen.

My course of action was clear—I would pursue this enquiry alone.

~ * ~

Bevan arrived on time, wringing a woollen beanie, smelling powerfully of aftershave and peppermints.

Once I'd served a slice of bara brith and tea, and he'd wiped any excess butter on a napkin, I showed him the restored photo.

'Seen lots of these, mind,' he said. 'Hundreds snapped that day with all them children waiting to be taken away. It was called "Operation Pied Piper".'

'So I've been told.'

'And this little one is you? Goodness gracious. So young.'

'Yes, but Mum was there, at least. Anyway …you said Southern trains left from several London stations. Is there anything in here to tell me which one?'

'Let's see. To be honest, it might be Waterloo. What makes me pretty sure, is the style of roof. It's called "ridge and furrow," see?' Bevan took the next five minutes to describe, in toe-curling detail, this architectural point of difference. 'Waterloo was one of the major meeting points for the September 1939 evacuation program. As the headquarters of the Southern Railway, it took passengers all over the south and west of London.'

'I'd love to see an old route map,' I said.

'I've a book of them at home. I'll drop by with it.'

'Thanks, you're very kind.'

He fidgeted. 'Did you say your mum died? Is that what these questions are about?'

'Partly. Gwen, my step-mum, always said we came straight from London to North Wales. But we can't have, can we?'

'No. For starters, the roof at Euston was entirely different in those days, made from iron trusses. It was a great innovation, at the time—'

'Sorry to interrupt, Bevan. I simply need to know where we might have gone.'

'I'm not going to lie—if you boarded the train there, you'd have gone to Dover or Brighton, Portsmouth, Salisbury, Exeter, Plymouth and all stops in-between.'

'So many possibilities. It's overwhelming.'

'I'm not surprised,' he replied. 'Is there someone else you could ask? Another relative or friend? Are you sure Gwen doesn't know? Seems odd to me.'

Quite! A vision of Morwen Davis popped into my mind.

Morwen was a frequent visitor to our cottage during my childhood days. Always kind, she took an interest in me, tolerating my questions and interruptions, becoming a valuable peacemaker and go-between when I hit my rebellious teens. Married early to a controlling man called Alan, she never fulfilled her goal to be a teacher. Our home, in the backwater of Bryn-y-Maen, became a bolt hole from her husband and life of domesticity. As a good friend to us both, she'd disapprove of my decision to circumvent Gwen, but the prospect of her recollecting our arrival in North Wales was hard to resist.

'You've had an idea, I'm guessing,' Bevan said, filling the silence.

'I have. Thank you so much, you've been an enormous help.'

'D'you still want those route maps?'

'Yes, please.'

'Right-o. I'll drop them in later.'

And with praise for the refreshment and taking several pieces of cake with him, he scurried home.

Six

I drove to Morwen's house the following Saturday, the first opportunity I had for a chat with her before we both visited Gwen in Bryn-y-Maen. As I stood outside her front door, I watched a stooped figure make slow progress up the hallway, distorted by a panel of decorative glass.

'Caryl, come in. I'm so pleased you phoned. Haven't seen Gwen for ages. Though it gave me a fright, to be honest. Thought the worst.'

I followed her into the lounge room, a coordinated confection of salmon-pink chairs and sofa, fitted carpet and ornate reproduction cabinets, nothing like her friend's rustic home. I took my usual seat on the end of the sofa.

'Sorry, didn't mean to scare you.'

She waved a hand and lowered herself into the chair nearest the heater. Like Gwen, she was grey, her hair cut in a no-nonsense style, but she'd avoided deep marionette lines, rendering her features less grim and morose. Nevertheless, her papery skin, wrinkles, and careful movements made her advancing years hard to ignore. 'Come on, fill me in. How's the family? What's little Chloe up to? How old is she? Must be time for a little brother or sister.'

'She's fine, thanks, a little poppet. Megan sends her love.' Some things were private even between good friends.

'And Gwen?'

'She's recovered up to a point. But her cough won't go away, and she needs to exercise more.'

'I know the feeling. Easier to take the lazy way out. You're sure she's up for a visit?'

'Oh, yes. She'd love to see you. Can you still come over?'

'No-one to keep me tied to the house these days.' She glanced at a series of family portraits on her bureau. 'So, why the chat? What's on your mind? I always know when you're fretting over something.'

I leant forward. 'I came across an old black and white of me with my birth mum recently, and it's brought up some questions.' I shifted uneasily. 'I'm hoping you might be able to help. You know Gwen. She's always touchy about my past. And, being sick ...to be perfectly honest, I'd rather not ask her.'

'There's a picture, is there?'

'Yes. I found it a couple of weeks ago in her garage. There's no doubt it's my mum.'

'How lovely, but ...the questions. I mean, what, exactly? This is awkward, if I'm honest.' She kneaded her swollen knuckles. 'How can I possibly help?'

'Can we try, at least? For instance, were you here when we arrived from London? How soon did she invite you over?'

'Why?' she snapped. 'You should be asking her about this.'

I bowed my head, trapped. 'She's struggling. The photo shocked her.' I played with the ends of my scarf. 'It might not sound like a good thing, but...'

Morwen sat rigid, as if coming to a decision. 'The truth is, she didn't let on for months. She bought the property in Bryn-y-

Maen and hid herself away. Later, much later, when she finally contacted me, she said she'd been grieving Paul and agreed to host the pair of you to provide her company and to do something worthwhile. Except, it all became difficult when your mum caught scarlet fever, which was perfectly understandable, I suppose. It hurt when she didn't tell me she'd come back.'

Prickles danced on my scalp. 'Come home? From where? So, the cottage was new? Not her original home?'

Morwen froze. 'There, see, that's why you should be talking to her, not me. This isn't fair.'

I inched forward. 'Please, Morwen. Where had she been?'

'Gloucestershire. When Paul was posted to the RAF base, she took a teaching position at a private girls' school.'

My stomach pitched. 'Gloucestershire?' Bevan had kept his word, delivering two hardbacks showing old Southern Railway route maps. In my mind's eye, a red dot made its way from Waterloo Station, south and west of London. I swallowed the familiar recounting of my life. Gwen had always, always, claimed we'd come straight from London.

'I assumed she'd stayed in her own home while Paul lived away, like most servicemen's wives. How long did she live there?' I asked.

'About twelve months, I suppose. Finished the year off, for the children's sake. There was no call to stay on after he died, especially with the money problems. He was a pilot, you know. Brave, brave man.'

'She's never told me any of this, except what happened to him. The move, the money problems, whatever they were. Why?'

'Probably because it was a difficult time in her life. The school went broke, and her wages weren't paid because she was a supplementary worker. She was married, so she couldn't be registered as a qualified teacher. Dreadful policy. Different these days, of course.'

I nodded robotically as my mind raced.

'Obviously, she was devastated losing her husband, but her pride was dented, too. Felt like the headmistress had taken advantage of her. That's the reason she bought a place in the middle of nowhere. They had a big house overlooking the water before moving away, but she couldn't afford anywhere in Llandudno, after that. Poor Gwen. She hated being deceived.'

I rubbed my temple, anxious I was losing important pieces of information. 'Sorry, I'm struggling with the dates. When did she leave?'

'The year the war broke out, 1939. Paul's posting began at the end of the summer, so she went with him to settle them into a new place before the start of the new term in September. Then, two weeks later, all hell broke loose. We were at war.'

'And the academic year would've finished the following July 1940. So, when did you first see her, after she came back?'

'Close to Christmas. I saw you a week before and was able to give you a little present. I rushed to knit a bobble hat for you, but the ribbing was too tight. You wouldn't let us help you, mind. Rammed it on and split the stiches. I had to take it home and mend it.' She appeared amused before her manner changed. 'Can't do more than crochet blanket squares for your refugees, these days.' She held up her arthritic hands.

'You don't have to. Buying a book of raffle tickets is enough.'

'Can't believe there's conflict in Europe. Didn't we learn anything? It's your story all over again, isn't it?'

She was right, but I couldn't help pushing for the details of our arrival. 'So, if you saw us around Christmas, we must have arrived sometime between July and December 1940, not 1939.'

'I never knew for sure, but yes, it must have been. We didn't receive many evacuees in these parts. They mostly went to Bangor and Harlech, the bigger towns. From memory, the majority had arrived the previous year at the outbreak of war, from Liverpool. You were latecomers.'

My lip twitched. Were we, indeed? 'It was quite a spell for her to be on her own, not seeing anyone, not even you, her oldest friend.'

Morwen's sour expression returned. 'She was dealing with a terrible disease. The doctor ordered her to quarantine. It must have been frightening for her. What if you'd caught it too? Or her, for that matter?'

'True. It killed Mum.'

Her scowl slid away. 'Such a tragedy. I wish I'd met her. No, she and Paul were both long gone before I was invited to meet you. Funerals over with and everything. You mustn't blame her for not being able to afford a headstone, either. She wanted to but couldn't afford one after what happened.'

'I wish you'd met her, too. But to be honest, I assumed all this happened much earlier. Probably a whole year earlier. Gwen always talked as if Mum and Paul had died close together.'

We sat in silence for a moment.

I pushed back in my seat. 'Can I tell you something now? The photo I mentioned shows Mum and me on a crowded London platform as if we were part of the first wave of evacuees in September 1939. I'm pretty sure of the date because it was something big and special, which is precisely why a cameraman was there to capture the moment.'

'You both came from London. But not then, surely?'

'It puzzles me, too. I spoke to my neighbour, Bevan, the railway enthusiast, and he thinks it was taken at Waterloo. There's a Southern train in the background. He says those routes went to the southwest, with branch lines to places in Gloucestershire. If Gwen was living in that part of the country at the beginning of the war, perhaps she gave us a home there first. I don't understand why she's never told me, or you, but it could be what you said before, about losing her husband, losing money and having to come back to Wales under a cloud. It probably doesn't mean much, but it's important to me.'

I didn't remind her of my belief I once had a brother and what it might mean in relation to our separation. The vista of new search possibilities, opened up by Bevan's route maps, were breaking through, like sunshine in a cloudy, grey sky.

'I don't know what to say, Caryl. She most definitely spent time in Cirencester, near the air base, but she's never said anything about you living there with her. It's not the story she told me.'

I sensed her confusion. My enquiries had hurt her.

'Why are you digging into this?' she demanded. 'Gwen loved and adored you, apple of her eye. You brought her such joy when Paul died.'

Chastened, I searched for an explanation, a way to preserve their friendship. 'I'm sorry. I didn't mean to upset you or spoil your visit. I do realise how lucky I was to be taken in by her. I also appreciate the stress and grief she must have felt at losing Paul. People say time bends when dealing with the loss of a loved one.'

She huffed and turned away.

An idea flashed by. 'Was it a nice house?'

'I never visited because of the wartime travel restrictions, but she wrote to say it was. On a quiet lane with other big houses nearby.'

'You'd have written to her, I'm guessing, like we did when I moved to Manchester to be with Stephen. It's become a forgotten art nowadays, hasn't it?'

'Yes, I used to love it. To the both of you and all my other friends. Gwen and I exchanged notes nearly every week. I missed her, you see.'

'And vice versa.' I plucked at my scarf again. 'You wouldn't have the address, would you?'

'Whatever for?' Her eyes flicked towards a sideboard.

'Please, Morwen. I promise I won't say anything to upset her.'

'I don't think I should. There must be a reason she hasn't mentioned that time in your life.' She drew back. 'I feel like I'm betraying her. She's my oldest friend.'

I sat silent, beaten. A lone dog barked, fretful, agitated.

'What will you do if I give it to you? It's just a house ...four walls and a roof. It won't tell you anything.'

I shrugged. 'I haven't had time to think it through, but I'd love to see it. If she doesn't know, what harm can it do?'

'But you can't be sure you lived there. Not for an absolute fact. You might be quite wrong.' She clenched her fists. 'I'm not sure, Caryl. God forbid, she finds out I've spilled the beans.'

She hesitated, staring into her lap. After several seconds, she pushed herself upright, steadying herself before taking slow steps towards the sideboard. The drawer screeched on unused runners. Rifling through the contents, she lifted a red leather-bound address book.

'Not a word, please. I'd never have started if I thought we'd end up here. Why I told you about Gwen's move after all these years...'

She found the page for Roberts and passed it over to me. Three addresses had been scored through; the remaining one was for Bryn Cottage. The first entry, I guessed, was an address in Llandudno, Gwen's childhood home. The second, another local address, was presumably her first home with Paul, before the outbreak of war. The third read 'The Willows, Marsh Lane, Cirencester'. It looked odd without a postcode.

'Thanks, Morwen. This means a lot to me.'

'A secret for two is soon a secret for nobody,' she replied.

I chewed my lip. 'Shall we get going?'

Seven

After dropping Morwen back at her bungalow, I called in on Megan to spill the news from my recent encounters. My resolve to work at my problems alone had vanished. We went into her kitchen where I perched on the edge of a bar stool.

'You can't go all the way to Gloucestershire in a day. It's too far.'

'I have to,' I said, tapping a shoe on the footrest. 'It might sound ridiculous, but I have to see "The Willows" for myself.'

'You're not going to let on to Dad, are you?'

'I'll say I'm going to Chester. He told me to buy a new dress for the hospital ball.'

'A lot further than Chester, and nearly all motorway,' she replied.

'Morwen wrote to her at that address in 1939, and Bevan's maps confirm the Southern routes went that way. I have to do something and I'm not ready to have it out with Gwen. Not yet.'

'But why would Gwen cover it up?'

'Morwen thinks she was grieving, embarrassed, but I still don't think that's enough reason to deceive me all these years.

And, if I find proof we lived with Gwen in Cirencester, it'll make me wonder about other things too. Already has, if I'm honest.'

'Like what?'

'Like Morwen never meeting Mum. Don't you think that's odd? I've always accepted Gwen's story, but now I'm questioning everything.'

'I suppose if you were all together in "The Willows," someone over there might remember Grandma Baker. Maybe even your brother.'

'That's what I'm hoping to find out.'

~ * ~

Masterminding a clandestine day trip to Gwen's old home proved more difficult than I expected. Stephen arranged to have my car serviced during the half-term holiday, on the very day I'd chosen to travel. Given how sensible the plan was, I couldn't object. Our road map of Britain was out of date, but by the time I noticed, my vehicle was high on a hydraulic lift at the local workshop. It meant a long walk into Colwyn Bay to buy a replacement in unusually hot and clammy weather. Fortunately, my Fiesta was returned in time.

As soon as Stephen left for work the next morning, I dashed onto the driveway, map book, flask and sandwiches in hand. A copy of my photograph was again tucked safely in my handbag. I pulled out after him but hung back until he'd turned off to the Glan Clwyd Hospital.

The morning sun glared through the windscreen then gradually travelled round to the passenger side. Traffic built as I approached major towns and slowed me down around Birmingham. I suffered moments of panic as I read unfamiliar signage and negotiated sudden lane changes, surrounded by thunderous, menacing lorries belching acrid fumes. Perspiration built on my forehead and armpits. After a quick stop at a motorway café, I arrived on the outskirts of Cirencester and began navigating the narrow country lanes. Unhelpful wooden signposts sent me round and back again before I finally arrived at Marsh Lane.

When I saw the road name, I pulled over, exhausted. Hot and sweaty, I was struck by how preposterous my journey had been, driving miles across the country, visiting a house where I might once have lived without any real prospect the current owners could offer useful information about my past. Poor Stephen, maybe his wife truly was a basket case.

After blowing my nose, I put the car into gear and drove on, a quote from Macbeth, the required A-level text for my students, ringing in my ears—*I am in blood stepp'd in so far that, should I wade no more, returning were as tedious as go o'er.* Putting aside the murder and bodily fluids, it felt apt.

My destination was half a mile along an attractive roadway. Most of the houses were detached, with big wraparound gardens. Well-heeled country homes, nothing like mine. 'The Willows' turned out to be much smaller, a pretty arts and craft bungalow, less grand than the rest. The garden displayed a profusion of cottage flowers arranged to merge and complement each other, shooting both bold and delicate flowers into the sunny air. Armies of bees buzzed happily amongst the bounty. Impressed, I made a mental note to attempt something similar back at my place.

I hesitated, a beat away from driving home, until a wave of indignation took hold. I had every reason to question my evacuation journey. Surely no one would object to a polite enquiry. I retrieved the picture and brushed my lips against my family.

The gate squealed on its hinges. Rehearsing my introduction, I knocked on the door. When a middle-aged woman answered, neat in expensive clothes, I gabbled the story of Gwen and Paul Roberts buying the house, and later, taking in a family of evacuees. I spoke of me, my brother and Kathleen Baker as if it were fact. Raising the photo of the scene at Waterloo, I was careful to present it at an appropriate distance.

'No, sorry. Those names don't mean anything at all. We're talking about the war years, aren't we?'

'They moved here in the summer of 1939, before the start of the term. Gwen had a job at a local girls' school; her husband worked at the RAF base. He died in an accident later in the year, and she left again in 1940.'

'We've only been here since seventy-two. The person we made the purchase from could've bought it from her, I suppose, but she'd be elderly now, and we don't have her details.' She clutched her pearls, twisting the strand around her fingers. 'I'm so sorry. Have you come far? Can I get you something? I could make you a drink, at least.'

I dithered, conscious of the time but suddenly curious to see what was probably my first home away from London.

'I'm Pam, by the way,' she said. 'Please, come in, and let me make a cup of tea.'

'A glass of water would be lovely, thank you.'

I followed her inside, straining to latch onto a familiar design or architectural feature. Noting the wooden floors, sleek lines and modern style, it was clear it had received a recent makeover. Even the view through huge bifold doors into the garden failed to spark any recollection.

Pam filled a tall glass from a water filter and handed it to me. 'You didn't say why you're here. Did you lose touch with someone in your family?'

I thanked her for the refreshment. 'I'm trying to find my brother, who I lost during the war. It might have happened when we were evacuated here. It's a long shot, silly, I suppose, but I had to try.'

'I'm so sorry I can't help.' She tilted her head to one side. 'What about next door? The big white one. It's owned by the Babbington-Careys. They've been here forever. The house passed down from one generation to the next, apparently.'

My spirits rose. 'Who's there now?'

'An old gentleman, Aubrey. He's widowed. His wife died about ten years ago, which is when his son, Ralph, and his wife moved in to take care of him. I expect they'll inherit the place when the old man goes.'

'Ralph? How old is he, roughly?'

'Oh ... mid to late sixties?'

Mental arithmetic was never my strong point, but I calculated a sixty-five-year-old would have been born in 1930—therefore, of school age when war broke out. A ripple of excitement rose in my chest.

She continued. 'I don't want to gossip, but I think Aubrey's going senile. I wouldn't believe everything he says.'

'Thanks for the warning. And Ralph?'

'Fine, but stand-offish. A buttoned-up kind of person. We've never had much to do with them. I suspect he considers my little cottage lowers the tone of the neighbourhood!'

I handed back the empty glass, thanked her profusely and put the photo away. As we said our goodbyes at the front door, she wished me luck. Yet I was already blessed. Reeling from the initial anti-climax, my mantra came back to me—the sun shines on the brave—as, indeed it was, drawing out the vivid colours in the gorgeous garden. My steps lightened and birdsong filled my ears.

Eight

Bracing myself for a second awkward encounter, I crunched on gravel around to the next driveway and walked up to the front entrance. Questions tumbled over each other.

I knocked, and a man matching Ralph's description opened the door.

It took me a moment to formulate a greeting. 'Hello. Sorry to disturb you. My name's Caryl Hunter. I was evacuated to "The Willows" at the beginning of the war. Were you and your family here at the time?'

Ralph's dark eyes bored into me, his face impassive. 'Yes. We've owned this house for generations.'

'That's what your neighbour said.' I paused, unsettled. 'This probably sounds crazy, but do you remember me, the little girl next door? Mum and I lived with a teacher called Gwen Roberts.'

'I'm sorry. I can't help. I have to look after my father.'

A figure appeared, pulling on the edge of the door, widening the gap. It had to be Aubrey. 'Visitors? Lovely. Who do we have here? Come on, Ralph. Be sociable.'

I launched in before I lost my chance, repeating the explanation for my visit. Ralph's jaw clenched.

'Gwen? Gwen? The teacher! Yes, yes. Tutored Oliver, the little scamp. Come in, come in. Lots to catch up on.'

With a surprisingly firm grip, he grabbed my arm and pulled me through a hallway laid with granite flagstones, the walls lined with portraits of family members. At the far end, a magnificent wooden staircase curved gracefully up and out of view. My footsteps slowed as I passed two carved doorways under the slope of the banister, the first and smallest snatching my attention with its triangular opening.

Aubrey guided me onwards through double doors into an enormous drawing room, replete with elegant furnishings, thick carpets and tasteful rugs, except for one lounge chair covered in throws and blankets. Soft classical music played from hidden speakers. Manicured lawns and neat flower beds were visible through the French doors and, separated by a hedge, the rooftop of the 'The Willows.'

'Ask Harris to make us a pot of tea, will you?' Aubrey told Ralph.

'No Harris these days, Fa. I'll do it, shall I?' He stalked out of the room.

The knot in my stomach eased.

'Come, sit, and tell me everything. Are you Gwen, did you say?'

'No, Mr Babbington-Carey—'

'Aubrey, please. No standing on ceremony with me.' He lowered himself into the blanketed seat.

I perched on the edge of a wing-back chair. 'Thanks. No, Gwen adopted me. I arrived next door at the start of the war with my mum and ... my brother.' The artifice came so easily second time around.

'Terrible business. Terrible. Did my best, you know...' His eyes glazed and flickered. I could only imagine the horrors he was dredging.

'I'm so sorry. This house must have been a sanctuary for you.'

He swung his fist in a shallow arc. 'Exactly! Afternoon tea on the lawn, badminton. The children! Children everywhere. And dogs. What marvellous times we had. Always people here. Julia, the most superb host.' His gaze drifted to the garden. 'Did I mention badminton? Lots of badminton.'

Ralph returned with a tray holding an expensive tea pot, cups, saucers and one plastic-lidded cup.

Aubrey continued. 'Marvellous times, eh?'

Ralph began pouring, confirming preferences for milk and sugar with hard-edged questions. The china rattled as I took it from him. He passed the beaker to Aubrey.

I pushed on. 'You said Gwen tutored Oliver. He's one of your children?'

Aubrey frowned, the beaker hanging at a dangerous angle.

Ralph stepped in, guiding the cup onto the armrest. 'Names aren't my father's strong point these days.'

I turned to the younger man. 'Is he your brother? A younger brother?'

'Oliver! And Lucy.' Aubrey slapped his thighs 'There, I did it. She had a friend, didn't she? Played with the dogs.'

I rocked forward. 'It might be me.' I dug the photo out of my bag and held it aloft. 'Do you recognise her?'

Aubrey squinted. 'Lucy, is it? With Gwen and Oliver?'

My arm sank down by my side.

Aubrey cut in. 'Bit her once, the little scamp.'

I seized the bait. 'I've always been scared of dogs. Was it me, by any chance?'

'Where's Harvey? Here, boy.' He surveyed the room, but no canine answered his call.

A vein pulsed under the skin of Ralph's neck.

'Sorry, I didn't mean to sound critical. I'm not here to sue.' A giggle erupted, bringing heat to my cheeks.

Aubrey blinked. 'Gwen, did you say? Terrific teacher. Tutored Oliver. Brought him up to speed.'

The neighbour's words were becoming crystal clear.

'I'm sorry, Mrs Hunter. You're welcome to finish your tea, but then I must ask you to leave. Dad's forgetfulness often descends into fits of temper. I'm sure you don't want a scene on your conscience.'

'No, of course not.'

'Are you ready?'

My cup was half-full, but the message was plain. I rose, said goodbye to Aubrey, who sat inert, contemplating the garden, and followed the younger man into the hall, my heels clicking on the stone.

Steps away from a front door—soon to close, both literally and figuratively—I summoned the last of my courage. 'Do you remember me playing with Lucy?'

Ralph's response was slow, deliberate. 'I was twelve when war broke out and only came home for the holidays. I certainly wouldn't have bothered with a couple of little girls.'

'Even though one of them was your sister?'

He reached for the doorknob. 'My father was hardly here during the war. Those stories you heard, the badminton and afternoon teas, are from a much earlier time. He had a high level posting in the War Office. Only came up on the occasional weekend.'

My shoulders slumped. 'Please, if you can help with anything at all, I'd be very grateful. I'm not here to make trouble. I only want to know if I lived next door before Gwen took me back to Wales.'

'Gwen helped Oliver and you played with Lucy. So, yes, you were here.'

'I was here. Oh, God, thank you. I was here, in your garden.' My hand shot forward in a gesture of thanks until I registered his horrified stare. It hung, momentarily, in the space between us. 'Sorry. Too much excitement. And my mum? And brother?'

Ralph pulled on the doorknob. 'Gwen's husband came home on leave from time to time, but I don't recall another woman living in the house.'

'And my brother?'

'What's his name?'

'I ... I don't know,' I said, voice thick, the flush returning.

'Then, I can't help you.'

A shuffle warned us of Aubrey's presence as he made slow, ungainly progress towards us. 'There was a boy. What was his name? Ate us out of house and home. Terry? No, Tommy. Everyone had to do their duty for England.'

Ralph motioned me outside with one hand and held out the other to his father. 'Come on, Fa. Mrs Hunter's leaving. Let's help you back to the drawing room.'

'Tommy?' I asked, my mind silently replaying the sounds, layering them over the image of my brother, yearning for a match which didn't materialise.

'He was my school friend, Fa.'

'Was he the same age as you?' I demanded.

'Thank you for coming. I'm sorry we couldn't be more helpful.'

Aubrey let out a sudden wail, sending my heart rate galloping. Clutching the back of his skull, pulling at the few remaining strands, he doubled over. 'The girl! Scarlet fever. She died of scarlet fever. "Leave and take your filthy diseases with you." Had to do it. Had to send everyone away.'

Ralph's features hardened as he stepped towards his father. 'Mrs Hunter. I must insist.'

'What does he mean? What's your dad saying?'

He didn't answer, his attention occupied by the distraught, unstable man, capturing flailing arms, manhandling him back towards the lounge.

My manners abandoned, I yelled, 'Was it Lucy?'

Without turning, Ralph replied, 'You must leave. Immediately! Close the door behind you.'

Nearly tripping over the step, I stumbled onto the gravel, slamming the door shut. Rooted to the spot, I heard Aubrey's mournful howl diminish.

I returned to my car, belatedly aware of my role in Aubrey's despair, a despair I'd created for a sick and vulnerable man. My visit had been of no benefit to him and hardly any to me, a jumble of possible facts crowding my mind. Ralph's words, painstakingly chosen to both inform and to fudge, muddled me. Craving Megan's company so we could examine the conversation together, I lay my head on the wheel.

I squinted at the digital readout: two o'clock. I'd need to leave straightaway if I were to arrive home without arousing suspicion. Imagining the return trip, the traffic, the stress, I wanted to curl up and disappear.

When the moment passed, I performed a U-turn in the narrow lane, took one last peek at the two houses, and pointed the car north, a kaleidoscope of images jostling for my attention.

Nine

The following day, Megan marched into my lounge room and threw herself onto the sofa. 'God, Mum, you look washed out. I knew it was too far to drive in one day.'

I flicked my hand, taking the armchair opposite 'I'll be better after a good sleep. Couldn't nod off last night with everything going round and round. Was Grandma alright?'

'Yes, fine. Chloe cheered her up, at least. So, what happened? Was the house there? What did you find out?' Her patience frayed, her countenance a study in anticipation and concern. 'Chloe's at a play date, but I don't have long. And, before I forget, can you look after her one Saturday night? Brenda's organising a hen's weekend and wants me to go. Not sure if it's my thing, these days, but I don't have much choice.'

'Of course we'll have Chloe! And Brenda's your oldest friend, so you must go. Just let us know when you have a date. Not that dad and I are likely to be out "on the tiles".'

'Thanks! Now fire away.'

Working hard to keep the story accurate and orderly, I recounted my visit, emphasising the most important detail of all—I did live in Cirencester with Gwen.

Megan shook her head, eyes wide. 'So, what was "The Willows" like?'

I sighed. 'The truth is, there was nothing familiar, not even outside. But if I hadn't gone, the owner might never have mentioned the house next door. Imagine?'

'And the other house?'

'I'm not sure. It could have been a trick of my imagination, but there was something about the garden. It's hard to describe ... warm? Happy? Ralph insisted Aubrey's memories of children and dogs running amok was from a previous time. And it did sound more like the years between the wars. I also had a jolt when I saw a cupboard under the stairs, of all things. There were two, one the perfect size for little children. I think Lucy may have brought me inside to play hide and seek.'

'Whether inside or out, one thing's for sure. Ralph confirmed you played with his sister.'

I crossed my legs. 'Assumed sister. Looking back on it, neither of them said, "daughter." Aubrey believed I was Lucy, then Gwen, which shows how confused he is, poor man. The way it all ended was awful.'

'Did you get any sense of how old Oliver and Lucy were in 1939?'

'Ralph said he was twelve when the war broke out, so the younger boy and girl would've been closer to my age.'

'So, there were three younger ones, you included, and Ralph and his friend. Aubrey's not far wrong about the number of children, is he?'

'And don't forget the dogs. You know I've always been afraid of them, but no one knows why. Gwen and I never had one. Is that relevant?'

'No idea, though if Grandma had been honest about you spending time with other people's pets, it might have helped explain it.' She stared up and away. Something was tugging at the edges of her logical brain. 'So, three boys. You don't suppose...'

'I know where you're going. Did I spend enough time with Ralph, Oliver or Tommy I presumed one of them was a sibling?'

'If you were there for nearly a whole year and saw a lot of them ... I mean, it's possible, isn't it?'

I uncrossed my legs and leant forward. 'Except for the photo, which leads to another possibility. It's far-fetched, I know. Much less probable than what you said just now. But if Aubrey muddled me with Lucy, could he have done the same with Oliver? Forget Ralph and his friend, they were too old, but what if there were four younger boys and girls and not three? Oliver, Lucy, me and my brother? You agreed the garden was full of children?'

She hesitated, reaching to adjust a cushion. 'Did you ask Ralph about another boy?'

'When I couldn't give him a name, he said he couldn't help. Blunt, just like that.'

'Oh, Mum!' Megan's face reflected my pain. 'What about Grandma Baker then? Did anyone meet her or confirm she was there?'

'Not really.' My head grew heavy. 'Come on, what would your statistical brain say?'

She gave the cushion one last pummel. 'Gwen lived in Cirencester in 1939, and people can account for you being there, including the very real chance Aubrey saw you in his garden playing with a dog which might or might not have scared you. They are the facts we can be fairly sure of. Here's the messy part: you didn't get your question answered about who met Kathleen, which is a little strange. Or, it could be a positive thing because it might not be so odd they don't remember your brother, either.'

Megan's mind was like her father's—a steel trap. I broke the tension by crossing to the mantlepiece and returning with the photo frame. 'This is going to sound dreadful, but with Mum gone, I'm less broken up about her than I am about him.' I stroked a finger down the length of the boy's body. 'Though it was great to hear people talking about me, there was nothing tangible about him. It makes me doubt myself.' I spoke to the little boy. 'Were you in the wrong place at the wrong time? Should you have been facing the other way, with your own family? Maybe I caused him to turn around, making a fuss about the kiss. I don't want to believe it, but I'm flipping backwards and forwards, unsure what's true and what's not.' I dropped back into the chair.

'I'm so sorry. Even I got excited earlier. So near, yet so far.'

'Story of my life. Up, then down.'

'So, that was it? Ralph didn't give you anymore?'

'Only what Aubrey said about a girl dying of scarlet fever.'

'I wonder who? I mean, you didn't die. You didn't even catch it, did you?'

'I don't think so, but I suppose I should ask Gwen, after all the other details she's left out of my past. If I caught and recovered from scarlet fever, why hasn't she told me?' I slapped the armrest. 'A person needs to know their medical history.'

'I agree.'

I continued, my body tense. 'What if Mum passed it on to Lucy before we went back to Wales? What if Lucy died too? It would explain Aubrey's distress. And why Ralph didn't want to talk about those years because his little sister had been taken from them. It's so appalling I can hardly bear it. Nearly drove into the back of a truck when that thought came to me.'

Megan gasped, her head bobbing forward. 'Don't scare me! Besides, it's pure guesswork, especially given the source—an old man with memory problems and an unhelpful son.'

'I know. It's like a never-ending nightmare. As soon as I get the pieces to fit, the picture changes.'

'So, what happens now?'

'The only way forward is to talk to Grandma again, which involves admitting I've been to "The Willows." How am I going to do that without dropping Morwen in it? I promised I'd keep quiet. And Gwen's not well. I'm not sure she's up to it.'

'We could at least list the questions, get them straight, in case the opportunity arises. She must know the photo has thrown up questions. She might be more prepared than you think.'

'I doubt it but go on. Where do we start?'

'Nothing about your brother. It'll set her off.'

'Agreed.'

She found a pen and scrap of paper in her handbag. 'Let's stick with the things we know. First, were you evacuated to "The Willows?" We know it's true, but it'll show her you've got information she needs to pay attention to. Next, did you play in the Babbington-Carey's garden? If she says 'yes,' ask about the dog. Were you frightened one day, and if she says she doesn't know, ask if it's possible one of their pets bit or snarled at you? Did you also catch scarlet fever? Why didn't anyone meet your mum? Probably enough to be going on with.' She pushed the note into my hand.

'Thanks, love. I couldn't do this without you. Dad's … you know.'

'I wouldn't if you'd stop, but you won't, will you? In which case, someone needs to keep an eye on things.' Her lip lifted on one side. 'So, Dad didn't twig?'

'Not that I'm aware of. I was late home for a day out shopping, but I said I'd met a friend and lost track of time. He seemed fine but disappointed I hadn't come home with a new dress. Don't tell him, will you? About any of it … including Bevan and Morwen. He thinks carrying on with a search will send me off my trolley.' I raised my palms. 'Honestly!'

Her agreement came with a familiar expression of concern. She glanced at the clock and jerked. 'Oops! Now I've lost track. I said I'd pick Chloe up at four, and it's ten past already.'

'You go, love, and thanks again.'

We both stood.

'Are you positive you want to keep all this from Dad?'

'Absolutely certain.'

She fiddled to locate keys in her huge handbag. 'Sorry, but there's another thing keeps bothering me. How did the photo end up inside the teddy bear?'

I frowned. 'Mum, I guess. She must've put it there.'

'Except there's an obvious flaw. If she left London the day it was taken, where did she get it from? No instamatics in those days. See if you can come up with an explanation. Or is it something else Grandma knows?' She raised an eyebrow.

'I doubt it. She was as shocked as me, and I'm quite sure her reaction was genuine.'

'I'll have to go, sorry. But I'll give it some thought, too.'

She trotted through the front door, turned back to wave and sped down the steps towards her car.

I sank back into my armchair, reflecting on Megan's last question. Part of me bridled at my oversight. I'd never once considered how the photograph had ended up tucked in the teddy bear's waistcoat. Still holding the frame, I examined the scene, comparing it to all the other images I'd seen of those days. Many showed children lined up under makeshift signs, the mustering points for their schools.

I shivered as a theory I'd always discounted, recurred. If I remembered him correctly, my brother was three to four years older than me. School-aged children were evacuated in class groups, a prudent decision given the unbreakable bonds between offspring and their parents. I'd once read the author of the scheme was a hard man who knew mothers, in particular, would be unable to leave their children with a host family if they travelled with them. We might have all arrived in Gloucestershire together, but he'd gone elsewhere with a teacher and his friends. Before the appearance of the photo and my visit to 'The Willows,' I'd swept the suggestion aside. Yet the boy had a label pinned to his jumper containing, no doubt, a name and other details. Had Gwen been right all along? Economical with the truth, but the core of my story unchanged: his teacher had found him a different home with a promise to send information to my mum. But, in the chaos of war, the system had somehow failed. Tears formed.

The front door swung open, and Stephen called a greeting from the hallway. Swiping at my cheeks, I rose and met him in the kitchen, his guileless smile pricking my conscience.

'Hi, love. Good day?' I asked.

'Not bad. You?' His brow creased. 'You're upset. What's happened?' His gaze darted between me and the frame in my hands.

I slipped it face down onto the kitchen table, my resolve firm—I would not, could not, share yesterday's adventure and have him pour cold water over my search again. 'It's nothing. We most probably lost touch because his evacuation was organised by his school.'

Stephen massaged his temple.

'What's wrong? Isn't it a possibility?' I asked.

'Please, Caryl, I don't want another fight. I'm tired. I've had a busy day at work, including a huge meeting about the HIV trial. But, if this idea puts it to bed for you, I'm happy.'

I opened my mouth to speak and slammed it shut. I wanted to hurl the information I'd recently uncovered about my year in Gloucestershire for the satisfaction of seeing his eyes bulge.

A long silence ensued before he straightened, looked at his watch and surveyed the kitchen. Instead of picking and preparing a home-grown salad, I'd been distracted again. 'I fancy fish and chips, do you? You get the plates, and I'll pop down the chippie. The usual?'

I nodded, head bowed. He was gone in seconds.

Pottering from drawer to cupboard, I collected crockery, cutlery, vinegar and various sauce bottles. Returning to the lounge to replace the frame on the mantlepiece, my daughter's question rebounded. How had Mum obtained the photo? I imagined the cameraman at the scenes of evacuation, followed by the printing process, remembering the images were most probably destined for newspapers, not individuals. The idea of photographers giving out their details or taking Mum's seemed impractical. I recalled Gwen had once ordered an official shot taken of me at a local event. It was possible my mother had done the same.

Peering through the curtains to ensure Stephen hadn't arrived back home, I reached for the phone.

Megan picked up after three rings. 'Oh, hi. Busy with dinner, to be honest.'

The words tumbled out. 'Mum could have bought it from the studio in London. Gwen did it once, for me.'

'Did your mum go back?'

'She must have done.'

'Another question for Grandma. But...' I waited for the axe to fall, the proverbial door to slam. 'Sorry, but if she left on the same day, how would she know which studio or even if it was published? Would you get London papers in the country?'

I swallowed hard. 'OK, I'll leave you to it and find the answer to that one.' The gaiety of my answer disguising my plummeting sense of hope.

'Sorry.'

'Yeah, I know. Talk soon.'

Ten

My fingers drummed the steering wheel as I drove to Bryn-y-Maen. Following my call with Megan, I decided I had no option but to approach Gwen. In my favour, her health had remained steady. She was mentally alert and feisty and had no excuse not to answer my questions. Even so, I was edgy. A leaden sky threatening thunderstorms bore down on me. When the cottage loomed, paint peeling, stained orange in places by rusty overflow pipes, it did nothing to raise my mood. I knocked and announced my arrival before letting myself in the back door.

'Up here,' she called, as if she hadn't remained in her room for several months.

'Shall I bring tea?'

'Yes, please. China cups, not mugs.'

When the tray was ready, I climbed the stairs.

'How are you?' I asked as I made my way towards the dresser, taking note of her appearance and manner. Pale, but animated, her hair had been brushed, presumably by one of the nurses. She smelled of lavender.

'Middling to fair.'

'That doesn't sound too bad.'

She huffed, pushing away a folded newspaper. 'Did you know? Our prime minister's resigned the leadership of the Conservative Party to distract us from the business of the European Union. He needs to tell us where he stands. In or out.'

'I'm more interested in the weather. Heatwave soon, apparently, instead of all this rain.'

She snorted. 'Won't bother us here.'

I passed her a cup of tea.

'What's the news?' she said.

'Could I ask you something about the photograph?'

She blinked slowly. 'Go on.'

'I'm puzzled by how Mum got hold of a copy. Did she ever go back to London? Or receive post from there?'

'I don't have the faintest notion. I was as taken aback as you.'

'A trip back home? Did she ever leave me with you for a short while?'

'I don't think so.'

'Letters? Did people write to her? From London?'

'Oh, Caryl, it was so long ago. What do you want me to say? I was working. I wasn't at home all day.'

'I assumed she'd have shown it to you.'

'Clearly not. Finding it the other week was a big surprise. It's not right to keep on like this, poking and prodding, going behind my back.'

I stiffened, calculating her meaning and whether she meant tidying her garage, finding the bear or worse.

She tugged at the edge of the bedsheet. 'Was it worth it? Standing outside a home you're too young to recall?'

Anger surged, loosening my tongue. 'Yes, especially now I know I once lived there. An interesting visit. Not so much your place, but the house next door owned, still owned, by the Babbington-Careys.'

Gwen's lips parted.

I pushed on. 'I met Aubrey and Ralph. I presume you know them because they know you, the Welsh teacher who lived next door and tutored Oliver. Why have you never told me? I don't understand.'

She took a careful sip of tea. 'What did they say about you?'

'Aubrey says I played in the garden with his children and dogs. Could it explain why I'm so scared of them?'

'Sarcasm is the lowest form of wit, Caryl. I never witnessed anything, so I never said.'

'Or you never said because you never wanted to admit living there. Again, why? And frankly, if you were so determined to cover up this period in my life, why not make something up about a dog bite, rather than allowing me to imagine I had an unexplained phobia all these years?'

She began rhythmically pulling at the sheets, her skin draining to putty grey. 'Aubrey would be very old now. In his nineties, I'd say. Did he have all his marbles?'

'Why are you asking? Ralph was there too, don't forget.'

'Mm, Ralph. Nasty boy. Did he grow up to be a nasty man? What did he have to say about his family and friends?'

'I caught them both on the hop, so the situation wasn't ideal. Neither knew if I was genuine, after all. But they both mentioned the younger two, Oliver and Lucy, and Ralph's friend, Tommy.'

'So, lots of children?'

'When I was living there, yes, assuming we can be sure of what Aubrey said.' I wanted to blurt out my hope that Aubrey had missed counting my brother or confused him with Tommy. Caught in a bind, I refused to diminish his testimony.

Unlike Gwen. 'So, he is losing his marbles?'

'You seem determined to undermine him. Why? What are you hiding, on top of this huge admission about living somewhere else first, before coming to Wales?'

'Nothing. Nothing, for goodness' sake. Please stop. You're getting upset. And, for what? It didn't change anything in the end.'

We fell silent. My head pounded. The air outside thrummed with the anticipation of thunder, the room darkening.

Her chin jutted forward. 'I should've told you, and I can see you're shocked. So, I'm sorry. I thought it best. At the end of the day, your mum died, and I took you in. Not out of obligation but because I cared for you.'

My list of perfectly prepared questions froze in my throat. I peered at her dark age spots, the knotty veins. This woman had taken me as her daughter, loved me in her own way, given me a safe and secure home. Despite everything that had happened since finding the photograph, my early childhood memories remained warm. And now she was dying. But I couldn't hold back entirely.

'It's true. I'm not happy you kept so much from me.'

'And, as I said, it meant nothing in the grand scheme of our lives.'

'Again, it's true, but—'

'But what? Tell me?' Her voice was hoarse.

'OK, but is there more? Are there other things you haven't mentioned?'

'Like what?'

'That's just it! I don't know.' I held her eye. 'When you realise someone has, let's say, been selective with the truth, it makes you question if they're keeping other things to themselves.'

'Oh, do stop this. Talk to me like I'm here, for heaven's sake. I'm not one of your difficult parents.'

The change of tone winded me. It took a few seconds to compose myself. I hardly trusted myself to speak.

Gwen shifted in her bed. 'Sorry, sorry. I do hate that way of talking.'

I was again holding the conversational ball, forced into another question when the flow had been lost, interrupted. 'I'm asking if there's anything else you ought to tell me. Not want to tell me, not choose to tell me, but need to tell me for my childhood to be an open book, complete, facts on the table. I can't put it any more plainly.'

Her thin lips pressed together. 'No, there's nothing.'

I sat motionless.

She clasped her hands together. 'Shall we have a top up?'

I rose unsteadily, collected the crockery and made my way to the dresser, holding back sobs I didn't understand, not knowing if I were truly satisfied or simply relieved, I could make no further progress. With shaky movements, I poured milk into cups, followed by tea, the china rattling as I handed over her cup and saucer.

'Thank you.' She took her time stirring. 'Morwen should never have mentioned the job at the girls' school. She phoned me to confess. Eating away at her. You had no right to ask, and she had no right to interfere, though I forgive you both.' She lifted her chin, the benevolent martyr. 'It's what started it all, and it's done neither of us any good at all, has it?'

I clenched my fists, sorry for the dilemma I'd set for a woman who was a friend to us both. 'The photo's what set things off.' A rush of sorrow overwhelmed me. 'I only want to find my brother. It's the first positive sign I've ever had. The business of us living somewhere else led on from there, but for me, it's all about him.' I put down my cup and turned towards her. 'I know you've always told me he doesn't exist, and I know I've never been able to trace him, but he's here.' Pressing a fist against my breastbone, hot tears fell onto my lap. 'It's never gone away.'

Gwen's gaze flicked in my direction. 'I'll say this. I believe you were fond of Oliver, Aubrey's youngest. I suppose if I'd been honest about living at "The Willows," I could've told you sooner. The whole year was so unpleasant, I wanted to pretend it had never happened.' She paused. 'Oliver was a couple of years older than you, so you idolised him, followed him around. When I was tutoring him, you played with Lucy. And the dogs.'

'Thank you.' I pulled a handkerchief from my sleeve and blew my nose, becoming curious about Gwen's interactions with the family. 'What were they like, the Babbington-Careys?'

'Aubrey wasn't there much. Worked in London. Julia was an unhappy socialite, who considered the war a monumental inconvenience to her social life. The younger two children were polite, well-behaved, hadn't lived long enough to become all hoity-toity. But Ralph, he was a snooty gentleman in the making.'

'Aubrey talked as if he was there all the time, playing games with the children, hosting parties.'

'Wishful thinking, I suspect. No, he had an important job in one of the government departments and travelled into London. He only came home on weekends. I presume they had flats for staff who needed to be on-call.'

'And Julia?'

'Hopeless. Swanned around complaining most of the time. Incapable or disinterested in being a parent. All too much trouble for dear Jules.'

'So, the kids were left to their own devices?'

'A lot of the time, yes.'

'Me too?'

'Not if I could help it. I always tried to be there.'

'What about Mum?'

Gwen lifted her cup, then stopped abruptly. 'I'm afraid she wasn't welcome. Working class, you see. Dreadful attitude, but the upper classes are such snobs. English upper classes, mind. But she was glad you had the chance to play with other children, Lucy especially, so I took you over there. And they were happy to see me because I was a teacher and could help Oliver.'

'Poor Mum.' I glanced sideways, imagining her humiliation.

'Quite. I'm afraid the well-to-do weren't always very welcoming. At least they liked you.'

'Even Ralph?'

'He was older, so he was above all the kiddie games and fooling around. Had a nasty streak, though. He could be spiteful to Oliver and once made you cry. I'd come through the hedge to tutor Oliver and didn't see what happened, and Ralph put the blame elsewhere. Something might have happened with you and the dogs. Maybe he teased one of them into snapping or growling. Ralph was a bully, a sulky, secretive child. No friends.'

'Except for Tommy.'

'What did Ralph say about him?'

'Aubrey was the one who mentioned him. Said he'd eaten them out of house and home, but they had to do their bit for England. Ralph told me he was one of his school friends, presumably from a family with a lot less food.'

'Yes. Tall, skinny thing.'

'And Ralph's age or thereabouts?'

'I think so, yes.'

'So, I'd have been in the company of Lucy and three boys, so I suppose … what you said earlier. Megan's suggested it too.' I couldn't say the words out loud—that I'd assumed a sibling relationship with one of these children. It made solid my doubts and shattered my most cherished dreams.

She remained silent.

I searched for a distraction. 'What did Mum say when I came home. Was she cross?'

'Cross?'

'About me crying, that time.'

'Goodness, Caryl. I can't recall her exact words.'

'But she'd have been upset. Probably wanted to go round and have it out with them?'

'I'm sure she was unhappy, very unhappy, on your behalf.'

'If only I could remember.'

'Probably for the best, as I said.'

My jaw clamped tight as I was out-manoeuvred once again. My cup remained on the dresser, cooling. I didn't dare lift it or take a sip.

As I reflected on my conversation with Ralph and Aubrey, an important anomaly surfaced. 'Goodness, I should've asked this first. Did Lucy die from scarlet fever, like Mum?'

Her body twitched. 'Whatever gave you that idea?'

'Aubrey said a girl died. He became very distressed, shouting about germs and disease and—oh, and sending people away.'

'He was probably worried about evacuees bringing infectious diseases with them from the cities.'

'But Lucy? Did she catch it? Did we bring it with us from London?'

'Aubrey's confused. As far as I know, Lucy didn't die of anything. But what happened after we left, I've no clue.'

'But I wasn't the girl he spoke about, so it must have been her, surely. He was distraught. It must have meant something.'

'I have no idea what he's talking about.'

'Did I catch it? Did he assume I'd died when we left for Wales? Or did he ask us to leave because he was scared we'd pass it to his family? Is that what he meant by sending people away? Is that why we came back to Wales?'

'Oh, Caryl. You're rattling me with all these questions.' She thrust her cup towards me. 'You'll have to let me rest. I'm coming over quite dizzy.'

I had no choice but to take her cup, breaking momentum, distracting me again. 'Please, Gwen. Why did Aubrey get so upset?'

'It was nothing in the end, but yes, you caught a mild dose. He was probably worried about it spreading to his children.'

'What? I had scarlet fever, too? Something else you've never told me.'

The tendons in her neck were taut, holding out loose skin like sails on a dingy. 'Because you recovered.'

'But it's important! Was I seen by a doctor? Did someone confirm it?'

'What are you accusing me of? Not caring for you properly?'

'Wasn't that Mum's job?'

'It would've been my responsibility, as host. It was nothing, Caryl, nothing to get so upset about. You were as right as rain in no time. It's your mother you should be thinking about. Your little episode was nothing compared to hers.'

I flinched. 'Please don't throw that guilt at me. Of course, she had it worse. All I'm trying to do is take in another important detail of my life which you promised, not ten minutes ago, didn't exist.' I squeezed my eyelids shut. My mouth went dry. 'Oh, God! Did Mum catch it from me? Was it my fault?'

'No. No. She caught it and died when we returned to Wales. It most definitely was not your fault. Please, stop it.' Her ribcage rose and fell. 'I took you in when I lived in Gloucestershire, not Wales, and not telling you was a dreadful mistake. And apart from your very mild dose of scarlet fever, which I'd almost forgotten about, it's the only thing different. When your mum died here, in Bryn-y-Maen, a billeting officer organised a search for next of kin and when no one could be found, I adopted you. And, whatever you saw in the photo, you did not have a brother.'

I hung my head, unequivocally advised the conversation was over. I tamped down on my rage until I could stand and move away. With a degree of concentration, disproportionate to the task, I loaded the tray and with a few brief words of farewell, I took my leave.

A few moments later, sitting in my car, I put my arms on the steering wheel and wept.

Eleven

Despite the cross words between us, my sense of responsibility and Gwen's decline forced me back to Bryn Cottage. Sitting at her bedside, weighing the scales of our life together, I persuaded myself to halt my bitter questions. Months of relative inactivity had produced the circumstance I dreaded: pneumonia. The wheezes and rasps made me flinch. She agreed to two courses of antibiotics but refused a third. A sign, surely, she was ready to go.

Her downward trajectory had obligingly coincided with the summer school holidays. In jarring contrast to the circumstances inside, the green fields had received their annual abundance of new life, young lambs prancing or sheltering under their mothers' bellies. In the hedgerows, poppies and cow parsley waved their fragile stems. Branches thick with growth made it impossible to evoke their wintry skeletal limbs. I wished she could make it downstairs into the garden, one last time.

One morning, after staying the night, I found her awake and animated.

'Good morning,' I said, yawning.

Unlike the guest room, hers faced the rising sun, and its glow burned through the window coverings.

'It's beautiful outside. Shall I open the curtains first or make some breakfast?'

'A taste of water will do. And you can let in some light, but not too much. Just the left side.'

I did as I was told, pulling on the heavy drapes, which creaked along rusty metal runners, sending a cloud of dust motes into the still air. Beams of morning sunshine lit up one half of the room, leaving her side of the wrought iron bed in shade. Even so, her waxy skin glimmered in unhealthy shades of beige and blue. I handed her a glass, and she took a few sips.

Her brow furrowed. 'You're tired.'

I made a small choking sound. 'That's rich coming from you.' I took the seat next to her.

'Is it being here? You don't have to stay all the time, you know.'

'It's fine. I'm on holidays. Would you like me to read to you? We haven't finished the Antonia Fraser.' I'd found the role reversal difficult to begin with, but reading to her had become a simple, engrossing occupation, removing the need for conversation. In happier times, it reminded me of reading to Megan, passing on all my children's classics to her.

'So why the long face?' she asked.

I hesitated. 'Being with you these last few weeks ... I lost one parent so early on and now...'

'You can say it. I'm dying and won't be here for long.'

I cringed. 'Exactly.'

Her eyes narrowed. 'I've done what I can by making my wishes clear, which is to have a cremation. You won't make me change my mind. I don't want to be buried.'

I gazed at her, deciding she didn't fear death. Gwen had lived a decisive life and would be resolute at its end.

'I know. But I'd like to ask the church if I can place two plaques in the churchyard at Bryn-y-Maen, one for each of you. I should've organised one for Mum years ago, but I was used to the way we mourned her. Placing flowers against the wall and sitting together on the bench ... I didn't need anything more. I assume that'll be okay?'

She sucked a ragged breath that grated and bubbled like a faulty radiator. I leaned over the bed and repositioned the pillows, watching her fight for air, her breastbone sharp against her nightdress. Sweat beaded on her forehead. It took several moments for her to relax.

'Shall I make some peppermint tea? Or do you want me to get a warm towel?'

'Tea ... peppermint tea ... thank you.' Each word and phrase needed its own tortuous lungful of oxygen.

'And can you manage some breakfast? Some porridge?'

'No ... just tea.'

I rushed downstairs, the initial pleasure of seeing her clear-eyed evaporating. The cruelty horrified me as I imagined her slithering down the bed during the night without the strength to turn onto her side.

I filled the kettle and put it on to boil. The kitchen and its chaotic, dusty contents prodded my recollections of one story after another. The time I broke her cut-glass sugar bowl, nearly vomiting with fright, only to be told she'd never liked it. The fancy teapot shaped like a Welsh cottage, a purchase so unlikely I could only ever see her making under extreme pressure. The furniture, dented, scratched and in need of repair, had supported me throughout my childhood as I drew, painted, sprinkled glitter across its surface, filled out homework sheets, read and studied. Lastly, the thick, misshapen goblet—it had insufficient refinement to be described as a cup—I'd fashioned during a spin on the art department's pottery wheel. I had to admire Gwen's tolerance—it was the ugliest thing I'd ever made.

By the time I returned, her cough had subsided. She lay back, staring at the ceiling, drained.

'How long have you been considering plaques?' she murmured.

'Only today. Why? Don't you like the idea?'

'Not really. I mean, is it necessary? I'd rather you scatter my ashes on the hill behind us—as I've asked—and leave it there.'

'We can, too. By the stand of silver birch?'

'Yes, that would do nicely. But not the other.'

'Why not? We need to put something in the churchyard. Paul's there.'

'He's buried, and I'll be roaming the hillside, so no, I don't see the point. Promise me not at Bryn-y-Maen. He shouldn't have been taken from me so soon.' She planted both palms by her hips, attempting to push herself into a sitting position.

'Here, let me help.' Between us, we managed a tiny slide backwards.

'Deganwy. The church there. It overlooks the water.'

'I don't know. Will it be allowed?'

'Try, Caryl. I'm very sure it's what I want if you insist on a plaque. They can be expensive, too. You've never needed one before, for Kathleen. And I'm very against having one for myself.'

'Alright, but in the meantime, I'll make enquiries. You've taken me by surprise.'

'Thank you. Good. I'm glad it's settled. Now, where's my tea?'

Twelve

Megan and I sat on a bench in Bodlondeb Park, pretending the weather was as hot and sunny as the papers had predicted. With bare legs and sandals, we sank into our cardigans, fingers pulled up inside our sleeves. My nose was so chilled it felt like December. Even my clarion cry, 'The sun shines on the brave!' had failed to amuse and she'd pouted in much the same way she'd done as a child, when offered wintry walks in woods or along the nearby shoreline.

From our bench seat, we watched Chloe race from climbing frame to roundabout to rocking horse, her hair a jet stream of curly, brown fuzz. Yelps and screams surged and waned. She'd want a push on the swings soon.

'Kind of weird,' Megan said. 'Why wouldn't Grandma want to be with her husband? Does she have a connection to Deganwy?'

'Not that I know of, but she did say the churchyard overlooked the water.'

'When has she ever bothered about water? Can she even swim?'

I stroked my temple. 'Am I going mad, or is this something else to do with Mum? Why do I have a sneaking suspicion, if I hadn't mentioned the two plaques, one for each, she wouldn't have made a fuss?'

'But why? Unmarked graves are entered into the parish records, so it's reasonable to have some sort of memorial.' She crossed her arms, thrusting her hands under her armpits. 'Grandma Baker is there, isn't she? You've checked?'

I crossed my feet at the ankles.

'Mum?'

'No. Why would I? I took Gwen's word for it. I've never spoken to the vicar or verified the records.' I caught her eye. 'I had no reason to doubt her, but with these new suspicions, maybe I should.'

'Do you want to find out for sure?'

My granddaughter charged towards me. 'Push me, Grandma, pleeeaaase.' Chloe posed, the archetypal supplicant, batting her eyelashes.

Standing, I whispered, 'Theatre studies?'

'Don't joke,' Megan replied, pushing upright.

'It's not a joke. I want a push. Please!' Fully confident we'd do her bidding, she turned and flounced towards the swings, my daughter and I dutifully following.

Megan turned to me. 'Let me go to the graveyard. You've got enough on your plate with Grandma.'

I lifted Chloe onto the seat, pulled it backwards, sending her high in the air. 'You don't believe she's there, do you?'

'Let me help. I'll contact the vicar.'

'Higher!'

I put my weight behind the seat again, pushing hard. If my mother wasn't buried in an unmarked grave in Bryn-y-Maen churchyard, I might scream and never stop.

'Higher!'

I pushed again.

'Hey, steady on. She's only little,' Megan said.

I took in Chloe's near vertical arc. 'Oh, God. Sorry, sorry. Hey, sweetheart, that's enough.'

'No! More. Pleeeaaase.'

'A couple more pushes, then Mum's taking over.'

Once Megan had established a sensible, if unwelcome, trajectory, Chloe startled us by leaping off the seat, landing perfectly and running to the climbing frame, calling to another little girl.

'If only I had her energy,' I said. 'About the grave? Yes, thank you. I don't know if I can face asking the vicar.'

'It's been a horrible few months, hasn't it? You need a pick-me-up. Something uplifting.'

'I can't plan anything at the moment.'

Chloe appeared from nowhere, throwing herself around my knees, nearly toppling me. 'Grandma, Grandma, are you coming back to our house?'

'No, love. Must get home to Grandad.'

She let go, squishing the toe of her sandal into a patch of soft mud. 'But I wanted to tell you something. Mummy's taking me to visit a Welsh school.'

Megan kicked one foot against the other.

I snatched a glance at my daughter before leaning forward. 'How exciting, sweetheart. Tell me all about it afterwards, won't you?'

Chloe nodded and reached for a stick, scoring patterns in the damp earth.

I pulled upright. 'Come on. What's wrong?' I asked.

'Rick's putting pressure on me to say "yes" but I'm not sure if it's the right thing. I don't speak Welsh and he isn't fluent. What do you think?'

'Go for a visit. See for yourself, then decide. Nothing's set in stone. If it doesn't work out, she can always change to another. Kids are remarkably resilient.'

'You went to a Welsh school, didn't you?'

'No choice, in those days. Did their best to turn a Cockney girl into a local. At least Chloe was born here so she's not having something imposed, exactly.'

Making full use of our continuing conversation, Chloe ran off towards the farthest piece of play equipment.

'Oh, God. Look at her. I'll never get her back,' Megan said.

'Come on, there's more.'

'Nothing. Only … this business of a baby, it's causing a few problems. Like I said, I feel I'm being bulldozed into agreeing to his choice of school, almost as if it's a punishment for making him keep trying. I know he wants a baby too, but it's become a kind of chore. Does nothing for the sex life, I can tell you!'

'You should take a break. It's your birthday soon. Could you get away for a night? We're always happy to babysit.'

'Thanks. I'll think about it.'

'On the subject of your birthday, what can I get you?'

'Don't worry about a present, honestly.'

'Come on … you must need something. What about replacing the dressing gown you lost at the hens' weekend? I presume the hotel never found it?'

'No, they didn't.'

'We had such a fun night with Chloe. Keeps us young. I told you she wanted the full sleepover experience, complete with popcorn and two full length videos?'

'Probably had a better time than I did.'

'And Rick's work? How's it going?'

'Yeah, good … actually, maybe not. Have I mentioned the secretive talks? The family's getting more and more worried about the mussel yields, just as new areas might be opening up in the Straits. They'll need money to bid for one of the licences but their income's down.'

'Are all the boat owners having those issues?'

'Not sure. It could be the seeding process or water quality. If the catch was graded A and not B, we'd be rolling in money.'

'It infuriates me our shellfish all end up in Holland and not in our local shops and restaurants. My friend's son owns The Ship bistro and complains about it, too. What will the family do?'

'Take stock, hope for a better yield. I'd like them to bring in an expert, but you know what these traditional worker families are like ... you'd think I'd suggested growing mussels on the moon!'

'Sorry, love. With all this on your plate, are you sure about the churchyard?'

She waved a hand. 'It's no bother. Right then. We'd better be off. Say hi to Dad. Now, where's that girl gone?'

Hollers and waving brought Chloe back beside us. After kissing me on the cheek, Megan bent towards her daughter and whispered, 'Come on, I'll race you to the gate.'

The two galloped away, leaving me to consider her offer to speak to the vicar and the lottery of the outcome. Was it fifty-fifty or less, considering all Gwen's lies? If the situation weren't so serious, I'd have laughed at the idea I was starting to think statistically like Megan.

Thirteen

Gwen passed away in her sleep a week later. Within hours, I was flung into the grim task of arranging a funeral. In the end, Gwen's objection to the plaque at the churchyard in Bryn-y-Maen turned into an irrelevance. We chose a service at the Colwyn Bay Crematorium and were informed that if a brass name plate were chosen, it would be mounted on one of the walls of remembrance within the chapel grounds. Relief flooded me. The prospect of explaining her odd request to an unknown clergy man or woman at Deganwy had filled me with dread.

It turned out to be a busy month for making arrangements, leaving us waiting ten days. In a rush of spontaneity and, I suspected, a longing for the return of peaceful relations between us, Stephen booked a last-minute trip to Paris, departing only three weeks after the service. For him, the sensible option was to begin sorting through Gwen's cottage before we left. For me, it was serendipity; I wanted to see her paperwork.

We set a day to begin, filling the car with the necessities to pack and clean. Sitting in the passenger seat, ready to leave,

Stephen reached across and patted my knee. 'Sure you're up to this?'

I nodded.

He stroked his chin. 'Sorry, but I need to ask—Gwen's paperwork—can we go through it together, please?'

'I'll make a start. If I'm not sure about anything, I'll give you a shout.'

'But—'

'For goodness' sake. It'll mostly be old electricity bills and bank statements.'

'I'd like—'

'What? If you're worried, I'll find something to upset me, I've been on the right track all along, haven't I?'

He sighed noisily. 'Let's go, shall we?'

He started the engine, put the car in gear and reversed out of the driveway.

~ * ~

With Stephen occupied in the garage, I strode towards Gwen's old oak desk, one of her storage places for papers and documents. It had deep drawers on each side, and I began on the left. Unlike modern filing systems, she had constructed a series of dividers from thick cardboard, which despite their simplicity, did a good job categorising the contents. The top edges were labelled, sometimes several times as her system changed and developed.

As predicted, there were sections for electricity, rates, phone, even one for the car she sold to Megan and Rick many years ago. Domestic trivia. I flicked through each pile, retaining the most recent utility bills and other important records.

Towards the back of the drawer, I came across a section titled, 'Caryl.' My insides flipped. A closer inspection revealed old school reports, some early drawings—stick women, yellow suns with starburst rays and neat two up, two down houses—and a selection of home-made Mothers' Day cards. The messages inside, sending lots of love to Mummy, made me wince.

I tugged at the right-hand drawer and found it locked. Searching a nearby mahogany writing box for a key, I came up emptyhanded. Returning, I yanked on the handle again. It stayed stubbornly closed.

I marched upstairs. Gwen's second hidey-hole was her dresser, holding more treasures, and with luck, the desk key.

When the drawer opened smoothly, I let out a whoop. Amongst a jumble of handkerchiefs and scarves, I retrieved several bundles of envelopes tied with ribbon. Inquisitive, I brought them back to the bed.

The first few were from Morwen, the Gloucestershire address neatly inscribed on the front of each. I opened one, reading about her dull life with Alan, reminiscing about her years at college with Gwen and how much she missed her friend. I swallowed. Invading her privacy sat heavily on my conscience. Slipping the envelope back on top of the pile, I paused, curious to know when they'd ended and whether they'd tell me anything about the timing of our return to Wales. Inspecting the chronology, the last was sent in August 1940, tallying with Morwen's understanding that Gwen had worked until the end of the school year. If Morwen hadn't known about our relocation, had she written more, receiving them back with 'return to sender' scrawled across the top? If so, she'd kept it to herself.

I tapped the envelopes on my leg as another thought surfaced. All manners evaporating, I ripped open each one. Morwen fulfilled my every need by commenting on Gwen's news, which began in August 1939. She expressed pleasure regarding the purchase of 'The Willows,' followed by excitement for her friend's new job, empathy for her anxiety in relation to Paul's training as a pilot, sympathy for his loss—November 1939, as it turned out—and, finally, outrage regarding the issue of unpaid wages.

By now, the pages were spread across the eiderdown as I plucked one, then another, turning them back and forth.

Corroborating Morwen's story, there wasn't a single mention of Mum and me. Though I knew it to be true, I had no explanation as to why Gwen had told her we'd arrived in Wales straight from our home in London, between August and December 1940. It still made no sense.

Stephen's footsteps grew louder as he climbed towards the bedroom. 'Caryl? D'you fancy a cuppa or, better still, something cold? I'm parched.' He rounded the corner and pulled up, staring at the array of correspondence.

'Morwen's letters to Gwen,' I said, dismissively.

'Oh.' His brow puckered.

'She's gone,' I said. 'Does it matter if I read them?'

'Morwen hasn't. Besides, why did they write? Haven't they lived here in North Wales all their lives?' He came forward.

My hands clenched, knowing any attempt to hide them would raise the alarm.

He picked up an envelope. 'Cirencester? When did she live there? Oh, 1939.' He glanced up, puzzled. 'Did you know? But hold on…'

Indignation pulsed. 'Exactly, 1939. Strange, huh?'

'I don't understand.'

'And look, through to 1940.' Brandishing another envelope, stabbing at the postmark.

Stephen cleared a space and sat across from me. 'What's this about? Tell me.'

'No!' I shouted, jumping up. I couldn't bear his intimacy, his false appeals. 'I'd rather you broke into the right-hand desk drawer for me. It's locked, and I can't find the key. Let me know when you're done.' I turned towards the dresser, grabbing a single envelope I'd left behind.

'I might damage it.'

'Do you want it? Will Megan or James? No. So, who cares?'

He stood, clenching his fists, before making his way towards the door. 'I'll see what I can do.'

The envelope shook in my grasp. Dropping onto a nearby stool, I studied the outside, plain and soft, as if frequently handled. Inside was a single sheet, folded in three with the title, 'Post Office Telegram,' an image of a crown sandwiched between the first two words.

The introductory lines, 'Dear Mrs Roberts, I regret to inform you...' broadcast its purpose—a death notification for her husband, the war hero I was too young to know.

Mechanic. I re-read the passage. '...served proudly as an aircraft mechanic. The tragic circumstances of his accident and the injuries caused to his passengers when he lost control of his car, will be investigated by the local police...'

The room spun. The howl I'd smothered for so long, broke loose.

Fourteen

'Caryl? Caryl!' The stairs shook as Stephen returned. 'Whatever's happened?'

I thrust the telegram into his hand. '"War hero," she said! Is there anything she hasn't lied about?'

Colour seeped from my husband's face.

I made a sound, halfway between a moan and a sniffle. 'Killed himself and injured others. Speeding? Drunk? Both? But no, he was a pilot. Died heroically in a ball of flames. Everything I believed I knew about him, gone. Just like that!'

'I don't know what to say. I'm as shocked as you.'

'No, not shocked. Not anymore. Did you open the desk?'

'Yes, but...'

I pulled upright, determined. 'Good. Let's see what's in there.'

'I'm not sure this is a good idea.'

Brushing past him, I stormed downstairs to the lounge room, Stephen cantering behind me.

'Have you touched anything?'

'Caryl, stop. Please stop. It's like London all over again.'

'Oh, no. This is facts and figures, not flights of fancy. You should approve.'

'I would if you were calmer. You're worked up, upset.'

I seized the first group of documents. Bank statements. The second—house insurance. Third—her copy of the will. Each sheaf hurled to one side, Stephen dipping and diving, retrieving the sheets landing on the floor.

'Caryl! Slow down.'

Next—pension. I stopped abruptly. 'Here, check these. See if Paul received an RAF allowance.' I shoved the papers at him.

Pushing towards the back—Gwen's exam certificates and teacher qualification.

'Well?' I asked.

'Only for her, from the Education Department.'

'Perhaps the money troubles weren't about unpaid wages but about him losing his entitlements.'

'Unpaid wages?'

Ignoring his question, I delved deeper. Nothing! 'They're not here, are they? My adoption papers. They're not ... bloody ... here!' I turned, my nostrils flaring.

'An absence doesn't mean they don't exist.'

'Always searching for an excuse, aren't you? She stole me, Stephen. With all the lies, I'm certain. She stole me.'

'This is why I wanted to be here for the paperwork.'

'What did you say?' I fired back.

'I wanted to help with these.' He plonked a disorderly pile on top of the desk.

'No, about absence not meaning something doesn't exist.'

He bristled. 'Don't twist my words. You said this was facts and figures.'

'No, you've contradicted yourself. The absence of evidence about my brother has always meant you didn't believe he existed. Do you want to know everything? Do you?'

He wiped a sheen of sweat off his forehead. Seconds passed. 'Can we, at least, sit?'

We moved towards the kitchen in silence. Stephen carried the untidy pile of papers to the table. As we sat and glared at each other, a crow cawed in a nearby tree.

'What d'you mean by "everything"?'

I took a deep breath. 'Let's start with Cirencester. It's where Mum and I went from Waterloo, not here to North Wales.' I explained about the words on the train in the photograph, Bevan's information and my visit to Morwen. 'So, I went. Told you I was shopping in Chester and drove to "The Willows".' His shock produced a twinge of guilty pleasure. 'The lady who lives there couldn't help, but she suggested going next door because the Babbington-Careys were living there during the war. They remembered Gwen and me. And, when I confronted Gwen, she admitted it. She said she pretended it had never happened because her time in Gloucestershire was so unhappy, though I have other suspicions.'

'I can't believe it. Why?'

'Can't you guess? She didn't even tell Morwen, which means something's wrong, Stephen, like I've always said. Gwen gave her the impression we arrived in Bryn-y-Maen late in 1940.' I pointed to the ceiling. 'Not one mention of the two of us living with her at "The Willows," when she wrote those letters up there.'

'What did the neighbour say?'

'It wasn't clear. Gwen says Mum wasn't welcome in the Babbington-Carey house because she was working class, and there was confusion about the children. The older man was hardly there during the war years and has memory problems, and the son was away at school most of the time and didn't want to talk to me.' I gripped my forearms, squeezing hard. 'Gwen lied to me again and again, and none of it helps find him.'

'I can't believe it. It's monstrous.'

'There's more. I caught scarlet fever. A mild dose, admittedly, but I could've passed it on to Mum, even to Lucy, the little girl next door. Gwen insisted I didn't, but what am I supposed to think?'

'Why did she keep it from you?'

'How will we ever know? That's the problem, isn't it? And, if I did give it to Mum, where were we? "The Willows"? Here? Megan's made me question her grave site, too. Convenient it's unmarked, isn't it?'

'Megan? What does she know?'

Heat rose up my neck.

'What, Caryl? Does she know about London? How long have you been involving her?' he whispered.

I held his eye, bubbling with rage. 'Don't you dare blame her! Besides, does it matter? Or is it more important I've had to do these things behind your back because, unlike Megan, you've never given me one iota of support.'

'Since the photo, obviously, so ... before or after London?'

'After! There, satisfied! And, no, she doesn't know about London. I didn't tell her.'

'You promised. You promised to stop.'

'Did I? And was it fair, extracting a promise when I was so out of sorts?'

'Out of sorts? God, Caryl, you were a wreck! That's why I begged you to stop. But you haven't, have you? Worse, you've drawn in our daughter when she's never seen what happens to you.'

I slapped a hand on the table. 'Can't you see I'm upset? Don't you care?'

He stared, teeth grinding. 'Oh, God, you try my patience. So, let me get this straight. She knows about Bevan's trainspotting? And Morwen's correspondence with Gwen? The cross-country jaunt to a house you once lived in? She's been in on all this? Before me?'

'Everything, yes. And she's checking the graveyard records for me.'

He stood and crossed the room. With his back towards me, he leant against the sink. 'I'm so mad I can't find my way out of this.' He hung his head. 'Everything I do for the best gets hijacked.'

I twisted my fingers. 'You've always taken Gwen's side, always. So sure, with your logic and scientific brain. Evidence, evidence. And, without your help, and with every reason to keep trying, which, by the way, made it impossible to keep the promise you forced on me, I discovered Gwen was a gold medal liar!'

Stephen turned back towards me, his cheeks flushed.

I leant forward. 'So, where does that leave my brother? Is he a figment of my imagination? Is Gwen an upright citizen who'd have searched for him, gone after him? Or was he an inconvenience? Maybe she didn't like boys. I don't know what happened, but something did. Something bad.'

'I need time to absorb it all. There must be an explanation.'

'There you go again.' I stood. 'You know what? Cancel the holiday. I'm not in the mood for Paris. The house can wait. I'll do it in my own time.' Would I ever step foot in Bryn Cottage again? 'Take me home, Stephen.'

'Not before we have this out.'

'I'll say something I'll regret.'

He beckoned to the chair. 'Please? Please sit down.'

'I don't want to. I want to go home.'

'Please, Caryl.' His features contorted with agony.

I sank back, shaking, heat leeching from my limbs. 'I'm so angry with you. So angry. You don't know what it's like to be adrift all your life, without a proper family. Your mum and dad were such a big part of our lives, coming to Conwy with us for holidays, being part of the kids' lives. Always there on birthdays to help blow out the candles. Your sister, as well. I've never had that, never.'

Stephen dropped onto a seat. 'I know, love, I know.' After a long silence he looked up, his chest rising and falling in time with mine. 'Can we stop for a moment? There's more than one thing going on here. I am angry about you going behind my back and involving Megan, but I suppose I can see how it happened. It's upsetting to be left out, treated like an obstruction, but my pride's getting in the way. More importantly, it's blurring the seriousness of the things you've just told me. And you're right, I've been lucky to have a close family, and can't really put myself in your shoes. I owe you an apology for that, at least.'

'It's a start,' I murmured, pulling a tissue from a nearby box.

'Will you, can you, tell me everything again, so I can understand it?'

Harsh descriptions of facts gave way to normal tones as I went through the story a second time, adding details and context in all its deceptive horror. Stephen sat motionless, listening attentively, asking the occasional question.

At the end, he pushed back in his seat. 'I'm stunned. I had no clue Gwen could be so dishonest. She's had me fooled all these years. I'm sorry, Caryl, believe me. I assumed I was a better judge of character.'

Vindicated, I was too exhausted to engage in further warfare.

He lifted the sheets, tapping them into a neat pile. 'Let's finish up, take home anything important and go through it together. And I'll cook tonight. Anything you like, your choice. I also want to see the photo again. I mean, why didn't I notice the words on the carriages?'

'You weren't expecting anything to change the story she'd always told you. Blinded, I guess.'

'Must have been. My world has shifted. I can't imagine what it's been like for you.'

My heart slowed its frenetic pace. 'It's come in dribs and drabs for me, not all at once. One individual shock after another. And the worst of it is, I'm no closer to finding him.' I searched

Stephen's expression for a challenge, a doubt. The muscles around his eyes twitched, a nervous tick I knew only too well.

'What shall I do? Collect the letters and put them in one of those file boxes?' he asked.

'Yes, thank you.'

'I only ever wanted to protect you from disappointment, you know that?'

'Worked wonders, hasn't it? Sorry, sorry.'

His body slumped. 'You've changed my opinion about Gwen, if it helps.'

I gave a soft snort. 'Part way there.'

We sat in silence, hostility swirling. As much as I wanted to, I wasn't ready to forgive. Too many years of resentment stood in the way. 'One apology isn't going to fix this, Stephen, but we're not achieving anything by staying here. I'm beginning to hate this place. Let's get this done and get home. We both need time.'

He picked up the file box and disappeared upstairs from where I caught a strangled sob of frustration.

Fifteen

The crematorium service over, family and friends spilled out onto the forecourt or took shelter under a nearby tree, before those staying took refreshments in the adjoining community room.

'Okay, love?' Stephen asked.

'Cried more than I expected to, after...'

'Yes, she had a lot to answer for.'

I wanted to fire back—so do you—but bit my tongue. Forced to change long-standing beliefs, he'd apologised many times since the day at Bryn Cottage.

'I suppose it's the finality of death, needing to publicly eulogise a whole life, not only the final weeks. With everyone here today from town, old teaching colleagues, friends ... my feelings are so confused, because all these people see her as an upstanding member of the community. I'd have said the same before I found the photo. What would they say if they knew?'

He shrugged.

I couldn't help noticing the parallels with Stephen. The lesson, it appeared, was to see my husband as a complete, flawed, human being.

James and his girlfriend Elle approached, on edge. I guessed they wanted to leave but were embarrassed to ask. I gave them my blessing, accepted a quick peck on the cheek from my son, before watching them take the path to the car park.

'Could have stayed for a cuppa,' Stephen grumbled.

Megan and Rick were next. My daughter linked her arm with mine. 'Lovely service, Mum. Beautiful flowers and she'd have appreciated the Treorchy Male Voice Choir.'

'Thanks, love, I know.' I put a hand on Stephen's arm. 'You've all been wonderful. I couldn't have done it without you.'

A stooped figure took careful steps onto the tarmac ahead of us, supported by her son. 'It's Morwen. Give me a sec.'

As I moved closer, her chaperone excused himself.

'Caryl. Beautiful service and I love hearing, "Gwahohhiad." Always makes me weep. Gwen would be so proud. Magnificent turn-out and having all of you here, her family. She treated you as her own, you know. I don't think Cirencester made any difference at all.'

Words stuck in my throat, as much for the liberties I'd taken with her letters, as her assumptions.

'I'll go to my grave wishing I hadn't told you.'

I grabbed her hand, causing her to wince. Apologising, I held her gaze. 'You've nothing to regret, I promise. Now, will you stay for tea and cake?'

'Did it, though? Did it put a wedge between you? Gwen hardly spoke to me these last weeks.'

'Not at all. She simply couldn't stand being caught out.'

'Are you sure?'

'Absolutely.'

A car pulled up beside us and her son helped her inside. I waved and beamed as it pulled away, anger bubbling again towards the woman who was at the root of all the lies, including the one I'd just told to a good friend.

~ * ~

Two weeks later, on one of the last days of the month, my husband, Megan and Rick accompanied me to the hillside behind Bryn Cottage. The crisp air smelt fresh, a day for bright summer-weight clothes. The stand of birch trees glistened in the sunshine, light reflecting off their silvery trunks, grey green leaves rustling in the gentle breeze.

Megan, dark patches under her eyes, was swathed in a large cardigan. Chloe had been deemed too young to attend the cremation, and we all agreed this last ritual would be difficult for an inquisitive pre-schooler. None of us could bear the idea of explaining how Great-grandma had ended up inside an urn. Once we'd arrived near the copse and complimented the beautiful location, expectation weighed on me. I hesitated.

'Are you ready?' Stephen asked.

'Give me a minute.'

'Take your time.' He handed me the container, a ghastly plastic Grecian replica.

I looked at my husband, then my daughter. 'Should we say something?'

'Up to you, Mum,' Megan replied.

'I'm not sure I can.'

My husband stepped forward. 'I'll do it. You concentrate on those.'

His words hung in the stillness as I tipped out a cloud of grey ash, sufficiently weightless to drift on the breeze. We stood in silence, rooted to the spot.

'A good end, love. You did well,' Stephen said.

A burst of fury fired inside me as I surveyed the remnants of her body, her secrets gently buffeted by the wind. My skin cooled. I took an unsteady step forward, craning my vision towards Bryn-y-Maen, another place of remembrance.

I clutched Megan's hand. 'Have you seen the records? It's been ages.'

'Please, this isn't the time.'

'Did you?'

'Can we talk about this later?' She peeled my fingers off her wrist.

I watched Rick turn and step away.

Stephen came up at my side. 'Caryl? What's wrong?'

'Nothing. Sorry. It's nothing.'

'Whatever this is about, let's get this over with and lay Gwen to rest,' he pleaded.

My anger exploded. 'What about my mum? Is she at rest? Did she get all this?'

Stephen froze.

My daughter stepped towards me. 'She's here—in you. And I'm part of you, part of the bloodline. And with Chloe, that's four generations.' She turned to her husband. They exchanged tiny nods. 'I wanted to wait until this was over, but ... perhaps it's the right time. We hope, we think, the fourth generation might be about to get bigger.'

I gasped. 'A baby? You're pregnant?'

'Early days, but yes.'

I rushed forward to hug her. 'Oh, that's fantastic, darling. Wonderful! I'm so pleased for you.' I pulled back and reached towards her husband. 'And for you too, Rick. Marvellous.'

My son-in-law blushed and beamed. 'Yeah, thanks. Bloody proud of ourselves, to be honest.'

Stephen shook his son-in-law's hand and slapped him on the back before embracing his daughter, kissing her lightly on the forehead. It was a miracle, a happy miracle.

I held back tears, making a deliberate choice to revel in this surprising and emotional news. Rummaging in my pocket, I found a tissue, and turned to my stricken family. 'It's ... everything. Sorry. I'm so happy for you both.'

Megan laid her arm around my shoulder and squeezed. 'I know. We understand. A death, a birth ... all we need is for someone to move house, and we'll have the full trifecta!'

I snorted. 'James, probably, with all his wheeling and dealing.'

'Sounds spot-on,' Rick said.

'So, when, love?' I asked, dabbing my cheeks.

'April sometime. I'm not sure of my dates, but it's fine. They'll work it out as things progress.'

I hunched my shoulders and clasped my hands. 'A new year, a new baby. I like the sound of that.'

'Early days, though. A long way to go before I'll let myself get excited. Don't say anything to anybody, please. Not yet.'

'I'll keep everything crossed for you both. Are you feeling okay?'

'Not the mornings, no, but I'm usually better by this time of day.'

'I thought you looked tired. Take it easy, love, won't you? Does Chloe know?'

'No! Definitely not. It wouldn't be fair, you know, if...'

'I'll keep quiet. This is such good news. Come on. Back to ours. I've a mountain of food waiting.'

~ * ~

The dining room hummed with relaxed conversation and shouts for top-ups of food and drink. With our duties over, the sense of release was palpable, my outburst forgotten or overlooked by my family. I tried my best but couldn't entirely disregard my inner turmoil.

New plans for our trip to Paris were eagerly discussed, and Stephen diligently described our proposed itinerary, flights, accommodation and daily schedule. Megan and I held a sidebar about her vision for a new nursery.

Rick collected Chloe from his brother's house, and we welcomed her back into the fold, the inevitable centre of attention.

But my focus regularly flew to my daughter, her exchange of glances with Rick, her downcast demeanour. I'd been anxious, too, during my first weeks of pregnancy and sympathised with her concern. Megan was carrying all our hopes.

Worried about her vulnerable state, when we cleared away the first course, I steered my son-in-law into the kitchen to gently enquire about the family business.

'I hope I'm not interfering, but Megan mentioned a few things about your work. How's everything going?'

'It's fine and not a secret. We've some serious decisions to make.'

'She said there are new licences on offer. Will you bid on them?'

'We have to if we're to survive. But we can't afford it with our current overheads, mind. Something needs to give.'

'Boats?'

'More likely people. One of us will have to step aside and find another job.' Rick sighed. 'It's all I've ever known from being a nipper, but if I get something land based, Megan will be happier.'

I struggled over whether to offer an opinion.

He watched my torment. 'Go on, she's said as much to you, hasn't she?'

'It's true, she worries.' My words offered a poor representation of her detailed risk assessments based on tides, weather and the distance Rick travelled from the river mouth. 'What would you do if you gave the mussel farming away?'

'Might skill up and learn to do the freighting. Get my HGV licence. There's an opening, currently, if they'll wait.'

'I'm so pleased. Sounds as if things are looking up.'

'The baby, new work and deciding against the Welsh school. I reckon we're tidy.'

Megan appeared in the doorway. 'You're taking your time. Can I help?'

'Perfect. Here, take these cupcakes for Chloe, please.'

We retook our seats, and Stephen launched in with a recap of the current political situation. 'Can't say I'm unhappy about Major regaining the party leadership. Smart move, something I can support. But will he stand up to the Europeans? The waste and regulation! Sticks in my gullet.'

Megan squirmed. 'Dad! Do we have to?'

'Megan's right. I don't want to discuss politics today,' I said.

Rick eyed his daughter, who was relieving a cupcake of its white icing, peeling it off with single-minded determination. 'Hey, Chloe! Ych a Fi. What are you doing?'

'It's not disgusting. I only like pink ones.'

'They all taste the same.'

She cocked one eyebrow, the author of her own opinions, and continued to pluck at the sticky fondant. 'Is Great-grandma in heaven?'

'Yes, she is,' we chorused.

'She went there from her house, didn't she? Mummy said. Except Great-grandma's house is a cottage.'

'Yes, darling,' I replied.

'Are there pink cupcakes in heaven?'

'Anything anyone could ever want,' I said.

'Like buckets of Smarties?' She stuffed the sponge in her mouth in two handfuls.

'Anything, sweetheart,' Megan said. 'Do you want to get down? Come on. Let's get you clean, and you can do some drawing.' She helped Chloe off the dining chair and led her towards the kitchen.

The conversation moved on, though I sensed Stephen's annoyance at having his topic scuppered. Rick unwittingly saved the day by commenting on the new vaccination for chicken pox, a subject which reversed the tide and gave Stephen ample opportunity to hold forth on his first love, medical research and innovation.

I listened as the men bemoaned the hiatus in the soccer timetable and their hopes for the next season. For all the cosy cheer, I couldn't help brooding on why Megan was holding back on her enquiries at Bryn-y-Maen Church.

Sixteen

With the dishwasher loaded, Rick, Megan and I headed into the lounge and sank into our habitual seats. Stephen remained in the kitchen dealing with a bulging rubbish bag. Megan yawned.

'You're tired, love. Don't overdo it. It's been a big day, one way or another,' I said.

'Yeah, I am. We'll be off soon. I'll see what Chloe's up to.' She made to push herself back up again.

With a movement akin to a police traffic officer, her husband thrust an arm sideways, barring her way. 'No, you rest. I'll go.'

On cue, my granddaughter skipped through the door and launched onto Rick's lap.

'Steady, Eddie,' he said.

She turned to him. 'I'm not Eddie. I told you.'

'What do you have there?'

'Oh, these are for Grandma.' She slid off his lap and came towards me, brandishing three sheets of paper covered in drawings.

'Super. Bring them here,' I said.

She laid them on the table in a line. 'So, this is Great-grandma in heaven, drinking tea.'

I smothered a laugh.

'What? She always drank tea.'

'Yes, she did. You're very clever to have noticed. She'll be glad there's a big pot up there.'

Chloe pointed to the next one, frowning. 'Oh, I did it the wrong way round. This is Great-grandma going to heaven from her cottage. This one should have come first, sorry.'

'Doesn't matter at all. And it's exactly like her house, so, well done.' A figure floated upwards from a home looking surprisingly like Gwen's.

'Cottage, Grandma.'

I picked up the third. 'Is this her, too?'

'No, that's Kathleen.'

I gasped. Had someone told Chloe my mum's name? We'd agreed to explain my adoption when she was older. Had it been brought forward by Gwen's death?

Megan gaped, diving forward, scooping Chloe up and away from me. Reaching forward, I was too slow to catch my granddaughter.

'Time to go. Where are your shoes?' Megan said, turning to Rick, seeking his assistance with a pointed glare.

Chloe wriggled against Megan's iron grasp. 'But I haven't told Grandma about Kathleen.'

My daughter threw me an anguished look, her neck red and blotchy.

I returned Megan's gaze and beckoned Chloe back to my side. 'Tell me quickly.' A sound like thunder roared in my ears. 'Tell me about Kathleen.' I looked again at the drawing, a figure alone in empty space.

Chloe leaned into me, her warm body pressing against my rigid torso. 'Mummy's very worried about her because she doesn't have a house. And, if she doesn't have a house, she can't get to heaven, can she?'

Megan and Rick froze.

'I'm not sure what you mean, love,' I said.

'Mummy told Daddy Kathleen has no grave, which must be another name for a house, mustn't it? Look, she doesn't have one, or a cottage like Great-grandma.'

My hands shot to my mouth. Chloe had interpreted her mother's words in a way that made sense only to a child. For the rest of us, the implication was clear. Kathleen had no grave. She wasn't buried in the churchyard at Bryn-y-Maen.

'Oh, God, I'm sorry. I didn't know she'd overheard,' Megan said.

Rick stood and gently pulled Chloe away, whispering quiet instructions to find her shoes.

I folded like a broken umbrella. Stephen appeared in the lounge room doorway and asked, 'Everyone alright?'

Chloe's little voice wobbled. 'What's the matter with Grandma?'

'Nothing, darling. I'm a little tired. The drawings are lovely.'

'Off so soon? I thought we'd all have a cuppa, first,' Stephen said.

Megan pushed off the sofa and knelt by my side. 'I'm so sorry,' she whispered, before turning to her father. 'Chloe's blurted something about Kathleen. It wasn't the way I wanted you both to find out, obviously. God, what a mess. It was the other thing I planned to tell you later. It felt wrong, today, on top of everything else.'

'What news?' Stephen's colour drained. 'Is this about the gravesite?'

I bolted upright, as disbelief rocked me. 'Is it true?'

'Yes, sorry,' she murmured.

'So, no brother and no mum.'

'She has to be somewhere. You didn't appear from nothing,' Megan said.

'What about Gloucestershire? Could she have died there?' I asked.

'I don't think so, sorry. I phoned several churches in Cirencester.'

'So, nothing? Absolutely nothing?'

'Everything hinges on where a death was registered, particularly the district name. If we had that, it may be possible to get a death certificate from the General Registry Office.'

Stephen came to my side. 'So, not the National Archives?'

'No, apparently,' Megan said.

He rubbed my arm.

I threw my head back, jaw rigid. 'We sat there, in the Bryn-y-Maen churchyard, at least twice a month.'

A howl from the next room pierced the white noise in my head. 'Is Grandma going to die as well?'

Chloe's words jolted me into the present—a confused granddaughter, but most of all, a distraught, pregnant daughter.

I breathed deeply and forced a smile. 'Enough excitement for one day. It's nothing I didn't expect, so no harm done, I promise. I was expecting this after the hoo-hah with the brass plates. Chloe did us a favour. Tell her I love her drawings.'

My husband and daughter exchanged puzzled glances.

'It's a big thing, though, isn't it?' Megan replied.

'Like I said, it doesn't surprise me after all the other lies Gwen told. It made sense as soon as you questioned it. I'm used to it already, really I am.'

Stephen peered at me. 'You're taking this very well.'

I waved a hand, dismissing their concerns. 'Practise, I'm afraid. Now, get yourself home, love, and off to bed. I'll phone tomorrow and we can have a long chat.' Standing on jelly legs, I gave Megan a hug and a kiss. 'Such marvellous news about the baby. It's made all the difference. All this other stuff is water off a duck's back, in comparison.'

Megan hesitated, anxious. 'Alright. If you're sure. Speak soon. Let me know if you need any help getting ready for your trip.' She turned and followed Rick and Chloe to the car. I went with them to wave goodbye.

When I returned to the lounge, Stephen was staring out of the window, rhythmically rubbing his palms backwards and forwards across his scalp. He beckoned me forward, enclosing me in a hug.

'Are you sure you're alright? Because I'm not. I've had time to think things over and although we've known Megan was checking, I never believed it would end like this.'

'Didn't want to upset her any more than she is already. Kids, eh? Out of the mouths of babes.'

'But how are you feeling? Deep down?'

I shrugged. 'It's partly true what I said about not being shocked. As soon as Megan asked about the burial records, something told me I'd been duped by that, too. But it will take time to get used to, not having a grave for my mother. She's nowhere, exactly like Chloe's picture. Did you see it? Did you see what she drew? A figure floating in empty space.'

Stephan nodded. 'Megan's right, though. She has to be somewhere.'

The emotion I'd held back to save my daughter, erupted. I let out a volley of gulping sobs. Breaking free, I stumbled across the room, took the photograph off the mantlepiece and clasped it to my chest.

Stephen guided us both to the sofa and turned to face me. 'When we were at Gwen's, and you told me everything you'd found out, like the lie about Gloucestershire, I didn't know what to think. As you said, Gwen told you it hadn't changed anything, and when I thought about it afterwards, at first, I tended to agree. Then there was the lie about you catching scarlet fever, which seemed strange unless you did pass it on to Kathleen, and Gwen wanted to protect you from knowing and feeling guilty. But this? The business of the unmarked grave? I can't forgive her.'

I gulped, releasing a hand to squeeze his.

'And, if we go back to the beginning, there's the photo of you with an older boy and all the certainty you've always had. You made me see the possibility, which is why I said we'd try again. But the thing is, love, you and I have searched, going way back to our days in Manchester when we bunked off to go to Kew Gardens. We couldn't find you and your mum with both your names, never mind a brother without a first. And, on the subject of names, you know I've always questioned the spelling of yours. Caryl with a "y" is Welsh, not English. You believed Gwen did it to help you blend in, but what if it's more than that? What if she changed other details, too? I mean, what extra hope do we have, when we know she deliberately covered her tracks? It's late in the day to come to that conclusion, but I really believe she has. Not in a small way, either.'

He stroked my hand. 'And we couldn't find your adoption papers, either, to verify your family circumstances. I know I made a promise, but to tell the truth, I'm petrified. It's hard to admit I made a mistake by not trusting your instincts, but I'm also damn sure, if he is out there, you'll never find him. Her behaviour these last few months has convinced me she was exactly what you said, a gold medal liar. She did everything to ensure you had no-one but her. I mean, even something straightforward like Paul's profession. What possible reason did she have for changing it except to be a social climber? Pilot indeed.'

'So, that's it? We give up?'

'No. Let's go to Paris and when we come back, we give it one last shot. Together. And, if we get nowhere, we let it rest. What do you say? Can you agree if we give it everything?'

107

I took a sharp breath. 'What if he's already dead? I'm frightened if I wait or agree to stop, I'll jinx myself. What if I'm too late?'

'Come here.' He pulled me into an embrace. 'We can't let ifs and buts stop us. One step at a time, eh? You've got Megan and me to help you.'

'He might have family, mightn't he, if he's gone? If we never meet, I'd be happy to know he'd once been with me, part of my family. Would it be enough?'

'I don't know, sorry.'

'And us? Will we be okay after everything that's happened?' I whispered.

'Paris? A new grandchild? We'll be alright, love, I know we will. And don't forget the ball on Saturday. I'm so proud of you, for your work with the orphans of war. Doing good to cancel the bad done to you. And we can dance away our worries, can't we? Will you, please, with me?'

I melted into his arms, aware of his heart hammering against mine.

Part Two

Seventeen

'Here are your desk and computer, Megan. And a few folders to get you started. When you're logged on by IT, I'll discuss your role and show you how our system's set up. There are some reference books and hard copy files on the bookshelf which might help orientate you to the organisation. Take your time. We're not expecting too much from you straight away.'

My new supervisor, Lesley, walks back to her office. She's young, uptight. Rays of insecurity radiate off her. I know what it feels like. I was once the young, bright star given responsibility for older workers. Rick's well-wishes and the phone calls from the girls come flooding back, lifting my spirits and confidence. I tell myself I'm a bloody good worker, team player or manager, depending on the situation. If necessary, I'll mount a charm offensive.

I pick up a cardboard folder with '70th Year Commemoration' emblazoned across the top, along with a date, September 1st, 2009, and location, St Paul's Cathedral, London. A quick glance inside reveals details of a service to commemorate seventy years since the first evacuations from London at the outbreak of World War II. I inhale sharply. My parents attended this event hoping to bump into my lost uncle, or anyone who might know him. It resulted in another disappointing dead end. I'm catapulted into Mum's life and story, and the awkward conversation we had when I told her about this job.

'Is this the charity we all joined in, what, 1996?' Dad asked.

'Yes,' I replied.

'The one I phoned and spoke with a very blunt woman? What was her name? Betty something or another?' Mum said.

'She probably didn't want to raise your hopes. I'm sure she was telling the truth when she said the charity had almost no information at the start. But she did put you onto the newsletter with the personal column.' The bi-annual newsletter contained a message board for people trying to contact lost family or friends. Despite repeated publication of her story, stalling as time and her own despondency wore on, she received no reply from her brother or anyone else.

'I thought we'd put this behind us, Megan,' Dad said, his voice firm. 'We both helped Mum after Gwen died. We brainstormed every avenue, turned every stone and all for nothing. Sorry, Caryl, but it's true, isn't it?'

Mum nodded; head low.

Dad had turned towards her, pained. 'I always assumed you were satisfied; we'd done our best.'

'I am, truly. Let's be honest, Gwen won.'

A long, tense silence followed.

Having already accepted the new position, I craved their acceptance, if not approval. 'It's only for eight months. I was tempted to say nothing, but we promised, didn't we, never to keep secrets?'

'Bit of a coincidence, isn't it, getting a job with them?' Dad said.

'Not particularly. There's a Facebook page these days. I joined up a while ago, so news of the project appeared in my Newsfeed.'

'But why take it?' he continued. 'Especially if it's temporary.'

'I need a change. I know I haven't said much, but I was very unhappy at my last workplace.'

He grunted. 'And what does Rick say?'

'Dad! I'm a grown woman. I can make my own decisions.' My husband's reaction, in truth, had been mixed.

Dad spoke to Mum again. 'You sure you're happy with this?'

She blinked and exhaled. 'It never goes away even if we don't talk about it or do anything, anymore. So, what difference does Megan's new job make?'

'But won't it get your hopes up?'

'No more than being a member of the charity. Those newsletters and the personal column, they're all online now, aren't they? He could still see my message ... one day.'

Dad's mouth hung open. I guessed he'd never realised she was still harbouring those dreams. 'I don't want anything upsetting you, what with ... you know.'

'Do stop fussing, Stephen. The doctors are taking good care of me. I'm much more excited about Lara's wedding than this.'

He'd held my eye, assessing the obvious paradox. Any excitement might set her heart on a dangerous gallop, yet this could be our last chance. 'I suppose, if your Mum's fine with it...'

He wasn't happy, not really, and followed up with a private phone call to warn me against sharing anything that wasn't rock solid. Totally unnecessary, but fair enough.

I return to the folder on my desk. Another sheet, a media release, encouraged members to contribute to the day either by attending the service or writing to the charity with stories of their lives as evacuees. Next, several typed pages detail memoirs from survivors of the great wartime scheme. Some are long and comprehensive, some short and succinct, though length doesn't appear to correlate with the tone. Scanning the shorter ones, I read both happy and sad experiences. At the bottom, a large envelope contains acceptances for the invitation to the commemorative service and a pile of photos taken on a September day eleven years ago—coloured images of women and men of my parents' generation, dressed smartly, chatting as they congregated on the steps of Wren's magnificent cathedral. I search for Mum and Dad, but they must have failed to catch the photographer's eye. With the materials spread in front of me, my role begins to take practical shape. Digitally recording and organising these documents is a priority for the charity and sparks my love of wrangling order from chaos.

Drawn to the books and larger files, I cross the room, taking in the view outside. The address I was given for the interview suggested a bleak industrial estate, not a converted Victorian house in a rural setting. The exterior is traditional red brick, four large bay windows and a date stone bearing the year 1899. The house is divided into four with two not-for-profit ventures on each level, the charity leasing the left half of the upper floor. Internal walls have been removed to create larger office-style spaces, but the black and white tiles in the hallway, some of the wood panelling, and several fireplaces have been retained. My desk is positioned along the exterior wall, facing inwards, close to sash windows which face west over farmland and wheat fields. Only one downer: coffee outlets are non-existent. Cravings are already taking hold, and I long to visit the kitchen to check out the facilities.

Turning, I notice the young woman Lesley had swept past earlier, with only a quick introduction. Presumably the charity's receptionist, she wears a headset and operates a complicated phone console. Her desk is turned towards the wall. Even from across the room, I can tell she has 'the gift of the gab.' Her body moves with the rhythms of her speech, her dark brown ponytail swinging and bouncing.

I return with a box file containing a pile of original handwritten letters sent by evacuees. Glancing over a few, taking note of ages and destinations, my sneaky mind examines the pages for any mention of Cirencester, the place Mum was first sent. I find other placenames in the Cotswolds but no mention of that particular town. What would Lesley say if she knew I was distracted by these personal matters on my first morning?

Caught out by a sudden arrival, I scoot forward, holding my pencil upright, eager to appear sharp and serious.

'You don't have to stand on ceremony for me.' The young woman I had seen earlier, thrusts her hand forward, a grin playing on her lips. 'Erin Hardcastle, pleased to meet you. You must be Megan?'

'Yes, Megan Williams.' I grab her hand, the fingers delicate and cool.

'I've been here a while, so if I can help, let me know. I can show you where the loos are, at least.' Her grin transitions into a blush. She has a sweet, heart-shaped face and bright blue eyes, like Lara, and around the same age.

'What's your role here?' I ask.

'Membership, mostly, and logging material for the archives.'

'Did you know a lot about the organisation before you took the job?'

'Very little. You?'

'I'd come across it before, yes.'

'We didn't even get taught about this stuff at school, so it was all new to me. What has Lesley asked you to do? The data management job?'

'Yep, I've done this sort of work before.' From what Lesley told me at the interview, the charity runs on worthy intent, without ever having the resources to impose order on their valuable materials. I'm positive with my eye for systems and detail I can make good on the trust they've placed in me.

'Mm, good luck. I suppose they want it all digitised?'

'I believe so. It'll be quite a job if they've never made a start.'

'They have a spreadsheet for membership.'

'Glad to hear it!'

'I've read some of the letters, the good, the bad and the ugly. What I find impossible to believe are the ages. So young! Some never made it back to their families.'

'I've heard that, too. Grim.'

'Others were adopted and did well. They say they probably did better than being returned to a bombed-out London. There are stories filed in those binders.' Erin points to the bookshelves.

'Thanks.' I'm acutely aware of the impact of adoption, of course.

'Are you logged in yet?'

'No, that's my next task.'

She turns sideways, tilting her head towards a private, partitioned office space. 'I can see Lesley watching us, so I'll get on. Come and get me when you want lunch. I'll show you the kitchen, though don't get your hopes up. I usually stop around twelve-thirty.'

'I will. Thanks again.'

I have an unexpected ally.

Eighteen

Erin's warnings about the kitchen are accurate. The room is stark and unwelcoming, filled with mismatched old furniture—a Formica table and pockmarked cork boards which appear to have been attacked by voracious insects. I catch a smell of decayed food and damp. Worse, no coffee machine in sight. I'll need to bring a plunger from home.

'Are you local?' I ask.

'Yeah, I live at home with my horrible brother. You?'

'About half an hour's drive away, in Bebington.'

'A bit posh, isn't it?'

'Not where we live. And not when we moved there, either. We've two girls and they were only little, then. We needed to be near Liverpool for my husband's job, so we took what we could afford.'

'What does he do?'

'Rick's a lorry driver. Got his heavy goods licence.'

'And the girls? Are they still at home?'

'No. Chloe's a nurse at the Sheffield Children's Hospital. She's the eldest. And Lara's an apprentice interior designer. What does your brother do? Is he older or younger than you?'

'Do? Don't make me laugh! Does slobbing on the couch for hours playing video games count? Jason's younger, seventeen. Left school last year and done bugger-all since. I try to spend as little time at home as I can.'

'Hobbies? Boyfriend?'

She blushes. 'Yeah, Luke, though I'm beginning to think he's a waste of space, too. I want to move things on, but he's not ready. Needs to "man up".'

'Chloe and Darren are the same. Been together for years but no sign of marriage. Lara and Felix, though ... my baby's tying the knot this summer. We're going dress shopping soon.'

'Wow!' She frowns. I suspect she's calculating my age. 'You don't look old enough.'

I thank her for the compliment, embarrassed but ridiculously flattered.

She continues. 'Does it mean your parents lived through the war? Were they evacuated? Is that how you know about this place?'

Smart cookie. It takes only a beat for me to choose a harmless white lie. 'No, they grew up in Manchester not London.' It's Dad's childhood story of living through the war period with his parents and sister, not my mother's.

'Only I wondered if...'

My phone vibrates in my pocket. Chloe. I point to the screen. Erin nods and begins washing her plate and cutlery.

'Hi, love. Can't talk for long. My lunch hour's nearly over.'

'Sorry. Wanted to wish you well for today. I only got home from night shift a minute ago. Held up by an emergency.'

'Thanks. It's going well so far. I'll tell you more when I see you next, once I've settled in.'

'Is Grandma coming dress shopping? Or is it too much for her?'

'She'd love to, but I think she's anxious about the long journey and a busy day, on top of all the medical appointments she's been to recently. I expect Grandad's had his say about it as well.'

'Bummer. Bet Dad wants to be there, too. The proud father?'

'Uh-huh. Talks about it all the time.'

'Thinking of Grandma and Grandad, d'you know if they've had their flu shots this year?'

'Yes, why?'

'Don't spread this around, but there's something happening overseas. A new virus, like SARS?'

'Will the flu shot protect them?'

'No-one knows for sure, but it can't hurt. The senior doctors are being called into meetings, so it must be something big. Anyway, it's business as usual my ward.'

'Glad to hear it. Let us know if you find out more, won't you? Sorry, but my boss wants to see me in about two seconds. Don't want to get off on the wrong foot.'

'Good luck and see you soon.' The call ends.

Lesley stands at the door to her office, inspecting her watch before beckoning me to join her. She's tall, slender with a neat bob and impeccable business attire. I smooth my trousers and hair, uncomfortable both styles are a decade out of step. Grabbing a pen and pad, I enter her private domain, the top half glass, the bottom solid. The room is immaculate with a modern desk and chair and coordinated office accessories. They even match an elegant reed diffuser wafting a mix of citrus and floral scents.

'Megan, how was your morning? Settling in, I hope.'

'Yes, thank you.'

'I notice you've met Erin.'

'Yes, nice girl.'

'Distractable, though. I'd appreciate you not adding to the problem.'

'Okay.'

'So, our information and materials need to be accessible on our system, not in boxes. I have some ideas, but I'd like to hear your thoughts.'

Recognising this as a tactic used widely in business to hide ignorance, I spend the next ten minutes describing ways of implementing a digital archive, catching her shadowy expressions. I'm right—she doesn't have a clue about these types of computer applications.

I begin the offensive, offering the olive branch. 'I could meet up with you each day to show you what I'm doing, if you like. 'Show you how I'm doing it,' I imply. The offer hangs in the air, then drifts away.

'Let me show you the photocopier and scanner and how the box files are labelled. They do have some logic. And I'll chat about the website sometime, too. I manage our social media, but we contract out the website work, so any changes go through me. We like to provide our members with regular updates and letting them know about the archive will be a good news story.'

When the orientation ends, I return to my desk and examine the edge of the box file I retrieved earlier. As Lesley had explained, it's dated according to order of receipt. This one reads Jan to May 1996, the year the charity first began operation. My professional training kicks in as I remove the letters a second time, identifying information currently unrecorded—names of evacuees, linkages between family members, approximate ages, point of departure in London, destination, length of stay, as well as the qualitative information about their individual experiences. The challenge grows.

At three-thirty, Erin taps me on the shoulder. 'Afternoon cuppa?'

'Love one.'

We make tea, leaning against the workbenches in the kitchen. My attention darts to a whiteboard damaged by telltale permanent marker. Erin challenges me to see if I can decipher the hazy pen strokes, a cheeky glint in her eye. Together we debate the nature of the company, business or team who'd discuss a phrase beginning, 'Find your inner...' The last word could be anything from canopy, to canary, to camera.

'I'm not supposed to distract you,' I say.

She wrinkles her nose. 'It's our tea break. We're entitled.'

'Not here. Back in the office.'

'Lesley, I suppose? I can't help chatting to the oldies when they ring in. They're like my own granny and grandad wanting a chin wag. They're lonely.'

'Just so you know.'

'Thanks. I'm used to it. She gets in a flap, then someone phones to say how friendly I've been, and it's all forgotten. What about you? Find anything interesting?'

'Making decisions about how to organise it all. And reading some of the stories has been a shock.'

'Yeah, I know. Except it was necessary with all the bombings.'

'True, but not even going with their parents.' Mum's good fortune, travelling with her mother had jumped out at me, contrasting with so many other tales.

'Couldn't trust them to do the right thing, apparently. If the adults had gone with them, they'd never have been able to leave them behind.'

'Yes, that's what ... a friend said, who was sent away and knows a lot about the scheme. I can believe it, too, especially if the new family wasn't to their liking. I'm not sure I could've coped either way, letting Chloe and Lara go without me or leaving them with someone I'd only just met. And no phones, only letters, assuming they were old enough to read and write. How did their families ever find out what was going on?'

'From what I've read, most didn't. Simply had to trust people. And it was wartime, so you know, people pulled together.'

'Not for all the kids.'

'True.'

We sink into an awkward silence.

'Treat tomorrow,' I say. 'I'm bringing my plunger and some ground coffee.'

'Oh. Retro.'

'Quick and efficient, though.'

'Don't people use them as fish tanks these days?'

'Don't believe everything you see in adverts.'

'Okay then. I'm game. Anything to beat this crap.'

We both freeze as Lesley calls our names.

Nineteen

I drive home, satisfied. Not a bad first day at all—new people I either instantly like or feel able to work with and an interesting project to get my teeth into. The stories I'm reading might interest Mum even if I can't find any mention of her brother. Not that we don't have enough to discuss with Lara's wedding, an event bringing her enormous pleasure. I sigh softly, knowing her decision to forego the trip to Manchester to help choose a bridal gown had not been of her choosing. We've promised to send photos instead.

The first few minutes of my new commute home are unfamiliar but pleasant, passing through flat expanses of farmland used for animal stock, cows mainly, and arable produce. Once I reach Chester, the route becomes commonplace, a mix of suburbs around Ellesmere Port and dual carriageway through more open fields.

As I take the Eastham turn towards Bebington, my handsfree phone rings, my friend's name, Brenda, appears on the screen. 'Hi, how's things? I'm driving, so I hope we don't get cut off.'

'Oh, are you sure you can talk?'

'Yep, fire away. Nearly home.'

'Great. Was it today? The new job?'

'Yes. Good memory.'

'My head's so full sometimes, it feels like a miracle,' she gushes. 'So, how'd it go?'

I fill her in on the organisation, work and people. 'I'm going to love it.'

'And Rick's forgiven you?'

'Not entirely, especially with the wedding and the worries he has about his work. No-one wants a short-term contract, do they? But you know how I hated my last job. It was a no-brainer. He's resigned to it now because he knows how much I'd love to help Mum, even if it's a long shot. He hated the lies Gwen told.'

'Every family has their secrets but, geez, she took the cake.'

'True. Harmless omissions are one thing, but Gwen...'

'D'you reckon there's any chance of helping Caryl?'

'There are boxes and boxes of letters and other documents. Who knows what I'll find?'

'How is she?'

'Fine, but slow and frail. She's waiting for a specialist appointment. Hopefully, they can do something. Dad and Chloe are sure medication will help. We must have her well for Lara's big day. Mum's so looking forward to it.'

'Suppose you find her brother. It'd be another miracle, wouldn't it?'

'A dream come true.'

'And your dad? Is he still mad at you?'

'Not mad, but he worries. I think he's trying to keep it to himself. Mum was surprisingly blasé.'

'I suppose that makes it easier. So ... I've got news! Bob and I are going on a big, fat Greek cruise for our twenty-fifth. What d'you think?'

Heat rises up my neck. Twenty-five years, as if I could forget.
'Super. Sounds amazing.'

'Can't believe I've been married to the old sod for so long! I remember every detail of our wedding day. Lots of people say they can't, but I do. Wish I could say the same for the hens' weekend! It was a corker till I passed out.'

'It was.'

'And we'll probably have a party, too. Get the old gang together and stay sober this time!'

'Uh-huh.'

'Did I tell you Tina and Phillip are moving back to be nearer his parents? They need support, apparently. Worried that his dad's developing Alzheimer's. Comes to us all, doesn't it? It'll make catch-ups easier when they relocate up this way.'

'I suppose so. Where are they looking to settle?'

'Somewhere near Liverpool to be close to the new practice. Might end up in your fancy suburb. Plenty of posh real estate in The Wirral for a rich lawyer.'

I choke, covering for myself by disagreeing with the term 'fancy' in relation to our modest home.

Her tone takes on a sly note. 'There were always rumours, you know, about what happened after I was carted upstairs.'

'And I've told you before. Nothing, absolutely bugger all. He was a perfect gentleman and showed me to my room. End of story.'

'Alright, alright! I only wanted to let you know I've been thinking of you and hope the job goes well.'

'Sorry. Didn't mean to bite. And thanks for phoning. Lovely thought. Have fun planning the cruise.'

'I'm sorry, too. Right, spray tan and bikini, here I come. I'm as white as a lily.'

We say goodbye, and the line goes dead.

Goosebumps form on my arms as the faces of the 'old gang' re-emerge, one in particular, who might soon be a neighbour.

Once I reach the outskirts of Bebington, my journey takes no time at all. Pulling into the driveway, I sit, head down, churning over Brenda's call. I jump when Rick taps on the side window.

His muffled voice leaks through the glass. 'Hey, everything okay? You look dead beat, to be honest. Hope nothing bad happened on your first day. Or was it the traffic?'

Grabbing my bag, I lever myself out of the driver's seat.

He kisses me and I summon a smile. 'Yeah, around the roadworks, but I'm fine. It's been a good start.'

'Let me make you a cuppa, and you can tell me all about it.'

Rick steers me towards the front door, giving me time to find a distraction, lock away my fears. I latch onto Brenda's comment about my house which I've never considered 'posh'—a 1930s semi with a front room bay window, but there's no doubt we chose an excellent neighbourhood by sheer good fortune. I remind myself it's been a happy home, mostly, made so by raising our two girls, even when they turned into bickering, obstinate teenagers. I've allowed nothing to shake Rick's trust in me and the kids. He loves us all but, right now, with Lara's wedding on the horizon, the idea of walking 'his little girl' down the aisle sets his heart aflutter. I know I'd do anything to keep his excitement intact.

We reheat leftovers from yesterday's Sunday lunch, eat and discuss our day. He's driven fresh food produce to Birmingham and back. I reply with the basics of the role, my first impressions of Lesley and Erin and begin to explain the current storage of important documents.

'How many boxes are there?'

'Loads. It's been their only method, so far. Which is good, in some ways. They've obviously kept everything. But there's no way to examine the contents, study patterns or see what happened in particular places. That will only be possible with a proper system.'

'And nothing about Caryl, I'm guessing. Too soon?'

'It is, but I've kept an eye out for any mention of Cirencester. I've only ever known her case, so reading all these other stories is teaching me new things. It also makes me question if she had it easier than some, being so young and going with a parent. Of course, I'm not downplaying the loss she feels for her mum and her brother. But for the older ones, the confusion of being plucked from their families, not knowing what was going on, must have been terrifying.'

'Our generation's been lucky, mind.'

'You can say that again. At least the charity's been there, in recent years, to let them talk or write about their memories and their past. Many start by saying they've never told anyone about those years. Imagine bottling it up inside? Though not all of them are sad. A couple of children ended up in big houses with housekeepers and nannies. Well-fed, chauffeured about in expensive cars. Most of the other host families did their best, especially women or couples who didn't have children of their own.'

'I wonder if we'd have fostered a kiddie if Lara hadn't come along when she did.'

'Maybe.' I scrape at my plate. 'Several evacuees kept in touch. One lady went to her "uncle's" funeral and was invited to sit at the front of the church with rest of the family. She even received a small bequest from the will, which was completely unexpected.'

'A nice touch, I reckon.'

'And the boys who went to live on farms loved the manual labour and fresh country air. Some found it difficult to go back to London. One boy asked to go back and lived in Devon while he was a teenager.'

'And you found out all this on your first day?'

'Fast reader. Most were short, one or two pages. And I haven't told you the bad ones yet.'

'Go on.'

'Awful, just awful. Unwanted, excluded, starved, beaten. Sometimes it wasn't the abuse but the homesickness and bewilderment, especially at the beginning. Many write about a veil of silence as they left London, so I presume families were encouraged to lie to their children so as not to cause mass panic. Most had no idea they were being separated and thought they were going on an outing. Makes me shudder. Some were as young as five or six! I can't picture it, can you? Would your parents have let you go? Or us, with Chloe and Lara?'

'Definitely not.'

'Even with bombs dropping on the house?'

'Let's thank our lucky stars we've never had to make that choice.'

We fall silent. Rick pushes his plate away. 'Oh, did Brenda get hold of you?'

I blink. 'Yes. Why?'

'Nothing. She pressed the wrong contact and said she'd try again. Just wondered if she got through to you, that's all. Something about a twenty-fifth?'

I nod, the plight of the evacuees melting away because, yes, Brenda's celebration, the exact passage of time, has most definitely got through to me.

~ * ~

I go to bed early but wake with a start, Rick's heavy arm across my right side. Our bodies are facing the window, spooning. I lurch forward, partly to avoid his breath on my neck. Mostly, it's a visceral reaction to the stirring of old memories and sensations. Squeezing my eyes closed, a kaleidoscope of black dots shimmer behind my eyelids. Nothing prevents me hearing the panting, grumbling, my nostrils twitching at the recollection of foul smells. I make a noise somewhere between a gasp and a moan.

Rick stirs and mumbles a question.

'Go back to sleep. Only getting water.'

Wrapped in my winter dressing gown, I pad noiselessly downstairs and put the kettle on. Rick, my darling Rick. Brenda's taunts, this time, have hit their target with force and precision. It seems the news of Phillip's imminent arrival in our area of northern England is messing with my usual tactics to justify and delude. Dazed, queasy, an invisible hand reaches inside me, twisting my guts up through my throat till I dry retch. Sweat beads on my forehead. I swallow and swallow against the dread of Rick's agony, a blow which will surely crush him. How could I have done this to my lover and best friend? How could I have kept this from him for twenty-five years?

Twenty

I go back to bed but can't sleep. I'm chilled, shaky, a headache beginning to bloom. It's my secret. My long-standing, guilty secret. I've been faithful to Rick for nearly thirty years, if I allow myself to swerve around what happened in 1995. I've chosen to believe it's reasonable but ... no amount of remorse has ever pushed me to confess.

Twenty-five years ago, at Brenda's country house hens' weekend, I met Phillip Harris. A once only encounter, yet he's been someone I could never forget. Most of my information about him comes from Brenda who keeps in touch with Tina, Phillip's wife, one of the girls who came up from London for the pre-wedding bash. I never attend get-togethers if they visit Phillip's family in these parts, keeping a mental note of my excuses, alternating with the occasional acceptance which I sadly and suddenly decline on the pretext of an emergency, usually involving Lara's asthma. I know Brenda assumes it's a more critical medical problem than it truthfully is.

Phillip and Tina have two girls a little younger than mine and they've been living in Tenterfield, Kent, where he works at Ridley and Harris, Solicitors. The office resides in a squat, double-fronted, Tudor farmhouse. That's Google Maps for you. I suspect it sounds flaky, but I'd flatly deny stalking him. To me, it's curiosity, a safeguard, the path smoothed by the ease with which my inquisitiveness can be satisfied.

Occasionally, I'd check the company website, his image appearing under a tab, "Meet our team". Professional, serious—the hairstyle shorter, the skin slightly less plumped and fresh, an irritatingly "distinguished" middle-aged man. The picture is small, but it has never raised red flags, which is why I check the site, stare at his fancy mug shot and convince myself I need only be guilty of a ghastly slip-up. My lapse would undeniably hurt my husband, but nothing more. This, along with the inconclusive events of the night, my irregular cycle, Lara's mild asthma and a myriad other quirks she shares with Rick—in other words, evidence and probabilities—have always implied I need not panic. Phillip is not Lara's father, Rick is. If only I could overlook the blond hair. Pin pricks of unease pierce my heart.

Reaching for my portable tablet on my bedside table, I search for Ridley and Harris. The beautiful farmhouse comes into view, followed by the list and photos of staff members. My familiarity with the page layout means I immediately notice the absence of his image. Returning to the home page, I scroll down.

It is with great sadness we announce the departure of Phillip Harris, who leaves us to be nearer his family in northern England. His clients have been personally contacted to discuss their needs and instructions. We wish Phillip all the best and thank him for his service.

I shut my search engine, tripping over Brenda's jest about The Wirral. It most certainly would be a perfect location for a respectable professional family. My Facebook icon displays a clock-like motion as it uploads an update. Phillip doesn't have an account on this platform, but Tina does, under her maiden name. She only posts about her life, not her husband's or the children. One of Rick's friends is a police officer who takes the same security-conscious view. If Phillip deals in criminal matters, or family disputes, it makes sense. I browse Tina's account, looking for any news of their house-hunting efforts. Nothing. I click to her page of friends, and freeze. A new profile for a young blond woman called Sienna Harris, catches my eye. I click again. Snapshots of an 18th birthday party, Sienna sandwiched between Phillip and Tina, all three beaming. I let my eyes lose some of their focus. Lara. Sienna looks just like Lara.

I bolt to the cloakroom.

Pushing back across the tiles, I lean against the cold, hard wall. An image of Phillip's face looms, the younger version, the charming junior lawyer who bought me cocktails, teased and amused. We sat, or rather lolled, on a deep feather-filled sofa in a dimly lit corner of the hotel lounge. I was tipsy, flirty, checking out of my real, wholesome life. Happy? Yes, happy. He said I was ravishing. A blush crept onto my cheeks.

'Ravenous? So kind,' I slurred.

He hooted with laughter, his blond curls bouncing, using my faux pas as an excuse to go upstairs and order room service. Levering me upright, a strong arm around my waist, I waved and blew kisses at the few remaining members of the hens' party who were conscious, including Tina. By then, Brenda had been absent for at least an hour. The last I saw of her, she was fighting with two other girlfriends against being taken to her room.

The inside of a lift offered Phillip and me our first private space.

'Are you up for this, babe?' he asked.

As he pushed me gently against the side wall, pressing urgent lips on mine, I could only think of the frustration of the previous afternoon. I'd left home in a furious temper, driving wildly, angry Rick was making work decisions without consulting me, pushing me on the issue of Chloe's school and the literal anti-climax of a dull hour in bed—a duty shag, you might say—which we'd stolen while Chloe played next door. It was a perfect opportunity, calendar and thermometer-wise, but Rick had grumbled, compounding my desperation, when I knew he wanted another baby as much as me.

So, when Phillip asked, seeking my consent with silky words and a velvety voice, I replied, 'Sure.'

He stabbed repeatedly at the lift buttons and crooned, 'Let's get this party started.'

The rush of desire was intoxicating. I giggled as we made our way along the corridor, stopping to remove my high heels. I didn't want a sprained ankle. My body was responding, I was ravishing no less; he was handsome, strong, confident. I wanted to be lustful, bawdy, for once in my damn conservative life. Fuck Rick. No, actually, fuck whatshisname. Phillip Harris, as I later found out, devastated and shamed by my behaviour.

'Yours or mine?'

'Mine.' Home ground, of sorts. I pushed away the niggle of doubt quivering up my spine.

'Key?'

I fumbled in my bag as I retrieved and brandished the plastic card.

'Here. Let me, Princess.' As he stooped to swipe it from me and across the lock, he planted another hungry kiss on the skin around my earlobe. Tension mounted. An exquisite ache rose from my loins to my navel.

Hormones tore through my system. I couldn't have pulled back if I'd tried. Besides, I didn't want to. I was all-in, reverting to my younger, sexier self. Wild, wilful, I returned those greedy kisses, groping at his hard-on with one hand, raking nails through his hair with the other. His hands cupped my breasts. Even through a dress and padded bra, his effect on me was clear to us both.

Gasping, eyeing the corridor for other guests, I pushed him through the door and onto the bed, wanton, nothing like my normal behaviour. With a confidence I thought gone forever, I unzipped my dress, stepping out of it with barely a wobble, and approached my stud, his pupils wide and dark.

Leaning over, my breasts bunched in my black lace bra. I held his eye as I undid his belt, slid it out from its loops, before slowing down, taking my time to caress his throbbing crotch.

He moaned blissfully.

In seconds, his shirt, trousers and our underwear had been hurled aside. He shuffled back and grabbed my hips, pulling me onto his naked lap. Invincible, desirable, I gave pleasure and received hot pulses of ecstasy in return. When his fingers slipped between my thighs, I climaxed there and then.

He grinned. 'My turn.' He lifted my knee and slid out from under me, guiding me onto my back. Burying his face into my shoulder, he entered, his beery breath tickling my neck.

Too late, I remembered. 'Condom!' I yelled.

'Fuck! Really? I assumed—'

'Yes, we bloody do.'

He pulled away and rummaged through the abandoned clothes, hunting for his wallet. Brandishing a foil packet aloft, he returned to my side. 'Quick. Help me, will you?'

For me, the moment of recklessness evaporated and it was clear his passion was leeching away, too. When he began again, his groans screamed effort, not pleasure, eyes tightly shut, plunging furiously until he reached his peak. A guttural cry sliced the air. Instantly sober and attuned to our contraceptive misstep, I pushed him away, drawing my limbs into myself, satisfied at least that the condom remained intact.

He stood back, head cocked to one side.

'I'll go, shall I?'

Nodding, avoiding eye contact, I felt something drop on the bed before the door banged shut.

Appalling images stung my eyes. It took several minutes to unfurl. When I did, my foot slid on the abandoned sheath, grey and slug-like. I watched with horror as the soft fabric of my dressing gown soaked up the stain. A dressing gown Rick had given me.

Yanking it free, I wrapped it in a ball with the condom inside, and flung it in the wastepaper basket. It wasn't going home to Conwy. No, this stayed here at The Nunsford Hall Hotel. Rick's lovely eyes—yes, the eyes that always held mine when we made love—came to mind, bringing a further rush of regret. I swept my clothes off the bed and snatched at the white sheets. Naked, mortified, they refused to budge. I wrenched and tore at them, finally swaddling myself, mummy-like, a poor substitute for my faithful husband's embrace.

The following morning, I paid my bill and trudged back to my car, the receptionist's words ringing in my ear. 'We hope you've had an enjoyable stay. Your party certainly looked as if they did. We pride ourselves on an experience you'll never forget.'

Forgotten, no. Shut and bolted into Room 23, yes. And Lara? One precautionary blunder, that lasted mere seconds?

Yes, I cheated on my husband. But, no, Phillip could not be Lara's father. For twenty-five years, I'd steadfastly turned from the possibility, the duty shag with Rick my logical, statistical saviour. The nightmares and guilt, my penance.

But now? The photo of his daughter? The daughter who looks so much like my Lara … my carefully constructed world frays at the edges.

Twenty-one

'Mum, what do you think?'

Lara beams. Swathed in satin and lace, she glides across the floor in front of us. The style—trumpet—is elegant and perfect for her frame, a sign of her excellent choice of clothes. Chic, understated, tasteful. My concerns about plunging necklines and sheer midriffs are put to rest. This is the third bridal boutique we've visited and by far the loveliest dress she's tried on today. I slug a sip of champagne, the bubbles tickling my nose. Expensive, too.

'You look stunning, love.'

'You haven't seen the back yet.'

She slowly spins. Acres of pink flesh produce a startled shiver. The fabric is held together by a series of intertwined satin shoestrings, a feat of costume engineering. I instinctively turn to Chloe, who reassures me with a nod.

'Stunning. Gorgeous. Is this the one?' I ask.

'Has to be,' Chloe says, her voice cracking, glass tipping at a dangerous angle.

I reach over and gently guide it upright, sharing a second glance with my elder daughter seated next to me on a faux Louis XVI sofa, as we simultaneously recognise this as a watershed moment. In unison, the pent-up emotions and expectations of the day are released. We each gulp air.

'Oh, don't,' Lara cries. 'You'll set me off. My make-up'll go everywhere if I'm not careful.'

The bridal assistant steps forward, whippet thin, her hair a sheath of shiny, platinum grey. 'Here. If I have to offer tissues, it's the perfect dress, believe me.' She offers a box encased in sparkly sequins and reaches for the price tag. 'A little over your budget. Is it okay?'

Lara's eyes widen. 'Mum?'

'It's not a problem if you're sure. Dad said you're to have what you want, so it's fine. You look gorgeous. Couldn't dream of anything better.'

'Grandma offered to help. It would cover some of it.'

I grip my glass. 'Don't worry. You can't walk away from that one. It's perfect.'

'I wish Dad was here. Look, the bride over there brought hers. Why didn't I invite him?'

'Tradition,' Chloe replies. 'Think how stoked he'll be when he sees you for the first time. He's going to burst, I swear.'

'A veil?' the assistant asks. 'What about a veil?'

The appointment continues. Lara is distracted by the new task as I picture my husband's pride. His 'little girl'. Two nights ago, unnerved by doubt, I spent the small hours scouring social media for every image I could find of Phillip's daughter, wishing I had attended those gatherings and watched her grow and develop. By morning, for the most part, calm had been restored. Lara's straight blond hair, like Sienna's, continues to trouble me but I'm less anxious about the other girl's features, which do not resemble Rick conclusively. Recalling that night, I swallow and blink, determined to cry happy, innocent tears today. My breath catches as I picture—and envy—Rick's reaction, a wholly uncomplicated one.

I bite my lip, banishing these thoughts. Instead, I torture myself with pound signs, and the very real worries about our financial situation. Mum's offer is tempting—they're comfortable—she and Dad are retired and not vulnerable to the new European politics. Brexit has recently been finalised, done and dusted, a thorn in our sides, a rift in the family. The concerns about my short-term contract were as much about our future in a post-Brexit world as paying for the wedding. Rick's work as a haulage driver will inevitably be affected by new border controls and customs regulations. It's all he and his colleagues talk about. My parents, always uncomfortable with Britain's membership of the European Union, seized the chance to vote 'leave.' My brother James took the same view, while Rick and Chloe were adamantly opposed. We all hoped it would crash and burn at the final barrier.

'Hey, you two? Veil? Headdress? Tiara?' Lara asks.

I wriggle upright, alert. Brexit! Not today. 'Try a few on and see if you like any of them.'

'Won't it depend on how you have your hair?' Chloe asks, ever the practical one.

'Oh, yes. What d'you reckon? Up? Down?' Lara begins pulling strands into a makeshift ponytail. Without a mirror, tufts of blond stick out at odd angles.

'Mum?'

'Your choice, love,' I blurt.

She lets the tresses go. Gravity brings the straight curtain of hair back down onto her shoulders. A quick smooth and she's Gwyneth Paltrow again. A tickly cough takes me by surprise.

'Do I need to wait?' she asks. 'Come back when I've decided?'

'I would,' her sister replies.

'I'd suggest trying a few while the dress is on,' the assistant says, displaying a look of mock concern I dearly want to question. 'You don't want to make a mistake. Brides always regret not achieving the full picture on the day.'

Lara appeals to us for guidance.

'Whatever you want,' I say. 'There's no rush.' In truth, I'd much rather savour the dress than anything above the neckline.

'A few different ones? To get some ideas,' she suggests.

The greyhound bows enthusiastically. 'Excellent.' She scurries to a different part of the shop, past more velvet couches, a reproduction French dresser and garlands of paper flowers in soft ice-cream tones.

Lara scrutinises every aspect of her appearance in a three-way mirror.

'The assistant ... pushy, isn't she?' Chloe says, legs crossed, her chin resting on an upturned hand. 'Pity we couldn't go on the telly, you know, "Say Yes to the Dress".'

'Is that the one where cameras watch your every move? Couldn't think of anything worse. I doubt the presenters truly enjoy it. What a job!' I sip the last drop of bubbles. 'Talking of which, how's yours going? Those kiddies are so lucky to have you.'

'Can't complain. The wins outnumber the sad times, thankfully. I couldn't do it otherwise.'

'I never stop thanking my lucky stars neither of you was ever seriously unwell. Only Lara's asthma, and that's never been a big deal.' I scratch my chin. 'It's a hereditary thing, isn't it, passed down from Dad?'

'Can be. Good genes, us. Welsh, English with a bit of Cockney through Grandma.'

'And what's news about the virus?'

Chloe fills me in on the latest, the spread across Europe, the first cases in England. 'Bottom line,' I ask. 'You're okay?'

'At the moment. Anyway, good of Grandma to offer to pay for something.'

'I'm sure we'll manage without it, but yes, I suppose. They've never had any money problems.'

'I'll take a photo and send it to her. This has to be the one.'

'Grandma'll love it.'

'I'll do it when she's jacked up.'

'Jacked up?'

'It's what they say on the TV show. You really need to watch it.' She grins, an expression identical to her father's, ever so slightly lop-sided. She's not even the one I'm worried about!

Movement catches our attention. Lara's hair is being expertly manhandled into an 'up do,' which is a considerable feat given her silky locks.

'So, your turn, tell me about your new job? How's it going?' Chloe asks as she fishes in her bag for her phone.

'Great. As I've said to everyone, it's precisely the sort of thing I love.'

'And the people?'

'Lesley, my boss, is a little standoffish. Wary of my age and skills for this type of project, I suspect. I'm working on it, showing her my progress so she feels involved. And there's a young girl, Erin, probably Lara's age. A real sweetie. She takes most of the calls and enquiries, can talk to anyone, which Lesley sees as a problem, unfortunately.'

'Sounds like a mixed bag.'

'Yes, but the work's going to be interesting.'

'Do you think you'll find Grandma's brother?'

'I very much doubt it, despite the volume of paperwork and what we may be able to do with it. We'll probably be stumped by the thing that's always held her back—her brother's Christian name.'

'Wouldn't it be amazing if you find the same photo of the three of them at Waterloo?'

'Amazing and utterly unlikely. My hopes aren't that high.'

'Mum? Chloe?'

I'm drawn to Lara's horror-stricken face before registering the rhinestone tiara balancing on her head.

'Not you?' I ask.

'God, no. Don't you reckon?'

Chloe stifles a giggle, her brown curls bouncing. 'Doesn't suit the dress. Not...'

The bride smirks. 'Yeah, I know.' She turns to the assistant and bends forward to have the offending article removed. They turn their attention to another option.

Chloe and I gabble on, ever the patient spectators.

The assistant claps. 'Entourage! What about this?'

We turn. My baby is wearing a plain veil, the top layer thrown forward, edged with a simple satin band which matches the straps on the dress. It falls into gentle pleats, the back cascading to the floor. A bouquet of silk flowers has magically appeared in her clasped hands.

I stand. Chloe leaps to her feet. The three of us hug as, yes, happy tears engulf us.

Twenty-two

'I want all the details.'

'Give me a chance. I only walked through the door a second ago.'

Rick guides me to the lounge suite and gently pushes me down. The sofa's age, characterised by alarming squeaks and groans, matches the rest of the dated room. It's ripe for a makeover, a cost we simply can't afford, but holds a warmth of our family life I could never risk disturbing.

'It's supposed to be a surprise,' I say.

'Give me something, please.'

'It's white and beautiful.'

'Did you take a photo? I bet you did.'

'No, stop. I promised Lara I wouldn't tell.'

'Megan! Come on … alright. I'll shut up. But it went well, yeah?'

'Not to begin with. She took us to a hideous place in a dingy strip of shops on a busy road. I wanted to smack her and hug her all at the same time. She's been on edge all day worrying about money. Apparently, Mum's offered to pay for some of it. I'm tempted, to be honest.'

Rick huffs.

'Let's see how it goes. Felix's parents want to chip in, too. It's quite usual these days for the groom's family to contribute. No one will bat an eyelid if we accept.'

'If I knew the ports were going to run smoothly, I wouldn't worry. They're saying the queues along the M2 down near Dover will be miles long. How's that going to work if it happens up this way too? If we don't deliver, we don't get paid. No one listened to us, but we always knew, mind.'

'I know, love, I know. But let's not spoil the day. Lara's going to make a beautiful bride, I promise.'

'No doubts there. My looks, your brains. The whole package, my girl. Felix is a very lucky man.'

I run palms down my thighs, smoothing the fabric, refusing to allow other thoughts to intrude. 'He is, he certainly is.'

'Come on, what else's bothering you?'

I mentally pivot. 'Chloe's worried about this virus. She says a group has brought it back from a skiing trip in the Alps. A family living somewhere down south. Brighton area, I think. They closed the doctor's surgery where they went for treatment, put them into isolation, then went back to thoroughly scrub the place down. Doesn't sound good, does it?'

'But Chloe's alright?'

'Yes. "At the moment," she said. The bosses at the hospital are going into meetings all the time.' Rick puts a hand over mine to stop my fidgeting. 'What if people get sick? Mum and Dad? Or ... what if it affects the wedding? The way Chloe described it, it sounded like one of those disaster movies. What was it called? *Contagion*?'

'I'm not being funny, but you're going way too far. It's not going to happen. I'm going to walk my little girl down the aisle and, somehow, hand her over to Felix. It'll be fine, I promise. Come on, you said it, let's not spoil the day. So, if Lara's sorted, what about you? I don't want you scrimping either, mother of the bride.' He squeezes my hand.

More money.

I turn. 'What if I asked Mum to help pay for my outfit? Kill two birds with one stone? A whole flock, when I think about it. She'll love helping me choose, Dad'll be proud, and it's one less expense for us.'

'Do you have to? Taking money from anyone else doesn't sit well with me.'

'They can afford it. And she's my mum. Isn't that what mums do? I've half a mind to phone while it's fresh.' I pause. 'Sorry. Do you mind me asking?'

'Go on. Can't hurt. I'll go make us a brew, yeah? Give you some privacy.' He stands, sending my posture off-balance as I sink into the dip he's left behind.

'Thanks, love,' I call over my shoulder.

Rehearsing my approach, I dial, hearing a click and fumble. 'Can you hear me, Mum?'

Once the line clears, we exchange everyday news, including an inordinate focus on the weather, which we both agree has been dreadful. I can't help questioning why we expect anything different when February is, without doubt, the most consistently dreary month of the year. She asks about the shopping trip, and I fill in the details. Her sense of disappointment is carefully shrouded but easy for me to hear.

I plunge in. 'I'm glad you saw the photo Chloe sent of the dress. Lara loved your reply.'

'Stunning, yes. A perfect choice.'

'Did you see the back?'

'I only hope she doesn't catch her death.'

'I agree, though it'll be August, don't forget.' I shake my head and suspect she's behaving the same way. 'It was a lovely gesture, offering to contribute, but we want to buy the dress ourselves. I hope you understand.'

'It's fine. Let me know if there's something else. Weddings aren't what they used to be with matching this, that and the other. They seem to cost a fortune these days. One of the ladies at the farm shop, her granddaughter's getting married too and wants the reception in a castle complete with butlers and a horse and carriage! Dad and I managed on a shoestring, but ... we can't help it, can we? Wanting the best for our children.'

'Exactly, like you did for Rick and me. We had a lovely day. Wouldn't have wanted anything different.'

'In which case, you must let me know if Dad and I can help. We'd like to.'

'What if you treated me? I'll need something to wear, too. If I picked you up, would you come with me to Chester? We'll take it slowly, stop for lunch. There are some lovely shops. Maybe just go to one or two?'

'I'd love to, and I know a super boutique, assuming it's still there. Haven't been for ages.'

'In a few weeks? Wait for the weather to improve?'

'Lovely. Something to look forward to. Thank you for this, Megan.'

'Dad'll be okay with it, won't he? Tell him I'll take good care of you.'

'Don't worry, I'll make sure.'

I swallow. With her heart problems, were delays of any kind sensible? 'Any word from the specialist?'

'No, not yet. They're very busy, I expect. Oh,' she adds, 'your job! How's it going?'

'Great. Right up my alley.'

'Computers, isn't it? Sorting out the records?'

'Yes. Creating a database.'

'So, the charity can put people in touch with each other?'

'With their consent and only if the details are there. It's voluntary, like it's always been.'

'You're saying mine will be, but not my brother's?'

'If he's never contacted them, no. Unless his name comes up some other way, I suppose.'

She sighs. 'I told Dad it didn't matter, but it's not true. I can't stop thinking about it.'

My insides drop.

'But don't worry,' she continues. 'I'll be fine. "The sun shines on the brave." Haven't I always said so?'

I stop my eyes from rolling. 'You have.' I drift to days on the beach, so cold and windy we dressed up, not down. Or setting off for a picnic and walk in the woods with rain pelting on the car windscreen. I'd cross my arms and scowl, reasoning the sun would shine on whoever sat under a system of meteorological high pressure and clear skies.

'So, you'll ring to make the arrangements?' she asked. 'I could look for an outfit too, couldn't I, like the old days?'

'Definitely.'

'I did miss you all when you moved to Bebington, you know. I always wondered if I'd said something out of turn.'

She wasn't the cause of our departure but, back then, I was rattled. 'We've had this conversation before. It was Rick's job. The fishing industry was in trouble and one of the brothers had to go.'

'If you say so. Not all sisters look alike, I know that. I shouldn't have said anything, but I thought … you know, IVF or something.'

I fight to quell my exasperation as these niggling doubts, the ones I tamp down again and again, return to confront me. 'It was nothing, Mum. She's ours, I promise.'

'That's what I mean. It was a terrible thing to say. I don't know what came over me.'

'It's fine. Don't worry. We've a lovely shopping trip to look forward to.'

'Righto. Oh, you've made my day. Bye, darling.'

I whip round to check whether Rick overheard. He's stirring teabags, tapping drops of excess liquid back into the pot.

Twenty-three

'I'm two minutes away from leaving, sorry.' My eyes dart back to the disturbing sights on the early morning news program as I chat to Chloe on my mobile.

'So, you're still having to go to the office?' she asks. 'You can't work from home?'

'As if yours isn't the one I worry about most. How's things?'

'It's all anyone can talk about—the virus, the virus, the virus. The secret meetings have gone ballistic. It's not only in faraway places now.'

I agree with her assessment. The disease has spread across Europe with alarming pace. Familiar cities have been drained of locals and tourists—canals, churches, museums and medieval piazzas emptied of visitors. Hospitals are overwhelmed by the sick and dying. It is like a disaster movie, no matter what Rick presumed.

'But you're safe on the children's ward? They're not going to move you, are they?'

'Not as far as I know.'

I exhale. So many brave medical staff are putting their lives at risk to treat their patients. The most in need are the elderly. I give guilty thanks for Chloe's choice of specialisation.

I watch as the reports move overseas to shine a spotlight on the indomitable human spirit. Footage from Italy shows opera singers practising their art on balconies instead of rehearsal rooms. In Spain, neighbours construct ingenious pulley systems to lift essential supplies into high-rise flats and apartments. Ancient village squares fill with conversation as neighbours call to each other across the deserted spaces.

'I've spoken to Lara and Grandad,' I continue. 'Lara and Felix only need a computer and internet connection to set up shop on their dining room table. They've done it before, so it won't be a stress for them.'

'Darren's the same. Spends his time tethered to a phone line, so he can work anywhere. And Grandma and Grandad? Grandad'll know what to do, won't he?'

'Yep. Taken his role up a notch, of course. I expect he's driving Grandma up the wall with all the rules. He must have mentioned "shielding" a dozen times. Luckily, they're not exactly "busy bees" these days. I'm glad I don't have to worry about them.'

'Which leaves you and Dad.'

'Dad's on the road keeping the supply of food and medicine going.'

'Which I understand, but I wish it wasn't him.'

'Me too. And I'm trying to finish off a few things.'

'Which you'll get done, when?'

'Soon.'

'Please, Mum. You have to look after yourself, too. Surely you can shift this kind of work out of the office.'

'As soon as it's a directive, we will. Lesley's organising things, so it won't be long. I know this sounds petulant, but I'm so close to having the test site ready. Lesley's agreed to the parameters, and she's allowed Erin to help because the phones have gone dead in the last week or so. Funny thing, though. It seems to be bringing us together. Did I tell you Lesley's started coming into the kitchen to join us for coffee? The other day, when Erin agreed the plunger was almost as good as café coffee, I whooped, making Lesley jump. Normally, she'd have glared, but we ended up giggling instead. First time I've seen her loosen up.'

'But you're wearing a mask, at least?'

'They're not mandated yet, are they? I thought we were supposed to save them for you, the NHS.'

'True, but you could make one, couldn't you? Or a scarf? Something, at least.'

'Sewing was never my forte. But I suppose I could try.'

'It's changing us all, in big and little ways.'

'When did you become so wise?'

'Don't put it off, Mum, please. I want you safe. Everyone's realising how important their families are.'

~ * ~

I arrive late at the office, making greetings and scant chit-chat. At my desk, I sort through a box dated June to September 2009, the months leading up to the 70th Anniversary Celebration at St Paul's. We've chosen this year as our testing ground based on the wide variety of material. It gives us numerous ways to sort and analyse the data. I scan, photocopy and annotate each letter, highlighting the relevant information. Erin enters a new record accordingly.

I lift up an envelope, studying the address. The postmark states it was sent from Chester and North Wales using both Welsh and English wording, transporting me back to my family holidays and young married life in Conwy. Inside, two handwritten pages in a style I've become used to, a leftover from a bygone schooling era, nothing like my hurried notes and shopping lists. I shuffle the pages to find the author. They'd come from a woman called Caryl Hunter, nee Roberts, nee Baker. My stomach drops.

42 Nant-Y-Garog Road
Colwyn Bay
Conwy
LL3 4XU
18th June 1996

To whom it may concern

My daughter has just found out about your charity and passed on the address. I had no knowledge of an organisation dedicated to the children of the wartime evacuation. I was one of those, leaving Waterloo Station with my mother, Kathleen, at the beginning of September 1939. I was three years old. I was called Caryl Baker back then, and we went to stay with Gwen Roberts, a teacher from Bryn-y-Maen, North Wales. Sadly, Kathleen passed away from scarlet fever when I was very young, so Gwen adopted me—hence my name change to Caryl Roberts and again to Caryl Hunter when I married my husband, Stephen.

My reason for writing is to ask if your organisation can help me find my brother. I have felt his absence all my life, yet I've been unable to find records of him, let alone what happened during the evacuation. Gwen had no knowledge of me arriving in Wales with a sibling, and my birth mum died before I was old enough to ask questions, so no joy there. My birth mother was unmarried, so I have never had contact with my biological father.

You may suppose this is a trick of the imagination, but I do have some evidence of my brother's existence by way of a photograph, taken that day on the platform. He's standing next to Mum and me. I'm quite sure he's part of our group. It turned up unexpectedly around fourteen years ago, but my attempts to find him failed, as they have on many previous occasions. But I suspect there are new ways of searching for lost relatives, and it's my life's dream to be reunited with him, or at least to know what happened.

Is this something you can help me with, please? You can write to me at the address above or find me in the phone book.

In the meantime, I'm sending a copy of the photograph taken at Waterloo which helps support my belief that my brother does/did exist.

I look forward to your reply with great anticipation.

Yours faithfully

Caryl Hunter, nee Roberts, nee Baker

I'd always known she'd written, yet uncovering her letter is more shocking than I expect. It opens the door to a wild, unpredictable possibility, something I've always doubted. With her correspondence in front of me, it proves the charity has taken care of their documents, allowing me to speculate on what else I might find.

'Are you okay?' Erin asks. 'You've gone very pale.'

'Yes, yes. Another one taking me by surprise.' I place my palms flat on the desk, bracing my upper body.

'Can I get you anything? It's nearly time for a cuppa.'

'Please, that would be lovely.'

Erin moves towards the kitchen. I'm glad of privacy as I re-read Mum's words, searching the envelope for the photo I know so well. Failing to find it, I begin a frantic search through the box, snapshots waterfalling between my fingers, before realising its absence means little. I don't need to see the picture to know this is my family history.

Erin holds out a steaming mug. 'Do you want it here or in the kitchen?'

'I'll take it here this morning. Sorry.'

She pouts. 'Suppose I'll stay too.'

'Up to you. But when you're finished, can you copy and scan this please? I'll mark up the details.'

'I'm good, you know. Not hard to pick out a name, station, town and all the rest.'

Cirencester. Mum didn't include details of her first destination. I want to grab a pencil and add the town name, yet I know I can't intervene. This important fact will remain unrecorded.

'I know. You're doing a fantastic job. It's just a process.'

She shrugs, unconvinced. I hand over the letter, hand shaking.

~ * ~

With news of the virus spreading, I'm scrambling to reach my first goal. Arriving at eight o'clock the next morning, I throw my padded jacket on the coat stand, replace it with my winter jumper and make coffee. Neither Erin nor Lesley is here.

My boss arrives at nine on the dot. She's wearing a mask, waves me forward and points to the floor just outside her pod.

'You've seen the news, I'm sure. We must begin social distancing and I'd appreciate you wearing masks from now on. Fortunately, we have lots of space, though that won't help if colleagues don't follow the rules. As you're the one in the open plan area, can I count on you to keep an eye on Erin, please?' Before I have time to reply, she scoots behind her desk and monitor.

By nine-thirty, I'm uneasy about Erin's lateness. At nine-fifty, she shuffles through the door, mumbling an apology.

'What happened?' I ask, part curious, part annoyed.

Her cheek is livid, raised, hot. The discolouration is worst over the bone. She's been crying.

'Oh, Erin. Are you alright? Here, come and sit down.' I guide her to a seat that's as far away from Lesley as possible and quickly fill her in on our new directives.

Sniffles are followed by a thick, croaky explanation. 'Jason! I hate him.'

'He hit you?'

'Not deliberately. It was an accident, but he did start the argument. Dad shouted at him and when he turned to leave the room, he crashed into me. Elbow, I think. Wrong place, wrong time.'

'You poor thing. Does it hurt? Have you taken paracetamol? Maybe a cold flannel if I can find one?'

'Yes, it hurts, yes already done, and I've brought one with me. Mum swears by witch hazel. Smells, though.'

'Give it to me, and I'll make you a cup of tea. Sit tight.'

With the cold, infused flannel in one hand and a mug in the other, I join her back in the office ensuring there's a decent gap between our chairs. 'Here, press this on your face. Are you dizzy? Is your vision fuzzy?'

'Nothing like that,' she murmurs. 'So angry ... and embarrassed.'

'I understand.' I pause. 'And it was definitely an accident? I can't turn a blind eye if it's more serious.'

'No, I'm sure. He's a pain in the arse, but he's not violent.'

'Okay. And you're positive you want to be here?'

'Better here than at home.'

'Come and sit with me or, at least, close-ish. We'll work on something together.'

The archive box is nearly empty. Keen to give my colleague time to recover, I take over her role, scurrying back and forth across the wooden floorboards to the printer, copying and scanning the next batch.

A beep and flashing light alert me to a problem with the photocopier. Opening various doors and trays, I locate the errant sheet, pleated by the internal mechanism. Smoothing the paper, I recognise the guest list for the service at St Paul's. I'd already found Mum and Dad, registered as Mr and Mrs

Hunter, but instinct tells me to look again. I run a finger down the lines, coming to a halt on Mrs. C. Baker. Female evacuees had their maiden name bracketed in the traditional way—nee surname—but here she is, registered under her birth name. Mum often told us about the blunt charity assistant. Had Betty something-or-other agreed to a double up in an effort to help Mum find her brother? My eyes dart back to the register. The entry is next to another Baker—Mrs. F. Baker, not a Mr, not a male sibling. If it was Mum's brainwave, it had come to nothing. I return to my desk, footsteps slow.

Erin sits quietly, working through the last of the contents. The contrast of her life with my mother's crashes into my consciousness, the irony hard to ignore. One woman has a brother, hates him and wishes he weren't part of her life. The other, denied his existence, has always wanted him and put her own well-being on the line to find him.

I find Mum's letter on my desk, ready to be re-filed. Her brief, incomplete story has been preserved in computer code, yet my goal of uncovering the key to her life story appears as unlikely as ever, the dead ends continuing to mount. My experience of working at the problem with Dad, and now at the charity, reflect her dogged searches, her unwillingness to settle, jumping at every possible opportunity to find out more—including this new attempt at the service at St Paul's— which have never borne fruit. It's the hero's journey of the children's classics, without the uplifting ending. Those characters prevailed, against all odds. Given the knockbacks of real life, I decide I was justified, as a child, in ignoring their other-worldly charm. To prove my view of the world, I latch onto a statistical question about the scope of the charity's contact with the evacuee population.

I call over to Erin. 'Question for you. How many members are currently registered on your spreadsheet?'

'Nearly three and a half thousand.'

'But they're not all evacuees, are they?'

'Oh, no. Anyone with an interest can join, like you did.'

'The service at St Paul's had a guest list of eighteen hundred and our Facebook page has around six hundred members, true? But again, they're not all evacuees.'

'Correct.'

'And the database. How many so far?'

'Less than five hundred.'

'Five hundred out of the one and a half million children displaced during the early part of the war. It's a drop in the ocean, isn't it?'

'Not like you to be so negative.' She flips down the lid of the file box with a sharp click.

Mum deserves so much more, a breakthrough, yet the odds are indisputably against us. We all suspect Gwen took other lies and inconsistencies to her grave, but none of us can identify the thread which will unravel the ball of deception. Her secrets are beyond our reach, wound tight, impenetrable. Except, I do have my suspicions, theories and concerns about Christian and surnames too awful to contemplate or share.

Dizziness sends me scuttling for a chair, where I sit with my contradictions. Here I am, taking a temporary job which risks the finances of my family, working tirelessly to put right the mysteries of the past because I see the damage each time I talk to Mum, and every time I contemplate the six-by-four montage of three people on a crowded London platform. Yet, despite the alarm bell ringing in my head, if I ignore the message that Gwen ruined a life with secrets, am I guilty of the same charge in relation to Lara?

But, what's the alternative? Phillip has never come calling to investigate the paternity of our child. Rick never doubts Lara is his. DNA testing was available in the 1990s when she was born but only if you made an appointment through a GP or medical practice. I'd have needed Rick's consent and, in the process, broken his heart. For what? A one-night stand?

But, what if I'm wrong? What if I've always been wrong? Who gets hurt? Like an aerial skywriter, the words 'my whole family' arc across my vision.

Twenty-four

Light from my computer screen casts a fraudulent warm glow, as the central heating slowly kicks into life. I'm in the home office after my confronting day, the weather obstinately cold and grey despite the promise of spring. I've texted Rick to pick up a takeaway, granting me precious time on my own.

My hands move with practised ease, clicking and bouncing from one site to another. Despite my previous certainty that there was no need, I've casually monitored the changes in DNA testing services since Lara's birth. I know they've changed, loosened their strict gatekeeping processes. What's shocking is they exist in such profusion. What does it say about the state of fidelity in the United Kingdom in 2020? Despite easier access, one requirement remains non-negotiable. As was the case in 1996, a request to test Lara's paternity needs to come from Rick with his consent and hers. It's obvious, of course. I should have anticipated these circumstances. Still, I'm crushed.

Inflicting further agony, I compare how technically straightforward it would be to clarify Lara's identity versus

Mum's search for hers. In contrast to the bounty at my fingertips, evacuees, even nowadays, have no single resource for examining their past, as a national register was never commissioned. I recall her stories of visits to records offices, red ledgers slapping on wooden desks, the use of gloves, all without a boy's Christian name to anchor her search.

The front door squeaks open. I open my browser history, removing the links. The last one disappears as my husband appears around the door. The screen contents are replaced by a webpage flashing breaking news of an important government announcement tonight, most probably limiting our freedoms. In an act of extreme subversion, I might break a twenty-five-year rule and have a second glass of sauvignon blanc.

We head into the kitchen.

'Plates ready?' he asks.

'No, sorry. Here, unpack the bag and I'll do the rest. It'll only take a jiffy. Was it busy?'

'Not too bad for a weekday.'

'I appreciate this. Thanks, love.'

We eat and discuss our days. Rick drove to Leeds and back through driving rain and endless roadworks on the M62, and is now in agony. He routinely reaches for his neck, massaging away the tension. At six o'clock, still seated at the table, we break another family rule and switch to the bulletin. Three familiar people stare, grim-faced, at the cameras.

Our prime minister announces the thing we've all dreaded— a partial lockdown. As he lays out the parameters and limitations, I wait to hear about marriage ceremonies. My teeth grind. No sooner are the words spoken than the phone rings. Lara.

'Cancelled. Can you believe he's cancelled weddings? All of them! How can he? What will Felix and I do? It's so unfair.' She snuffles back tears.

'Postponed, not cancelled.'

'It doesn't help. All our plans. My dress. My beautiful dress,' she wails.

'Which you'll wear one day soon. Oh, Lara, love. I'm so sorry, but if you've spoken to Chloe, you'll know it's the right thing, even if it means this.'

'You're making me feel guilty.'

'I didn't mean to.' I push back my hair. 'It's the worst possible timing. I'm so upset for you both.'

'And for how long? He didn't give a time limit. What about the things we've booked? I can't even arrange a new date.'

'Can I help? Do you want me to make some phone calls, take some of the load?'

'Thanks, but you don't have the contacts. It's probably easier for us.'

I keep my tone steady, though my exclusion from the arrangements has hurt. 'True, but I'd like to help. Talk to them as soon as possible. They'll be dealing with this for all their brides and grooms. It's in their best interests to be flexible, so I'm sure they'll be helpful. They'll need your business even more.'

'Except they'll probably have brides already lined up for later in the year. How's that going to work?'

'I don't know. You need to talk to them. Can Felix help? Is he there?'

'Yes.'

'Good. Take notes, keep emails—'

'Ever the practical one. You and Chloe get it from Grandad.' She's less sad, sulkier.

'It's a shock, love. Give yourself time before ringing anyone. And it will happen, I promise. You'll have your special day soon.'

She tuts.

'Could be true. You never know.'

Rick's phone trills. He turns the screen, 'Chloe.'

'Will you be okay? I'll ring tomorrow, see how you are after talking to Felix and decide if there's anything I can do. D'you know what will happen at work?'

'We've been told to wait for a phone call. Both of us. But with this news, we're sure to be sent home. Done it before, at least.'

'Yes, good. And he'll be staying with you?'

'Yes, Mum. He's never at his flat these days.'

'I'm glad. Better to be together in a lockdown. Listen, Chloe's talking to Dad. Can I ring tomorrow?'

We say our goodbyes as her tears come again. Rick passes his phone to me.

'Chloe, love. Sorry, I was talking to Lara. The wedding's off. She's in bits.'

'Has to be done. I know it's a bummer for Lara, but I'm relieved, to be honest. The sooner the better. Should have been done weeks ago. She'll get her chance sooner or later.'

'That's what I said.'

'It's such a worry—lethal and spreading. If we don't stop people moving around and mixing with each other, it'll overrun us all. Hospitals are already at breaking point. You've seen the news, haven't you?'

'Of course. We're as worried as you. What's happening on your ward? Are you still treating the kids?'

'Infection control's ramped up, but we're running short of masks and gowns. Word on high suggests we've been slow to order supplies, and we didn't join in with a big contract organised by the EU. Bloody politicians. If this is about Brexit...'

'Is your ward short? I mean, how at risk are you? Probably a good thing we haven't been wasting them.'

'We're fine, I promise. It's the poor buggers in ICU and the adult wards who churn through that stuff and need a good supply.'

We turn the conversation to the impact on the family, Chloe worrying about Rick's parents. Rick's mum and dad live with his sister in Crewe, so I do my best to reassure her they'll be in good hands, too. I sense the responsibility she bears for us all.

'How's Dad taken the news about Lara? I didn't get the chance to ask.'

I catch my husband's attention. 'Chloe wants to know how you're feeling about the wedding.'

'Gutted,' he replies.

'Did you catch what he said?'

'Yes. Not surprised.'

He leans across the table towards my handset, his jumper scraping the top of a sauce bottle, leaving a blood red smear. 'Not being funny, but I wouldn't be so fired up if you and Darren had done the decent thing. You should've been first.'

I throw him a death stare and turn away. 'Don't take any notice. He's winding you up.'

'Just my little joke, mind,' he shouts behind me.

Chloe snorts. 'He bloody isn't, is he? Why can't he accept how we choose to live our lives?'

'He does, honestly. He's upset, we all are, not that it's an excuse. Come on, give me something which has nothing to do with Lara or this virus.'

'We had a good weekend at our friend's place. They live in Macclesfield, so we took a drive into the Peak District. It was flipping cold, but we managed a walk before bolting into a pub for lunch. Glad we arranged things when we did. Won't get the chance for a while. Actually, Pete and Abby are getting married. When this is over, I'll get them to send Dad an invitation, shall I?'

'Very funny. You know, all of a sudden, I wish you weren't a nurse, even on a children's ward.'

'We have to keep going. Health issues don't stop because we're in a pandemic. Kids carry on burning themselves or falling down flights of stairs, unfortunately.'

'I know, I know. You do an amazing job.'

159

'Not always. One poor mite came in with a nosebleed which wouldn't stop, so the docs ran all kinds of tests, worrying about haemophilia. Thankfully, it wasn't anything serious, but because he's an unaccompanied refugee, social services had no clue about his medical background, which is unheard of these days, with pre-natal care being so good. I don't know how we managed beforehand.'

'The boy's alright? No harm done?'

'This time, yes, but what else don't they know about him? Like Grandma not finding out she had scarlet fever until she was an adult!'

'Uh-huh.' I massage my temple, the story sparking a consequence I'd never considered.

'Sorry, I need to go. I'm due at work in a couple of hours. Promise me you'll follow the rules? If Dad wants advice about how to stay safe on the job, with masks or hygiene, he can call me anytime. And, if you speak to Lara again, tell her I'm sorry.'

We end the call. Telling Rick I have work to do, I return to my study, Chloe's anecdote about the refugee child igniting an insistent question. If I'm wrong, and she's Phillip's child, what don't I know about Lara's health? I, too, recall Mum's fury about her brush with scarlet fever.

I slump in my chair, zoning out of my complicated world. Lightheaded, I'm transported, floating trance-like into a warm blue ocean. My arms and legs are nudged by a flotilla of slimy, flabby, grey-green blobs. I scoop up a specimen, assuming it's a jellyfish, only to find it's a condom, bursting with frogspawn, dragging fiery, sparking tentacles. The stings arrive. Floundering, I pull myself upright, scanning the horizon for an end to the invasion. The burning prickles accelerate. One here, one there. Two together. I'm gasping, losing oxygen, sinking.

Twenty-five

Mum's apprehensive tone unsettles me.

'This video whatsit. So, we click it at seven o'clock?'

'You'll be fine. If you have any trouble, phone me and I'll talk you through it. More importantly, tell me about the specialist appointment.'

She describes her phone consultation with the cardiologist from the Glan Clwyd Hospital, Dad's old workplace. Fortunately, her EEG, blood and stress tests were done before the 'stay at home' orders came into effect. The results are promising. She's been diagnosed with tachycardia, a rapid heartbeat, and started a course of betablockers. Already, she feels better. I'm delighted, relieved.

'Yes, it's good news. For Dad, too. He's been worrying.'

'You can tell everyone later.'

'True. But couldn't we have used the other one? You know ... sky, something.'

'It's not designed for a group of people. This is the latest thing. Everyone's using it.'

'Okay, if we must. I'll probably leave it to Dad.'

Chloe had suggested an online family chat. Sadly, it didn't occur to her that none of us would be physically present to help her grandparents—the motive, ironically, for bringing us together in a world of isolation. I suspect it will cause anxiety and hope they connect and manage the slight time delays, variance in microphone volumes and occasional freeze frames. After all, it was new to me only a few weeks ago, the result of a turn of events none of us saw coming.

Rick and I eat dinner, anxious about how to manage Lara's despondency. We clear the table and retire to my study. I slam shut a notebook bearing several charts containing combinations of three letters of the alphabet—A, B and O. Rick glances at me.

'Follow up from the project,' I say, taking in his baggy, pilled sweatshirt, a comfortable work favourite. 'Um, you'll be on camera, you know.'

He stomps out of the room to get changed.

At seven, I click the link and wait. Chloe set up the meeting so she's responsible for letting us all into the virtual space. After a short wait, my screen splits in two with me in one half, Chloe and Darren in the other. Before I have chance to say hello, Lara and Felix join us. Rick returns, dapper in a cable knit sweater.

'Hi, everyone,' Lara calls, waving.

We return the hellos and hand gestures before breaking into a series of questions, concerned for each other's wellbeing.

I raise a hand. 'Hold up! We should wait for Grandma and Grandad, otherwise we'll be going over the same ground.' A black, blank box appears, dividing the screen into four rectangles. 'I think it's them. Oh, God, I hope they manage.'

Rick and I wait. The other couples gape. A picture materialises, Dad's head obscuring the screen. When he moves back, I see Mum's bewilderment, her lips moving, but no sound.

'Can you hear them?' Chloe asks.

'No, they must be on mute.' I play charades, attempting to communicate the problem, indicating the button at the bottom of their screen. Lara and Felix giggle as I do my best impression of a pop star, pointing furiously at my imaginary microphone.

'I'll ring them,' Chloe says. 'You keep going, Brittany.'

Mum reacts, picks up and mouths into her phone. A tense discussion takes place with Dad, and there's more pointing at the screen. Finally, their voices come through.

'Bloody technology!' my father grumbles.

'We can hear you,' his granddaughters tease in unison.

Their grandmother fans herself with a magazine. 'I'm so hot and bothered already, I can't think straight. How is everyone?'

We repeat the basic pleasantries, typically British and stoic, underplaying our anxieties. Chloe is particularly guarded, yet gently probes about our routines and habits. Moments of dissonance occur, mostly in the first few minutes as we all learn to manage the new medium. Mum finds it the hardest, frequently talking over others, followed by apologies which further interrupt the flow. It's a double-edged sword—enveloping yet strained, stilted.

'What's happening at your hospital?' Lara asks.

'We've passed the peak of admissions, but we're stretched. If our PM has done any good, it was getting sick himself. Shocked people into realising they need to follow the guidelines.'

Rick stirs. 'Couldn't have happened to a nicer chap, mind.'

'That's harsh,' Dad replies. 'Could have died. He's doing his best.'

'Is he?' Chloe wriggles. 'Testing numbers are nowhere near good enough, the messaging keeps changing. I know everyone's worried about the economy, but there won't be one if this thing rips through the country.'

'We're in a much better place now he's taken us out of Europe.'

'Dad!' My warning comes from too many family rows over Brexit. I grab Rick's arm to quell any further unrest.

He pulls free. 'Fine for you to say, but my job's in trouble because of it.'

'Oh, stuff and nonsense. All this border and customs rubbish has been blown out of proportion. It might take a little time for things to run smoothly, but we have the whole world at our feet. We can make trade deals with anyone.'

'We need overseas workers to staff the NHS, Grandad. They're vital. The system would collapse without them,' Chloe says.

'British scientists will get us out of this, you'll see,' Dad replies. 'The Oxford team. I'm keeping up with things. After SARS and MERS, they knew we'd be attacked by another virus at some stage. Halfway there already, I expect.'

'I doubt it'll happen quickly,' Chloe grumbles.

My mother leans forward with a question. 'Megan? Tell us about your job. Any news?'

'Um, making progress,' I say. 'Starting to analyse the details. I don't want—'

'What about the wedding?' Dad butts in.

'Nothing, Grandad. There's been no change,' Lara replies.

Mum pouts. 'I hadn't finished,' she says, glaring at Dad. 'Have you found my letter yet?'

'Yes, I have. Sorry, I should have told you earlier.'

'That's good, isn't it? Means they've kept the things people have sent in.'

'True. If people have written to the charity.'

Her face falls. 'I know, I know. Thanks, love.' Her smile is twisted, insincere. 'Sorry, Lara. I interrupted. What were you saying?'

'There's no news of weddings being allowed here in the UK, but ... we did find out about these quick ceremonies abroad. Gibraltar, for example. You only need a day's notice, and they'll do it on the spot.'

I gasp.

Rick bolts upright. 'You're not robbing me of the chance to walk you down the aisle, are you?'

'No!' Chloe yells. 'You can't.'

Lara bristles. 'Fine for you to say, when you and Darren have never done anything about it.'

Chloe runs a hand through her soft curls, a picture of remorse. 'No, I mean, not now, not with this virus going around. Packed into an airplane? It's the worst thing you could do. Especially with your asthma. And, yes, we want to be there, too. Celebrate as a family. Don't we?'

Six people in three boxes nod vigorously.

Rick wrings his hands. 'Please, Lara. Don't do this to me. I'm so excited ... so proud...' He's trying not to beg. My heart rips open.

Chloe leans forward, peering to her right, presumably to the quadrant of the screen where she sees her sister. 'Please, Lara. For everyone's sake.'

'It's not only the wedding. We had plans. Plans to start a family. I know we could but ... I wanted this first.'

Stunned, the hairs on the back of my neck rise. A baby? So soon? Alongside me, Rick's posture stiffens. I'm jolted when I see misery in my younger daughter's eyes. 'Oh, Lara. We understand how upset you are, but can you be patient? For a little longer?'

I gulp. It's not about Lara and Rick anymore. Chloe's recent patient without a medical history is no longer a portent for the future, but a soon-to-arrive member of our family. I'm back in the ocean, thrashing.

'Is it getting any better, Chloe?' Lara weirdly glances left. I'm disorientated and disturbed by the dynamics as much as where the conversation has led me.

'The numbers are coming down, yes, but a lot of people are sick. If I had a crystal ball—'

'Can't you organise something in your garden, Megan?' Mum asks.

The four young ones stifle a look of irritation.

'There's a blanket ban on any sort of get together, even outside, remember?'

'Oh, yes, sorry. Being in the fresh air, you know, I thought it might help.'

Dad folds his arms, glancing sideways.

I want this conversation to end, too, for mine and everyone's sake. 'Come on, something positive to end the call on. Anyone?'

'I'm better now I'm on my new tablets,' Mum says.

Her statement is followed by words of gratitude and relief from us all. The conversation stalls again.

'I reckon you can't go past Captain Tom, can you?' Dad says. 'A true English gent, veteran army officer, pushing himself to walk round his garden for charity. And all the money going to hospitals on top of the millions we've clawed back from the EU? Remarkable. That's what the NHS needs, Chloe, good old British grit.'

My elder glowers. Nevertheless, there's a collective round of praise. Darren mentions talk of a knighthood for this extraordinary man. Felix says Captain Tom Moore reminds him of his own great grandad who lived to be nearly a hundred. Before we say our goodbyes, our moods are marginally lifted.

~ * ~

Rick pounces the minute the video call ends. 'Did you know Lara wants a baby?'

'No. It's a shock, isn't it, in this day and age?' I reply.

'Can they afford it?'

'I've no idea. Lara's a junior, so I don't suppose she earns very much. Felix is older, with more experience under his belt. His wage might be better.'

Rick clicks his tongue. 'And rich parents!'

'That, too.'

'Even so, it's a big decision. What about her career?'

I flap a hand to wave away his objections. 'It's up to them, isn't it? Where there's a will. Pity we're not near enough to help with childcare. Fancy moving to Manchester? I'd end up going full circle, like Mum.'

'Seriously?'

'Of course not. Definitely not at the moment. She's not pregnant yet, so there's no point worrying. You know Lara ... it may only have been a thought bubble, and she'll keep us waiting years.'

'Imagine ... a grandad too.' His voice falls away in the contentment of the moment as I crave his ability to innocently fantasize. Conversely, I imagine Lara on a hospital ward, baby in her arms, confusion written over her face as the child's medical history veers from her own. The alarm bell rings again. Will it every stop?

He pulls up, surveying the transformed office. 'Sorry, meant to ask earlier. How's the new work regime?'

To prevent any difficult questions, I jump to relay the latest developments. I tell him that when Lesley confirmed the news we must work from home, she returned to the office one last time with packing boxes and the services of a delivery driver. By lunchtime, I had my work laptop, a home office multifunction printer/photocopier/scanner, my in-tray, stationery and several file boxes. With these items came a draft article for the website concerning the new database; instructions for accessing the work system; a calendar for teleconference calls; and a process for claiming expenses for paper and ink cartridges.

I continue. 'We've proved we can carry on with Erin and me talking by phone or email. But I'm frustrated too. There was something I wanted to check for Mum, but it involves searching for old diaries and I can't do that from here. I think someone tried to help her at the seventieth anniversary church service by putting her on the guest list under her maiden name. I want to find out, for sure.' I pause. 'Plus, there's Erin. She's chirpy at the moment, but I don't know how she'll manage being at home day in, day out. I think the office is her sanctuary.'

'You worry too much.'

'Probably. Anyway, today we did our first mini-trial. We sorted fifty-eight names into groups, according to the train or bus station they left London from.'

Rick frowns.

'Well, it rocked our boats. Erin was ecstatic. So great to see her involved and committed. There's more to that girl if she's given opportunities. When I told her she could finish early and I was going to phone Lesley with the good news, she nearly exploded.'

'Good, love. I'm pleased.' He glances at the clock.

'And how's your new regime going?' I ask. He and Brenda's husband, Bob, have arranged to watch a soccer match, simultaneously drink beer and talk on their phones, the nearest alternative to being at a game together.

'Tidy! Though it's not the same. Mind if I go next door? The game's about to start.' He stands to leave and turns back. 'Shall I tell Bob?'

'Tell him, what?'

'About being a grandad soon.' His eyes are full of mischief, eyebrows raised. My gut clenches, rock hard.

Once Rick leaves, his stunt propels me to re-examine my notebook, the one I didn't want him to see, and review the combinations of letters which make up blood types. I toyed with these charts long ago. They might be a poor and inconclusive substitute for a proper genetic test but, at the time, they offered some comfort, and certainly no warning signs.

I'm probably stressed, or frightened Rick will catch me, but today, they swim and make no sense. Chloe could interpret the codes better, but I can't possibly ask her. Twisting my wedding ring, I consider for the first time my elder daughter's qualifications and superior knowledge in this field. If I don't ask for her help, what happens if Lara ever needs blood or a transplant? What if unknown medical issues are passed on to her babies? I scrutinise the combinations with dread, sure there's a permutation which would catch me out. A distant roar from the lounge room disrupts my train of thought. Rick's team must have scored.

Rick! Lara! Grandchildren! I touch my forehead, moist with perspiration. Yet, it's no good pretending—I can't continue to ignore this uncertainty. Modern services and facilities provide the means to solve it. I chew on my thumb. So, what next? Hair samples? My throat constricts, and I find I can hardly breathe.

Twenty-six

Picking up my phone, I notice a missed call from Lara.

I press the screen icon, sinking into my favourite armchair. 'Hi, love. How are you?'

There's a long break. 'Fine. Good. It was fun, the other night, wasn't it?'

'Weird, but fun. Glad Grandad got to grips with the technology in the end. And how are you coping? This business with the wedding must be so hard. If it's any consolation, Brenda's plans to go cruising for her twenty-fifth are in pieces, too. She was in tears the other night.'

'Yep. Groundhog Day. I can hardly bear to listen to the news. At least your friend succeeded in walking up the aisle.'

'True. And listen, love, I hope you're not mad at Chloe for coming down hard on your plans about Gibraltar. Her concern was to do with travelling on planes, staying safe overseas.'

'I know, but she can be so full-on. I know it's her career, but—'

'She's worried. I hope you don't end up with an overseas service because you think it's your only option. You've said it before, they can't be cancelled forever. People want to move on with their lives, start families. Which, by the way ... the news about a baby ... I have to admit it took us by surprise. So many couples wait years before deciding to have children. How long have you and Felix been thinking of this?'

'Um, a little while.'

'And he's fine with it too?'

'Sure.'

I find a loose thread along the seam of the chair arm and weave it through my fingers.

'We're over the moon it's part of your plans but don't rush into it, will you? You're young. Take your time. It's a big decision, life changing. I know everyone says the same, but it's true. Wonderful, but true.'

'It's a mistake, isn't it?'

I sit straighter, the thread tightening around the tip of my thumb 'No! Not a mistake. It'll be amazing when the time is right. You and Felix can work out when's best for your careers.'

Silence.

Maternal instincts kick in. I'm ashamed of my words and change tack. 'And as soon as you're pregnant I'll be round to your place in a flash, so I can take you shopping for prams and cots. We'll have to start a baby fund.'

'Oh, God. Mum ... I ... we're so sorry.'

'What? What's wrong?' I pull upright.

'The baby. No time for a fund, I'm afraid.'

'You mean...'

'I couldn't tell everyone, not when we were all together, especially with Grandma and Grandad there. It's why I dropped the hint.'

I inhale. 'Are you ... pregnant?'

'Yes.'

'Oh my God. Lara! Pregnant!' I freeze, then flop backwards, the cushion moulding to my shape.

'Are you cross?'

'No, goodness ... it's ... it's super news, but such a big, bloody shock.' Swamped by both unease and excitement, I laugh and cry. It's a done deal now and deal with it, I must. 'Oh, love, I'm so happy for you.'

Muffled sobs come down the line.

'Oh, sweetheart, don't. It'll be fine. I promise you'll be fine. And Felix? How's he taken the news?'

Words, rapid-fire, arrive between sniffles, granting me precious recovery time. 'Shocked, to begin with. I guess he's worried how we'll manage with money, like you said.'

'You'll find a way. And we'll help any way we can.'

'Thanks. I've been so worried about telling you, disappointing you. And what'll Dad say? And the others?'

'Everyone will be delighted. And don't worry about Dad. He'll be down the pub celebrating before you know it. Ah, no, he can't, can he? But he'll glug down a few cans at home, raise a toast, I can assure you. When will you tell him? He's not here at the moment. Off on a job across the Pennines today.'

'Can you let me know when he gets back, and I'll ring?'

'Absolutely. Can't keep this to myself.' I rock stiffly, my free arm across my middle. 'So, how many weeks? Have you seen a doctor yet? Oh, ante-natal care? What's going to happen about those things?'

'It's complicated by the virus. I've seen my GP, and she's calculated I'm about nine weeks. I knew earlier from a home kit. I'm on the list at the hospital maternity unit, but if things go smoothly, I'll probably have most of my consultations by phone or video call. The saddest thing is I might not have as many ultrasound appointments as usual.'

'What a shame. But I'm glad you're not being expected to travel and attend the unit. Sounds like they've come up with some good plans. So, everything's okay so far? The doctor's happy?'

'The only thing is my blood group. Are you Rhesus negative? Was it a problem for you when you had us?'

'Sorry?' I'm on my feet, striding into the study. 'Hold on, just a tick.' My free hand scatters work materials as I hunt for her baby record book, though I'm sure I know her type. I'd only ever fretted over the combinations of A, B and O, not the pluses and minuses.

'If a woman's Rhesus negative, and I am apparently, they have to monitor the antibodies in your blood during pregnancy to make sure the baby's healthy. If it's tested regularly, everything's fine, but it can be an issue if it's not discovered early on. Did you have the same thing?'

'No.'

'It must be Dad who's negative.'

I drop onto the hard office chair. 'Are you sure? Could we both carry that marker?' I'm reading the charts, squinting, my ability to process information locked. I don't want her to ask questions. She mustn't ask questions until I can figure this out myself. 'Don't say anything, love. He'll only worry if he thinks he's passed something on to you. You know what he's like.'

'It's not a problem. They picked it up straight away, like, routinely.'

'All the same. If it's not a problem, why upset him?'

'Alright, message received.'

I drag a hand through my hair. My expectation I could work at my own pace has been shattered by the most female of milestones—a pregnancy and an antenatal blood test. Neither Lara nor the baby need be unwell or requiring urgent medical care for my secrets to be revealed. I inhale sharply. Chloe! She'll pick up any inconsistencies in a flash. 'Will you tell your sister, or shall I?'

'Can you do it? She'll only get her knickers in a twist about my care, and I'm not sure I can handle Florence Nightingale right now.'

'Done. Leave it with me. I might not ring straight away, until you're clearer about what's going on. A week won't make a difference, will it? She'll be excited, being an auntie. And I'll tell Grandma and Grandad, shall I?'

'Shall we wait for them, too? I'm only nine weeks, you know, if...'

'I agree. We'll hold off. Sensible for everyone's sake. Let me know when you're ready.' I hear a man talking in the background. 'Is Felix there? I should say something to him, as well.'

'He's scared shitless about what Dad'll say.'

'I'll try to put his mind at rest. Here, pass him over.'

I hear fumbling, followed by a new voice. I congratulate Felix and reassure him of our happiness and support. Nevertheless, he expresses anxieties about speaking to Rick. As much as I try, I can't entirely vouch for my husband's kindness, however much he wants to be a grandpa. I suspect he'll put his son-in-law-to-be through a little discomfort.

Lara returns. 'So, you'll text when Dad gets home?'

'The very second, before we eat.'

'Thanks Mum.'

'Congratulations, again.'

I hear a giggle which sounds like anxious pride.

~ * ~

I bolt for the bathroom. Rick rarely uses a hairbrush, having a style which requires little in the way of maintenance. A quick comb and the occasional dab of gel is enough to control his mane. Nevertheless, I hunt for a stray hair around the sink, hoping I don't muddle it with one of my own. Once a single specimen is detached from its owner, it becomes almost impossible to identify. I decide to search for one on his clothing to avoid a mistake.

As I slide hangers across the rail, searching for a jacket or jumper, anything with the texture to entrap—ha, ha—I acknowledge that until today, I might have continued to delay requesting a DNA test. A phrase always scorned by me, returns: the universe is making you pay attention, Megan. I slam the cupboard door shut, then pop two brown strands in a plastic Ziplock bag. On the rectangle designed for labelling, I write my husband's name.

I walk down the corridor and push open the door to Lara's old room. It's had a superficial makeover, including the removal of wardrobe stickers, teen-idol posters and coffee-stained beanbags, yet there are sufficient reminders of her teenage self in the colour scheme, curtains and flowery string lights woven into the headboard.

I already know where to find a second sample. Removing a shoe box from the top shelf of her bookcase, I find the treasures saved from her childhood. I did the same for Chloe and presented their personal collections on their eighteenth birthdays. Christening cards, their first pair of shoes, special baby toys, even a box of milk teeth. The last item was received with horror, and in hindsight, I conceded it bordered on the macabre. Importantly, there's a lock of hair I cut and kept when she was a toddler. Opening a velvet box originally designed for earrings or a ring, I tease free a few strands and prepare the second bag.

I turn towards the door and stop, running a finger along the spines of her favourite children's books, the jacket covers hard and fragile. They were Mum's once, passed down first to me and onwards to Chloe and Lara. My decision to leave them unread was, in turn, repeated by my elder. Lara, on the other hand, was glad to have them as part of her collection, taking refuge in mystery, faith and the supernatural. I pull out *The Velveteen Rabbit* and read the back cover, the story of a stuffed toy who becomes real. I'm beginning to wonder if I might be wrong about them, too. If I believed, pleaded, for Rick to be Lara's father, would my wish be granted? At this moment, I'll trade my rational touchstones for a miracle.

Returning to my desk, the two plastic bags tucked inside the notebook, I search amongst the profusion of DNA laboratories who advertise on the internet. Reading the 'how to' pages, which explain process and show examples of necessary documentation, my insides plummet. Besides the issue of signatures, one other major obstacle presents—I need buccal swabs, not hair. I grimace, blaming my naivety on TV crime shows and can't help but wonder if they ask for buccal swabs because they'd be impossible to explain as anything other than a DNA test, making sure the participants know what is being requested.

I type new words into the search window: 'secret DNA tests,' 'DNA tests with hair.' Finally, I find a small number of labs willing to take 'non-standard' hair samples, preferably with the follicle attached and with caveats, warnings. This type of sample produces less accurate results, though only marginally. As a consequence, they cannot be used in a court case. I smother a snort. The odds are good enough for me. I already know, deep down, I'll risk forging the signatures. Memories of Phillip's occupation makes my scalp prickle. He's a lawyer. If anything goes awry, he'll crucify me. I shake off the thought; how would he ever find out?

When I re-examine the samples, Rick's meet the requirements—there's a miniscule bulge at the end of the shaft. Lara's, chopped off when attached to her scalp, won't do. I drum on the desk; aware I can't even make an excuse to visit her now we're confined to home.

A memory flies back of our visit to the bridal boutique. The wedding dress needed alterations and remained on the premises. I brought the veil here so Felix wouldn't see it. I pray the comb snagged a hair.

Storming into the kitchen, I grab a new Ziplock bag and pound up the stairs, falling on my knees at the end of her single bed, sliding a large, shallow box forward. Parting layers of netting, my hand closes on something rectangular, hard and spiky. Two blond strands are caught in the plastic. Teasing them free, noting the crucial follicle bulge, I'm saved, elated, until the enormity of what I'm undertaking makes my stomach pitch. Along with falsifying official documents which carry the offence, 'fraudulent receipt of personal information,' I can add 'violation of an exquisite symbol of innocence' to my list of crimes. I close my eyes, disgusted by the reasons for my actions.

Forms printed, my hands sweaty, I forge the signatures of my loved ones. I thank my lucky stars I have my own bank account for the payment. I check when the results will be back, noticing the pandemic has wreaked havoc here, too. Staff absences have extended the turnaround from two weeks to four. I begin a mental countdown. The results will arrive one week after Lara hits the safe, twelve-week pregnancy mark. I'm already thinking of ways to delay her announcement to the family.

When addressed, sealed and stamped, I thrust the envelope deep inside my bag and jog to the post box. The few neighbours brave enough to step outside their front doors are unaware of my wrongdoing. I'm respectable Megan Williams, not a lawbreaker, guilty, mortified. I ram the paperwork into the chute, knowing there's no stopping the outcome I've set in motion. I cannot un-see the results.

As I approach our house, I spot Rick's car in the driveway. I turn the lock and step inside, reluctantly accepting a hug. When he goes upstairs to change, I send Lara a short text.

The hairs on my arms lift. The computer. I race into the study to check the monitor, finding it empty of incriminating words and graphics. In the background, Rick answers the phone to his younger, pregnant daughter. There's a holler of something I hope is positive. I collapse onto my chair, until the appreciation of being alone sends me spinning back towards the screen. In haste, I make several irritating spelling errors but manage to compose a question: can Rhesus alleles reveal misattributed paternity? Scanning the results, I find nothing to support the terror which set off today's actions. Lara's status as a Rhesus negative mother cannot include or exclude Rick as her father. I summon the sound of the envelope as it plopped into the post box, now the property of the Crown, irreversibly destined for a laboratory in Birmingham and question, if I had the chance to take it back, would I?

Twenty-seven

Lesley phones to say we've been allowed back to work, provided we continue wearing face coverings and maintain appropriate social distance. I'm relieved to leave the house and everything to do with my private life. Erin is ecstatic. Lesley's response will be interesting.

After weeks indoors, my journey today is in technicolour. Summer has arrived with its lime green foliage and hedgerow flowers. Lambs frolic on the edge of watchful, sedentary flocks of adults, mothers renewing their energy with lush shoots of grass. Putting aside my personal dramas, as the Victorian villa looms in the distance, I inhale deeply, sure in the knowledge that working from home is not for me. Most importantly, being back in the office means I can follow up on Mum's contact with the charity administrator, Betty.

Erin rushes at me as I step through the door before pulling up, her face covered by a bandana. 'Oh, no, we can't hug, can we?'

'No, and I haven't put mine on yet.' I fumble in my handbag to locate a mask and secure it around my ears. We offer our elbows, instead.

'Weird, isn't it? At least we're back. I couldn't have stood another day at home.' Her speech, muffled by fabric, loses some of its exuberance.

'How are Jason and Luke?'

'Jason's the same as always. As for Luke ... he ditched me ... by text! At least I know where I stand and won't carry on making a fool of myself.'

'I'm so sorry. What a coward's way of ending it. How are you feeling?'

She grimaces. 'I don't want someone who cuts me off then dumps me without the guts to say it to my face.'

'I agree. You deserve better. And your bruise? I can't tell with that thing on, but I'm assuming it's gone.'

She slides a hand over her cheek. 'Yeah, it's fine. Jason grunted an apology last night.'

'That's progress.'

We continue to discuss our lockdown experiences, especially our loneliness. We turn as Lesley arrives.

She comes forward, impossibly glamorous and coordinated in her smart mask. 'Hi, it's good to see you both,' she gushes. 'Well done for all your hard work while we've been away. And thanks for keeping me in the loop, Megan. I'm grateful. I've had a play with the analytics. It's exciting, isn't it, to be able to examine specific elements?'

Erin and I stare, stunned by her rare compliment.

'Thanks. Yes, Erin's been fantastic,' I reply, after an awkward gap. 'How's lockdown been for you?'

'I live on my own, so...'

I've never been comfortable to ask personal questions. 'I didn't know, sorry.'

'Me neither,' Erin mumbles.

'Shall I make a pot of coffee for us all? If it's okay by you, Megan?' Lesley asks.

'Go for it.'

She walks towards the kitchen.

Erin and I exchange looks of surprise. She speaks first, with astounding wisdom, 'Never make assumptions, eh?'

~ * ~

When our coffee is drunk and our chatter dries to a halt, I return to my desk next to the window. As with my morning journey, there's simple joy in using my long vision, scanning the field towards the distant horizon. Lines of cloud streak the sky, moving slowly, north to south. The wheat, thigh high, moves in rippling waves, green and healthy.

Erin, hunched over her keyboard, catches my eye and grins. Lesley has orientated her desk closer to the doorway of her glass cage. We're following the rules to maintain distance, yet we've never been closer.

Reflecting on the improved atmosphere, I speculate whether it's more than our forced separation and collective anxieties surrounding the pandemic. Involving my boss in the construction of the database has boosted her confidence and improved her prickly manner. By supporting Erin to appreciate her potential, I've brought her value to Lesley's attention. Erin churns through the file boxes, managing her own allocation of paperwork and doubling our productivity. Maybe I can do something right after all. And, if I'm ever to advance my search for Mum's brother, it's now. The attitude and skills of my colleagues, along with the progress made with the records, means it's never been a better time. And, for me, it will be a sanity-saving goal. I decide to talk to Lesley.

At ten-thirty, we stop again. Lesley points to the phone, declining our invitation to join us.

'So what did you do to keep busy?' I ask Erin. 'When you weren't slaving away at our project, of course.'

She giggles. 'So, I spent heaps of time in my room, as you know, to get away from everyone. Wasn't much besides my phone, except for my collection of books. Re-read loads of my favourites.'

The hairs on my arm tingle. 'Like what?'

'*The Hobbit*, the first of the *Narnia Chronicles*, *The Secret Garden* and, my all-time favourite, *The Velveteen Rabbit*.'

I swallow, recalling my visit to Lara's room.

'You have been busy.'

Animated, she talks about magical themes, the quests, the hurdles, always leading to happy endings, a perspective I'd always rejected, then in desperation, toyed with, mere days ago. When Rick was away on an overnight job, I had returned upstairs, sat on the bed and read *The Velveteen Rabbit*, snapping at the coincidence that both the toy and my mother's teddy bear were discarded because of their owners' encounter with scarlet fever. I imagine Erin turning well-thumbed pages, the dust covers bent and frayed, the opposite of my encyclopedias, *Pear's Dictionary* and other material full of facts and figures. I want to tell her I've read it too, but remain silent.

'How's Lara?'

My back stiffens. 'What about Lara?'

'The wedding? Is there any news?'

'No, nothing new. The restrictions haven't changed.' Exhaling, pushing aside the ridiculous idea Erin can also read minds, I skim the surface of what it's like to manage a daughter riding a rollercoaster of emotion, omitting any mention of mine. Several days have elapsed since her phone call. Rick's reaction, pure and untainted, differed according to whom he was speaking. Lara was lavished with love and congratulations. Felix received the same only after stern words about commitment and responsibilities. I'm alternately prone to goofy grins as I picture a tiny speck of life growing and developing in my daughter's womb, or scared out of my brain about the DNA test results. Each time the last thought rises, I react as I've done for twenty-five years—I package it up, bury it deep, distract, divert, deflect.

'Are you alright?' she asks. 'You seem miles away.'

My family upheavals spur me to make a suggestion. 'I'm thinking about you and Jason.'

'Why? I try hard not to. Arguing, grumbling, being a prize dick.'

'My two had their moments, though I suspect girls are quieter about it. Boys let it all out, I believe, from what friends have told me.'

'Sounds about right.'

'And they do get better, apparently, only it takes a while.'

'I'll be out of there before then, I reckon.' Her mouth sets in a hard line.

'Can I tell you about my mum?'

She frowns. 'Sure.'

I keep it simple. 'She was adopted and never had the chance to know her brother. In fact, she doesn't even know for sure he existed, except for one black and white photo, which suggests a boy was once part of her family. For all that, she's loved him her entire life and has tried everything to find him.'

'So, what? I should be grateful?'

'Hard, isn't it, when he's a dick?'

Her chin dips. 'I'm sorry about your, mum but...'

'Something to consider. Chances are he'll be a different person in a few years' time. So long as the black eye was what you said, an accident, it might be worth waiting to find out.'

She shrugs, avoiding my gaze, before washing her mug and returning to her desk. With renewed impetus, I walk to Lesley's pod. She's off the phone.

'Come in, come in,' she says, indicating a chair which has been pushed the mandatory two metres from hers. 'What can I do for you?'

'Long story. Do you have time?'

'Yes, a little.'

I make my case by telling her the full version of Mum's story.

She arches an eyebrow. 'Did you apply for the job in the hopes of helping her?' The old, spiky Lesley.

I blink.

'Sorry,' she says. 'Uncalled for.'

'I knew about the charity because we'd come across it back in '96. Since then, I've regularly checked the website, and I joined the Facebook group when it formed. It's how I found out about this job. It was a perfect fit for me, skills-wise, and a chance to try to help, in my own time, of course. I love this project and I hope you're happy with what I've done so far.'

She nods.

'To be honest,' I say, 'I had serious doubts there'd be anything here, but I've since found a letter she wrote in 1996 and she and Dad are on the guest list for St Paul's. It's made me seriously consider whether there's anything new to find.'

'She wrote to us here? You didn't say.'

'Nothing much came of the letter, but there is something interesting about the guest list. It could be a clerical error, but she appears to have been listed twice, once as a single guest with her maiden name, Baker, and again as a couple. Someone here tried to help her, I think, when her letters in the personal column led nowhere.'

'Sounds irregular. And, no other Bakers, I'm guessing.'

'One, but she was female.'

'Was her brother older or younger? If she's in her eighties, would he be alive?'

My lips press tight.

She shifts awkwardly. 'Being practical, sorry. But I don't see why we can't keep a look-out whilst the data's being entered and we're running reports.'

I exhale. 'I was hoping you'd agree, thank you. And there's something else. The woman Mum spoke to was called Betty, but she can't remember her surname. Do you have records of who worked here around that date? I'd love to know if Betty made the double entry on the guest list.'

'Those kinds of records would be on my computer. HR, you know.' She taps away at the keyboard. 'Yes! A Betty Bloch worked here from February 1996 until December 2009. She retired after the big church celebration.'

The name Betty conjures a kindly lady in a tweed skirt and sensible shoes, but a surname like Bloch? I hope her character turns out to be different. 'Would her emails be accessible?'

'We wouldn't have kept messages from so long ago, I'm afraid.'

'What about diaries? Message books?'

'Possibly. I'm not sure where they'd be.'

'Erin's desk? Can we check and do a bigger search at lunchtime?'

'If it's in your breaktime, I don't see why not. Within the guidelines, of course.'

I stifle a groan. 'Great. Thanks. I'll get the ball rolling.'

'No goose chases, please. I don't want Erin distracted again.'

I remain silent.

'No, it's true. She's worked hard. If you can give us both the details ... like, what's his first name again?'

'We've never known. Master Baker, aged seven or thereabouts. Assuming we've got the surname right. But I think I know where he was sent first. Cirencester, in Gloucestershire.'

'Pretty place. Well, good luck with the search and let me know where it leads.' She wraps long arms around her middle, as if she's holding her emotions in.

'Great. I'll tell Erin. She'll be stoked.'

Twenty-eight

'Are you kidding? I'd love to help!'

'Thanks. It'll be quicker with two.'

'But I am cross. Why haven't you told me the full story? You said your mum spent the war in Manchester.'

'I know, sorry. Dad lived there, not her. It was the first thing that came into my head. I didn't want anyone questioning my motives. Plus, there was her letter. Gave me hope.'

'If the letter's our starting point, we need the date.'

I retrieve it from the box labelled June to September 2009, noting Mum wrote on June 18th.

'So, we're looking for Betty's diary or message book,' I say. 'Shall we start with your desk?'

Erin conducts an extensive search—me watching, socially distanced, frustrated—but no books of importance are stored inside.

'What about the cupboard in the hallway? Is it ours?' she asks.

'Let's find out.'

The wooden cabinet hunkers against the panelled walls, with two enormous knobs and a hole for a key. Grabbing the handles, bracing for resistance, I pull hard. The two doors groan open, leaking dust and a musty smell. It's packed with hardbacked notebooks of several colours and sizes.

An upright group in a neat row catches my eye, the word 'Diary' with a date written in gold script on each spine. Removing a pile, I rifle through until I find 1996. Examining the inside cover, I find no name, so there's no way of knowing if it belongs to Betty. I flick from page to page, reading entries for meetings with lists of participants, to-do lists, days scored out for annual leave and bank holidays.

'There are plenty of other names in here, but none are hers. Logic says it must be Betty's.'

Erin flaps the letter. 'Come on, what's written on June 18th?'

'Nothing important, but that's the day Mum wrote, so it'll be after that.'

I progress forward, slowly—19th, 20th, 21st. Weekend. 'Look!' I turn it towards Erin. 'June 24th, "Call Caryl Hunter." Bingo!'

'Now what? I can't see any notes so...'

'It's a start.'

Returning to the cupboard, I pull out a second pile, larger in size, lying on their sides. The first is a correspondence book with records of phone conversations. It's not the right year, but my heart leaps.

'Here. Take some of these. See who's first to find June '96!'

'What's the prize?'

'A hug and a doughnut.'

She rolls her eyes. 'Just the doughnut then.'

We move towards my desk, sit on opposite sides, eyeing each other competitively. With swift movements and vigilant scanning, we work through the books.

'Here! Got it, or at least I think I have,' Erin says. 'Yes, June 24th.' She holds it across the breadth of the table so we can both read.

24/06/96. Caryl Hunter. Phone call. Provided additional information as per correspondence. Doesn't know her brother's Christian name. Explained scope of charity and inability to conduct investigations. Enquiry closed.

Erin frowns. 'God, so mean.'

'Her experience every single time.' The disappointment gnaws at me.

'Nothing else?'

'Enquiry closed,' I say. 'Sounds pretty firm to me.'

'Let's hope we have better luck with the database.'

'The odds are against it, I'm afraid.'

'You have so little faith,' Erin replies, eyes drifting towards the kitchen. 'Sorry, there's nothing more, only … have we finished? I'm starving.'

My sandwich, probably damp and squishy, brings a rush of nausea. 'Sorry, yes, you go ahead. I'll eat mine at my desk.'

'Cheer up. The journey's not over yet. Not in my book.'

I'm unconvinced by Erin's optimism. Betty Bloch, in my imagination, segues into a sour, disobliging spinster wearing dowdy clothes and flat leather lace-ups.

I begin collecting and ordering the diaries and message books when a label and date catch my attention. Erin's mention of Mum's letter took us down a redundant path. My current quest relates to the cathedral guest list, not her original contact with the charity. I grab the correspondence book labelled 2009. When I pull it from the pile, there's another one underneath. Two volumes, a busy year.

I read as fast as I can, finding notes relating to the announcement of the commemorative service at St Paul's and the follow-up it generated. Though a simple acceptance of the invitation was the only requirement, Betty had received a flood of questions and enquiries. Fortunately, her recording system is consistent, rigid. Perhaps she'd have been a kindred spirit after all. I run a ruler down rows of dates, attending to the messages on the right, my lips moving in time with each name. 10/07/09. Caryl Hunter.

10/07/09. Caryl Hunter. Phone call. Questions regarding guest list and concern the use of "nee" open to error, especially if member attending with spouse. Request made to be listed separately under maiden name. Agree to discuss with manager but suggest caution. NB: member very emotional. To be brought forward immediately.

Flicking forward nearly a week, I find a second entry.

16/07/09. Caryl Hunter. Phone call. Passed on decision, given her anxiety, the charity is willing to list her separately under her maiden name. Details reviewed and confirmed—Mrs. C. Baker, host town: Cirencester. NB: Background—previous contact with charity June 1996. Member expressed deep gratitude.

Betty has risen in my estimation and the guest list is explained. Could my poor mother have done anymore, persevering, over and over? As interesting as all this is, it leaves me empty. There was no Mr Baker at the service, despite all her hopes and manipulation.

My finger runs down the page and Mum's name comes into view again.

17/08/09. Thomas (Tommy) Barker. Provided an account of his life as evacuee. Host town: Cirencester. Link to Caryl Hunter (nee Baker)? Spelling error? Enquiry investigated and resolved—negative. Thomas Barker's name not misspelled.

I fold over, gutted on Mum's behalf.

Twenty-nine

Rick and I grunt at the TV, knowing the very idea of a holiday this summer is moot. The news is awash with rules, changes to rules, risks of quarantine and encouragement from travel companies for Brits to travel abroad. In many ways, it's preposterous, given the last few months of widespread illness and death. Yet many amenities and businesses are functioning normally again, the Queen has been seen outside in public for the first time in many months for a socially distanced performance by the Welsh Guards, more and more people are returning to work and the rules around the mixing of households has slightly relaxed.

We can't meet as a whole family, but we've either visited or hosted each household—Mum and Dad, Chloe and Darren, Lara and Felix—since the restrictions have changed. The lack of a full 'gathering of the clans' has brought unexpected benefits. Lara and Felix have been persuaded to keep news of the pregnancy private. In the meantime, we have phones and all manner of internet services to keep us connected by voice or video. The chance to hug, or share a meal and a conversation close up, has never felt more important. It's a national wake-up call to cherish the simple things.

A distant ringing sends me galloping into my study. I swipe up my phone as the old-fashioned alert tone stops. Lara. A beep and message. 'Call me.'

I find her number and ring.

'Have you seen the news? They're on again. Weddings. He's just said. I'm fit to burst!'

'Was there an announcement?' After all our time glued to the TV, I can't believe I've missed this vital information.

'This afternoon. They can start again from July 4th. I've contacted the venue and because ours was booked for August, we can go ahead.'

'That's marvellous, love. I'm so happy for you both. The best possible news.' August! August! How soon will the pregnancy announcement have to be made? The DNA results are still a week away.

'It won't be how we arranged it. Only thirty people, because of social distancing.' She's downcast beneath the excitement.

'But you'll have a service? A reception?'

'Thirty for the service and very strictly organised. The rules around receptions are even more complicated. It's two households indoors or six people from different households outdoors. It won't suit us or any other family. The woman at the venue was very blunt, asking if it's what we want.'

I'm calculating the numbers and combinations without even considering Felix and his family. Nothing works. It's worse than heartless. 'You seemed so sure.'

'I don't know. Part of me says it's the service and the vows which matter, with thirty of our closest family and friends, but part of me still wants the big day.'

'What about the baby? Should you consider him or her, too? How are you, by the way?' Lara is past the danger zone. I've been silently counting off the days and weeks on the calendar at home and at work, wishing the laboratory website was wrong and the arrival of the results would overtake this pivotal milestone.

'I'm fine. Much better in the mornings.'

'That's a relief. And the appointments?'

'Going well. Easier than traipsing to the hospital.'

'So, August. You'll be...'

'About twenty-four weeks and showing, probably. I suppose we ought to tell the others.'

Logically, the timing of the announcement makes no difference, yet my brain screams to know the outcome of the paternity test before word spreads to the rest of the family. 'Oh, I don't know. Should we? There's no rush, and you've some big decisions to make. Going back to the venue, for instance, do you need to decide straightaway? Has the owner given you a deadline?'

'Yes, Friday, close of business.'

'So, take it slow. Write down the pros and cons with Felix. Whatever you decide is fine by us.'

'Thanks. I guess the biggest thing ... oh, God, he'll be so upset ... Dad won't be able to walk me down the aisle.'

'What?'

'Another regulation. We have to sanitise our hands before and after exchanging rings, too.'

'Oh, Lara. What a carry on.'

'It's not worth it, is it?'

'You have to decide, love.'

'And Dad?'

'If he can't, he can't. End of story.'

She sighs heavily. 'What if we legally marry in August and had the proper event, later?'

'Would that satisfy you?'

'I'd have to talk to the venue. They might not be too happy if we don't have a reception of some kind.'

'So, maybe keep the venue on-side for the future, and Dad can have his moment later on.'

'Maybe. Oh, God, it's so complicated. I'll talk to Felix.'

'I guess you'll have the best of both worlds—married first and a proper wedding.'

'True, leave it with me.'

'Great. Um ... I might not mention anything to Dad yet.'

'Sure, especially if we go for Plan B. No point upsetting him if we can still offer the big day.'

'Agreed. I'll wait to hear from you. And we'll put off telling the others about the baby for now. Yes?'

'They're going to be so mad with us.'

'Don't worry. I'll take the heat for you.' In more ways than one.

~ * ~

I don't know where I caught the virus, but I started to deteriorate, a test came back positive, and I'm at home, Rick caring for and scaring me. Through a haze of cotton wool thinking and lightning bolts of pain, I offer feeble warnings for him to keep his distance, wafting my arms ineffectively, coughing with the effort. I worry his wrinkled brow will set firm if he's not careful. I can't eat but force myself to drink—water, plain and warm—and slug tablets that go down my gullet like golf balls.

After three days of restless stupor, my dreams so vivid I wake sweaty and terrified, my world refocuses. I can sit up and talk, but I've lost my sense of taste, which makes food unpalatable. I do my best for my husband's sake, recognising he'll have struggled to cook. Though not strictly permitted, he sits on a chair at the farthest end of the bedroom, masked and gloved on Chloe's strict orders, leaning forward with tension and concern, monitoring every rise and fall of a spoon or fork. He passes on news of all the phone calls he's received, especially from Chloe, who's coached him through the crisis with calm words and common sense.

The following weekend, I'm far more alert, less woolly-headed. When Lara phones to check up on me and relay the latest news on the wedding arrangements, Rick and I listen on speakerphone. Afterwards, we eagerly discuss the exciting developments, talking across the length of the room.

'So, the venue booking's on hold, and she'll have a civil marriage service at the registry office in Manchester, in August. Not a bad outcome, mind,' Rick says.

I give silent thanks for not disclosing the meagre arrangements they might have made. 'Civil marriages can be quite straightforward, you know, especially if restrictions are still in place. Remember what she said about sanitising hands before exchanging rings? I think you need to get used to the idea you might not give her away until the later ceremony.'

'Let's wait and see, shall we? We need to get you better and back on your feet, first.'

'You've been a saint. And Chloe. I bet it's her advice which has stopped you catching it, too. Either that or I've been lucky and had a mild dose. Feel sorry for the poor buggers who had the full Monty.'

'I hope it's not your way of saying you're going back to work anytime soon?'

'You heard what Lesley said. Despite being free to ditch isolation on Friday, she wants me to take another week off. I expect she's terrified I'll pass it on but a whole seven days seems too long. Plus, I'm worried about Erin. Lesley was very non-committal when I asked after her.'

'Think of yourself before your colleagues.'

Our metal letterbox flaps open and closed with a loud thwack, followed by a thump on the tiles. Rick goes to collect the post. He climbs back upstairs, rounds the door, looking puzzled.

'Something for you.' He forgets the rules, walks forward and holds up a package.

My body cools. The Birmingham postmark is my clue. I let out a faltering breath as I note the lack of names and logos on the envelope. The laboratory promised anonymity and has kept its word. More importantly, the results have arrived before Lara's big announcement. I want to rip the parcel out of his hands.

I wave him away.

'Everything alright?'

'Too close! Get back,' I yell. He retreats. 'And it's nothing important. Nothing worth catching the virus for.'

'Looks official.'

My foggy brain grasps for an explanation. 'A while back, I contacted an old colleague about the best way to do something with the database. I bet it's that, you know, technical stuff. I gave my home address because I was working here. I can't be bothered with it now. I'll take it with me when I go back to the office.'

'I'll put it on your desk, yeah?'

'Thanks, love.'

He disappears with the paperwork which could change his world.

Thirty

With a great deal of persuasion, Rick returns to work, offering to cover the weekend shifts as a means of making up for his long absence. I curb my eagerness to see him go. He calls regularly whilst on the road, as do Chloe, Lara, Mum and Dad. I'm embraced by love and care, turning me to jelly every time I consider slicing open the envelope sitting, accusingly, on my desk.

As the sound of his diesel engine fades away, I stride into the office, snatch it up and rummage in the drawer for my knife opener. My phone rings. Jaw clamped, I check the name on the screen before throwing the package to one side.

'Hi, Megan, it's me, Erin.' She sounds flustered, ruffled.

'Must be something important.'

'I've been worried about you and the virus, obviously. Are you better now? Lesley says you're coming back to work.'

'Yes, much better, thanks. Still tired but no fever and the cough's almost gone.'

'Phew, I mean, what with you being older.'

'Thanks!'

'You know what I mean. Oh God, sorry again.'

'It's fine and perfectly true. So, what about you? How's work? I'm sure you've carried on splendidly without me.'

'Yes and no.'

'Come on. What's up?' I recall Lesley's lack of engagement about Erin's work.

'Do you have a minute? Several, in fact?'

I lean back in my chair. 'Fire away.'

'So'—Erin's swallow carries across the phone line—'I was making a routine entry about a guy called Thomas when I thought I'd found something to help you. The letter said he was evacuated with three siblings. They wanted to stay together but were split up because no-one wanted to take all four. The eldest, Michael, ended up with a horrible family. Thomas was next in age and had a different experience altogether, some good some bad. And the younger two—a boy and a girl—were kind of skipped over. They'd gone somewhere else, together, but Thomas's words made it clear he never saw them again. To make it worse, he lost touch with Michael, who blamed himself for not keeping the four of them together, which is why Thomas wrote in 2009 ... to have one last go at finding his older brother.'

The skin on my neck tingles. 'Did he have any idea what happened to the eldest?'

'Thomas knows Michael ran away from his host family as soon as he was able, probably around sixteen, refused to go back to London and went to the West Country to work on a farm. The family had an address for a while, but when Thomas was old enough to search for him, Michael had moved on without leaving a forwarding address or any trace of his whereabouts.'

'And the younger ones?'

'He never saw them after they were first split up.'

'A boy and a girl? How old?'

'Thomas was twelve at the start of the war. The younger boy was eight and the girl, three.'

'Where did all this happen?'

'Cirencester.'

I inhale saliva, setting off a ferocious coughing fit. Erin fusses over the phone. It takes several minutes to restore calm.

'What was his surname, this Thomas chap?'

'Barker.'

My head jerks. 'That's only one letter different to Mum's surname, Baker! Hang on. Thomas Barker, did you say? Betty Bloch was onto this, too. Oh, Erin, I'm so sorry. There was a note. Betty wondered if there'd been a spelling mistake, but she marked the outcome as negative. I could've saved you the trouble.'

'I wish I'd known.' There's a note of deflation in her tone. 'But you can't blame me for trying, can you?'

'I'm so sorry. I'm assuming you believed the younger two were Mum and her brother? I might have wondered, too, although there's never been any suggestion Mum had three brothers. But Betty sounded pretty sure she'd got to the bottom of it. I got the impression she phoned and spoke to Thomas herself.'

'She did.' Erin waits a beat. 'And so did I. I mean, what harm could it do? Until it all went wrong.'

'Hold up. Names! Did he name his younger siblings?'

'Yes. Gerald and Karen. Karen Barker.'

My eyes pop. 'How close is that to Caryl Baker?'

'Which is why I wanted to talk to him. To try to work it out. Luckily, he'd provided a number.'

I remain silent while I overlay Thomas's story on my mother's. No wonder it caught Erin's attention, even assuming it possible to overlook the mismatch in sibling numbers. 'No more interruptions. Tell me about the phone call.'

'Lovely voice, posh but with a bit of Cockney. He was surprised when I told him who I was. That's when he said he'd been contacted before, by someone at the charity. Betty, obviously, but he couldn't remember the name. So, anyway, I gabbled on about being interested in all the stories and quoted a few lines from other people's cases. He was reserved at first but finally said he'd never told a soul about being an evacuee until he saw the invitation in the local paper around the time of the Seventieth Anniversary and decided to make one last attempt to find Michael.' She pauses. 'I asked if it had helped, but he said it hadn't, which was a bummer. He didn't attend the service, either, which wouldn't have made any difference, because when I checked the guest list, there was no Michael Barker. The biggest problem was he didn't want to talk about the younger two. Everything turned icy when I asked about them. His words were "No, I don't think so. Nothing will bring those two back."'

'Poor man. Something awful must have happened to them.'

'I assumed so too, but I have to admit, I was bursting to keep going. He went on to say how everyone knew about the men at Dunkirk, the pilots, the Blitz, which was only fitting for courageous men and women to be honoured, but only he and the others knew what it was like to be evacuated. He acknowledged it was probably their own fault for not speaking up. With all the celebrations at the end of the war when families reunited, no one wanted to dwell on the bad times. When you're a child, he said, you tended to accept things. In his case, by the time he was old enough to do anything, it was too late. That's the reason he kept it to himself all these years. He seemed finished with what he was prepared to talk about, so I said goodbye.'

'No harm done, surely?'

'Not then. But I couldn't leave it alone, could I? Left it a few days, then rang again.'

'What did he say, second time? Was he cross?'

'Not raging. More irritated, I think. So ... I told him about the database.'

'Why is that a problem?'

'I kind of exaggerated.'

'What do you mean? We'd only have what he gave us ... his and his siblings' names recorded as arriving at Cirencester.'

'I was trying to help you, so I told him we could do more with the program by analysing the information. I was deliberately vague, but I gave him the impression it might help if he told me about the younger two, Gerald and Karen.'

'Oh, Erin.'

'Don't, please. I know I shouldn't have done it. Lesley's furious, saying my future's under consideration.'

'How did she find out?'

'He asked to be put through to my manager. I put him off the first time, but he rang again. She shut the door once the conversation turned tricky, so I don't know what was said.'

'I'll talk to her. It's my fault you're involved.'

'No, Megan, please.'

I drag a hand across my forehead. 'Nothing good ever comes from delving into Mum's past. I know from bitter experience.'

'Could be true. As well as things ending badly with Thomas, I found out something which might close off this enquiry, good and proper.'

'What d'you mean?'

'To encourage him to talk, I told him a little three-year-old girl from the same town was adopted, and she'd written in, too, hoping to find her seven or eight-year-old brother.'

I gasp, pulling upright.

She continues. 'I could tell he was shocked because he repeated her name, like he was in a trance. Obviously, it made him believe his little sister might be alive. I was excited, too, so I carried on about this girl leaving London and being billeted with a woman living in Cirencester, first, but when her mother died of scarlet fever, she was adopted by her host and moved to Wales. I said she was called Caryl Baker, and pointed out the similarity to the name Karen Barker and with the location and right age, could she be the missing girl? I couldn't bring myself to say "sister".'

'What did he say?'

'That's the problem. As soon as I mentioned the girl travelling with a parent, the shutters came down. He swore it couldn't be her because their mother didn't go with them, stayed behind in London, which is why she told the eldest, Michael, to make sure they were kept together. But once he knew it couldn't be her, he became really cross and blurted out the story of what actually happened to his younger brother and sister. They were involved in a car accident when their host father ran off the road into a river. Everyone was presumed drowned but only Gerald and the man's body were recovered. Karen's wasn't. That's why he jumped at the possibility she'd survived and been taken in by another family.'

'Oh, God.'

'Don't make it any worse. I feel bad enough already.'

'No, I meant the accident and how it would've affected Thomas and Michael, especially Michael if he already felt bad for not keeping them all together.'

We fall quiet.

'And the two of them both being so young,' I continued. 'Karen was only three. I always believed preschoolers went with a parent.'

'I said the same thing, but we were wrong. They assumed families would be kept together so little ones did leave with their older brothers and sisters. He said he'd come across plenty of examples in his search for Michael.'

My pulse races, my head wedged in a vice. Erin had rushed to a catastrophic conclusion on my behalf, causing this man great distress.

'This is all my fault,' I whisper.

'I told him I was sorry. Said I'd probably lose my job, should lose my job.'

'What did he say?'

'Said, yes, I deserved to be reprimanded. I'd been careless and unprofessional, and I couldn't play with people's lives, especially giving someone hope that their missing sister had come back to life. But then, he murmured something about my regret being genuine. I finished by saying I'd take it all back if I could, and he said he believed me.'

'So, the call to Lesley might not have been so bad.'

'But she's not telling me anything, so I don't know.'

'Be patient. I'll get back as soon as I can and sort this out. Lesley knows I started this whole thing, so I'm going to make sure she understands you did it for me, with good intentions. I don't know if it will be enough, but I'll do my best.'

'Thanks.'

'And, when we come across the Barker family, we'll know to put them to one side.'

Erin's voice is a whisper. 'Yes, most definitely.'

'See you soon, and try not to worry. If Lesley agrees, I'll ring him and explain about the little girl being my mum. It might help if he understands how personal it is for me, and why you tried to help.'

I'm about to ring off when Erin says, 'There is one thing ... a good thing of sorts. This—all the talk about brothers—has made me think about what you said before about Jason. You know, family ties. No family's perfect, right? Rifts happen all the time in my favourite stories, so I've decided to give him some slack and see what happens.'

I blink, hearing a mixture of uncertainty and determination. 'Absolutely. Good for you.'

'See you soon. Bye.'

I swing my chair towards my monitor. The screen goes blank. Yet, a glimmer of positivity shines through. Erin's admission about Jason stuns and overwhelms me. One cautionary tale from me, and she's opened herself to new relationship possibilities. I'm amazed, proud, envious. Inspired by her courage, I pick up the knife and slit open the package.

Thirty-one

Giddy relief lifts me out of my office chair. I'm invigorated and alert, as if a fresh, sweet wind has blown away storm clouds. I study the paperwork again, checking and rechecking. The hair samples show a ninety-eight percent probability Rick is Lara's father. Thank God. It's as good as it gets with 'non-standard' samples and good enough for me. The nightmare is over. I can return to my straightforward, solo guilt.

Regrets about my fling are no less acute because I have an answer. Does every cheater feel the same? Do we all wake up the morning after, mystified but instantly aware of the enormity of our misdeed, the lives damaged, including our own? Wondering why we did it, what insanity made us jeopardise our happiness? How saying words like, 'I love you,' sour on our tongues for months, years, never mind the stab when those endearments are repeated by our husbands or partners. Neither before, nor since, have I been tempted to stray. The knowledge Rick will never know is a false comfort, shaky grounds for absolution. Yet sparing him this anguish fills me with gratitude.

I replace the pages in their envelope and pump the air. Yes, yes, yes! Lara is Rick's little girl, her blond hair some kind of ancestral throwback. What, on earth, made me doubt it? I peek inside the package again, elated my anticipation of a grandchild and Lara's eventual big day will be unspoiled. Despite the overwhelming relief, my chest hitches with latent dread. I pluck a tissue, dab my face and allow my heart rate to settle.

My phone chirps. Brenda. Exquisite timing! I'm primed to put her in her place, putting a stop to the rumours surrounding my behaviour with Phillip at her hens' weekend.

'Megan, hi. How are you? I've been so worried about you.'

'Better, thanks. It's out of my system, so I'll be back to work soon.'

'Are you sure?'

'Lucky, I reckon. Small dose.'

'And Rick's well?'

'Unbelievable, but yes. Chloe had him trussed up like a supermarket chicken. And you? What's news of the cruise and party?'

'Don't ask. Same as Lara, I expect. Yes, no, yes, no. Even Bob's sick of it.'

'Must be making it hard for Tina to house-hunt, too.'

'Wow! You really are worried they'll move in next door, aren't you? I was kidding, you know.'

'Absolutely not. Phillip and Tina can do what they like. He and I might have had a sneaky kiss, I'll admit, but it went no further. And I'd appreciate you not bringing it up, please. I know I made light of it last time, but it's becoming a bore, frankly. And it isn't only me who might get hurt by loose talk.'

My shaking hand creates ripples in my coffee cup. Anyway, it's cold and disgusting. I put it back on my desk.

'Alright, alright. It was only a joke.'

'A joke which is no fun for me or'—I stop myself before mentioning Lara—'Rick ... or Tina.'

'Sorry, girlfriend.'

'Because if they do move near us, the opportunities for a blunder multiply, don't they?'

'Yeah. Sorry again.'

I hear a key in the lock. 'I have to go. Sounds like Rick's home early. Hope he hasn't caught it, too.'

'Speak soon?'

'Of course. Bye.'

The call finishes as Rick walks through the door. He glances at the opened envelope. I stop myself shooting a hand towards it. Fortunately, the contents are hidden.

'This is a surprise. What are you doing here?' I ask.

'I could say the same, mind. You need to be resting, not sneaking in here to work. Come on! Back to the sofa. I'll put something brainless on the TV for you.'

'Why are you back so quickly?'

'The lads reworked the schedule so I could do a local run. They could see I was worrying about you.'

'How considerate.'

His arm encircles my waist. He doesn't need to manhandle me but, riding high on a wave of relief, I welcome the sparks of pleasure prickling my skin. I take in Rick's lovely face. The man who looks at me as if he can't believe his luck when we make love, the man I've trusted to share intimacies. I plant a soft kiss on his lips, a different kind of tension blooming.

'Steady Eddie! What's this all about?' He catches my eye. 'Really? You feeling that much better?'

My lip curls playfully. I am well enough. And I want him.

'Right!' He loops one of my arms around his neck and slides one of his around my knees. 'Up we go.'

We aren't a couple for romantic gymnastics. Rick tried to carry me over the threshold on our wedding night, but the gesture ended in a mound of intertwined limbs on the prickly door mat. Today, he heaves and stumbles, bumping my hips against the desk. I find my feet as my half-drunk cup of coffee tips. Liquid spreads across the surface. Rick grabs the cup and thrusts it at me as I reach for the paperwork. I miss the baton pass, and the mug crashes at my feet, the last drips arcing across the rug.

'Ych a fi. You deal with that!' he shouts, pointing at the floor.

I watch in horror as he peels open the soggy envelope to extract my important 'work' papers. The letterhead proclaims the laboratory name in large, unmistakable characters.

'What's this? Tests? Is something wrong with you?'

The rollercoaster ride I presumed finished, takes a sickening switchback turn.

He flicks the limp page open and reads, his expression darkening. 'Important work stuff, you said. When were you going to tell me? In fact, why? Why are you checking whether Lara's mine? Or is that too obvious?' His voice is raw.

'I don't know what to say.' I'm numb, my stomach taut.

'Explain, or I'll walk straight back out the door.'

'No! Please, I'm so sorry. Can we sit down?'

'I'd rather stay here, to be honest.'

I reach for his hand, but he snatches it away. 'It says what I've always known. You're Lara's father. It's just—'

'I'm not an idiot. The only reason you'd arrange a test is if you had doubts. So, say it. You cheated on me!'

'Once, kind of.'

'Don't you dare try to excuse yourself. A kiss and a cuddle wouldn't cause this. I didn't imagine you even capable of that. So what happened? Who is he? Do I know him? I'll bloody kill him.'

'I slipped up at Brenda's hens' do.'

'So, who? A friend of hers? A stranger? A stripper?' Veins pulse at his temple.

'He knew Bob and met one of Brenda's girlfriends there. A few years later, they married. They live, lived, down south.'

'Are you keeping in touch? How do you know all this? Does he know you've sent off for a test?'

'I never see him. I know this through Brenda! And no, he doesn't know.' My eyes flash. 'I made a mistake, Rick, a terrible mistake, and I've never believed he was the father, until...'

'What?'

I wring my hands. 'They're moving back up this way because his parents are getting old. I went on Facebook to see if they were house-hunting. I didn't want them in our neighbourhood without any warning.' I'm rambling. Rick's brows knit together. 'They've never posted photos of their girls, but one of them turned eighteen and there were birthday snapshots of her.'

'And?'

'I'd never seen his daughter.'

'So, what, she looks like Lara, does she? Seriously? There must be thousands of girls who look like Lara! Although stalking this guy bothers me. Bothers me a lot, mind.'

'I haven't stalked him! Brenda talks about them. It's been once or twice in twenty-five years. I didn't want him on our doorstep.'

'Twenty-five years? Lara's twenty-four and we had trouble conceiving her. All adds up, doesn't it? Was it a mistake, or did you assume I was firing blanks? A quickie, away from the hubby, pregnant, Bob's your uncle!'

'Don't, Rick, please. It was nothing. And there's the results. You weren't firing blanks. It was probably me.'

'So, who is he?'

'It doesn't matter, does it? Blame me, but don't ask for details.'

'Come on. I need the details. If he's a friend of Brenda's, how can I not? I'm not bumping into him at a party and having him smirk at me. Or has it already happened?' His nostrils flare. 'If I've been in the same room as him, not knowing, I'll ... I'll...'

'You haven't. I've made sure of it.'

'Who is he, Megan? Or do I have to ask Brenda?'

I fold in on myself, rigid shock turning to limp misery. 'I'm sorry, I'm so sorry.'

There's a long silence. 'Were you ever planning to tell me?'

I can't find the words to be truthful without condemning myself.

'That's a no, then.'

'I've never wanted to doubt. But with Lara pregnant, there's been questions about her blood type and Chloe mentioned a little boy with no medical history. If I'd been wrong all these years, it could've ... it rocked me enough to check. But it's fine, isn't it?'

'You can't honestly think this can be swept under the carpet, can you? And why were you so sure he wasn't her father? What happened between you? You said you slipped up, kind of. I hope you used a bloody condom.'

'Rick, please.'

'No, you owe me an explanation!' he yells.

My chills are replaced by burning heat, rising up my torso. 'Can't you see what this is doing to me? You're being cruel. Have you forgotten what was happening? We weren't happy, Rick. Arguments all the time.'

He flicks his hand, dismissing my pathetic excuses. 'Tell me.'

'When I saw the picture of his daughter, I wondered if the condom had worked. They're not infallible, after all. There, satisfied.'

'Hardly. Was he?'

'No, not really.'

'Good.'

I wait for him to ask about my pleasure, anticipating the blow.

He pauses, chewing his lip. 'No, sorry. Not enough. Start at the beginning. If you don't, this'll eat me up.'

We bat the demand back and forth. I'm beaten by his rage, defeated.

'I drove off angry, like I said, except we'd snuck upstairs for sex, remember, and I reckon that was the time we did it. You and me, Rick! Like it says in the report. So, I get there, unpack and the bubbles flow. There was a big indoor spa in the basement, so we met up down there.'

'With him?'

'No, just the girls. And it was only us at dinner, too. In fact, these three chaps didn't turn up till much later in the evening. I'm not even sure Brenda saw them because she had too much to drink and was taken to her room quite early. As I said, they were Bob's friends. Though he wasn't there, obviously.' I stall.

'Come on, Megan. Spit it out.'

'One of them took an interest and offered to see me to my room.'

'What, like Brenda? Drunk? Took advantage, did he?'

'Tipsy!' I blurt, cheeks burning. 'We went inside and … and it happened. It was rubbish and the condom put him off his stride. I can't say any more, I simply can't.'

'If you're lying…'

'I'm not.' I hold his gaze, aware my blush, at its absolute peak, will cover my white lies, my moment of abandon.

'So, nothing for him to gloat about?'

I shake my head.

'Good.' He drags a hand across his brow. 'And it was only the once?'

'Yes! God damn you,' I growl.

A beat away from lashing out, he's curbed by my anguish. 'One photo, mind? Not real life, even. Lara looks like fifty different people, depending on how she's dressed or the expression she pulls.'

'I know. I only wanted to do the right thing.'

'Bit late. In the meantime, I could've had a cuckoo in the nest for twenty-four years. Didn't do it for my sake, did you?'

'You're her dad. Always will be.'

'Easy for you to say. And us? What does this do to us, Megan? How can I ever trust you again?'

Exhausted, my insides roiling, I have no answer to a question I hoped always to avoid.

He spins towards the door. 'I'm going back to work. Don't wait up. I'll make up the spare room when I get home. Sheets and stuff in the usual place?'

I dive forward. 'No, Rick, please. Don't do that.'

'Better than the Premier Inn.'

I grab at his arm. He pulls free.

'You've hurt me, Megan. I never expected this.'

His tears brim before he walks away.

Seconds later, the front door slams.

I swipe the keyboard off the desk, wincing as it crashes and bounces on the carpet. Folding my arms, I lean over, weeping, until my throat aches.

Thirty-two

I take a further two days sick leave, partly to ensure I'm fully recovered but more because of the real possibility I've driven my husband away. I welcome any distraction from the echoes of an empty house. Rick and I play happy families at opposite ends of the couch when Lara calls on Skype to discuss the marriage service and her ante-natal care, including a side-on view of her perfectly flat tummy which she insists is as big as a whale. When Chloe checks in on us, she reports on her work and the tentative hopes for a return to normal life, while covertly checking up on me and my recovery. If not for their calls, I'd be bereft.

On the day of my return to the office, I'm steadier and healthier, taking a ridiculous amount of time to choose between two outfits which neither Lesley nor Erin will notice. Grateful for the resumption of an absorbing pursuit, I concentrate on the next steps in the development of the database and protecting Erin from Lesley's censure.

My colleagues are at their desks when I arrive. Erin throws me what I assume is a beaming smile from behind her bandana and waves from her desk by the window. Lesley rises and beckons me into her pod. Erin's face falls.

'Megan! I wasn't expecting you so soon. Are you sure you're well enough to be here?' She frantically adjusts her mask, testing the edges for gaps.

'I can assure you I've had the "all clear." I'm not infectious. It's more about stamina and ability to concentrate.'

'Good, but please don't overdo it. And the guidelines remain firm. Distance, hand washing etcetera.'

'I'll be very careful.'

She crosses her legs. 'I suppose you know what Erin's done?'

'Yes, she told me.'

Lesley is poised to pounce, but I raise my hand and blurt my own regrets and offer to apologise to Thomas. In the end, Lesley admits she doubts a formal complaint will materialise.

'And Erin?' I ask.

'A warning, but I'm leaning towards letting her keep her job.'

'Does she know?'

Lesley bristles. 'My job, my timeframe, Megan, thank you.'

I walk away from her, aggravated after less than five minutes.

~ * ~

Our breaks revert to a two-horse event. Erin isn't off the hook yet, so she's unusually careless and overreacts to any kind of problem. Only when we sip coffee together, at a safe distance, face coverings held under our chins, does the tension ebb away.

We've nearly emptied the file boxes and have searched the office for any remaining material misfiled or stored at a time before the current system was in place. We come across a large stack of correspondence from when the charity first launched, several years prior to the 70th anniversary celebration. The accounts provided by the evacuees never lose their power to move us, bringing the need to regularly debrief, especially after reading something grim. We agreed, weeks ago, to counterbalance a 'bad' story with something 'good.'

Today's lunch hour is no different. Erin bounces through the kitchen door and stops dead. 'Go on. Spill,' she says.

'It's nothing new. We've heard it countless times. But why did they line children up in village halls and have host families go up and down, choosing? It makes me feel sick, especially if I imagine it happening to my girls. Hadn't they ever read stories of slavery? Horrible rich people inspecting teeth and biceps? Or men choosing stock in cattle yards? They did the same thing.'

'I know what you mean. Doesn't take much to put yourself in the children's shoes, especially if you were last to be picked. Like me, with sport. Maybe the grownups assumed it was fine because the kids were young.'

'Or the adults didn't like having to take in strangers, but they didn't have a choice.' I sigh. 'Come on, your turn to tell me something good.'

'One girl told her mother she had ladybirds on her pillowcase, when in fact, they were bed bugs!'

I shiver. 'Not good!'

'Made you squirm, eh? And … one kid was so bored she kept herself amused by folding and refolding her underpants!'

'Again, sad and not good.'

'Sorry. It's the detail, isn't it? Fancy harking back to those little things. Makes you appreciate what an impact it had.'

'It does … but, back to it. If we keep this up, we'll be done before we know it.'

'Hold up. You haven't said anything about the family. How's Rick?'

I blink, mute.

'Oh, God, is he alright? Shouldn't you be with him if he's caught it too?'

I clear my throat. 'No. Just some bad news. On his side of the family.' Almost too true. 'I'd rather not discuss it.'

'Sorry.' With two hands she rotates her mug back and forth.

'Come on. What is it?'

'The database. You need a distraction. Let's check the arrivals for Cirencester.' She sees my alarm. 'Why not? You can't upset anyone by verifying entries on a computer screen.'

'You need to be careful, we both do. I haven't discussed it with Lesley, but I doubt she'll continue to give my search her blessing after what happened with Thomas.'

'So we keep it quiet.'

'Erin...' My parental tone embarrasses me.

She peeks around the door, turns back and grins. 'Lesley's busy, so we're fine. Come on, Megan. It's the last thing, isn't it? I mean, where else are you going to find the information we need? You can't leave this stone unturned. What we need is a little luck on our side.'

We're startled by movement. Our boss stands in the doorway, eyeing us suspiciously. 'My mother's not well, so I'm taking the rest of the day off and probably won't be in tomorrow, either. She lives on the south coast, so I can't get there and back without staying overnight.'

'Not the virus, I hope,' I say.

'Hopefully not, but it's hard to tell.'

'Sorry,' Erin mumbles. 'Hope she's okay.'

Lesley's gaze flicks between us, settling on neither. 'Thank you. I'll make a move straight away and call you tomorrow to let you know my plans. I hope you can hold the fort, Megan. I'm sorry this is happening when you've just arrived back.'

'Please don't worry, we'll be fine. Plenty to do. This is far more important.'

She retreats, eager to get away.

Erin winks. 'What did I say?'

Thirty-three

As well as a database search, Lesley's absence gives me an opportunity to make amends on Erin's behalf. It's a risk, but I'm confident I can explain her actions to Thomas Barker and ask after his intentions. If he plans to make a complaint, a chat will give me a chance to talk him out of it—rather my head on the block than Erin's. I'll make the call after she leaves.

By mid-afternoon, after another painstaking session of data entry, Erin has a list of boys who arrived in Cirencester on the evening of September 1, 1939.

She flaps the page. 'There are six, three we know about and three others, two about the right age.' Excitement oozes from her pores. Since Lesley's departure, my spirited, energetic colleague has returned.

I shift papers and point to the opposite side of the desk. 'Scoot your chair over there, and I'll turn the monitor. This should meet the rules.'

While Erin relocates herself, I read the names: the Barker siblings, Michael, Thomas, and Gerald; Alfie Parker, Jerry Miller and Robert Wilkins. Erin shivers as we agree to put the Barker family to one side as we know, to her cost, my mother isn't Karen and Gerald isn't her brother. Clicking the database, I bring up the record for Alfie, hastily scrutinising the details. It's a short, succinct missive. At eight years of age, he was billeted with the Davis family. Within a few months, he returned to London due to severe homesickness. He said his family were so glad to have him back, and vice versa, he was never sent away again.

I click to Jerry Miller.

'Hey, steady on,' Erin says. 'I haven't finished.'

I comply, forcing myself not to tap my pen. She nods and we progress through the records again. Jerry was seven years old. Stating his destination as Cirencester, yet most of his letter describes being billeted with Alice and Bernard Thompson in Reading, where he enjoyed a happy childhood resulting in his adoption by them. My brow twitches.

Finally, Robert Wilkins, twelve years of age, was sent to a family who owned a small factory. Used as cheap labour and treated badly, he was extremely unhappy. The lack of food, warmth and care are described in painful detail. It takes a moment before we can speak.

'Well? Is it one of them?'

The two younger boys are the only serious contenders. 'Alfie Parker. Gerald Barker. Caryl Baker. I can't believe there are so many similar surnames.'

'But, Alfie, going back to London 'cos he's homesick? It might explain why your mum lost track of him.'

I narrow my vision, concentrating. 'Three things. Firstly, this surname business—misspelling wasn't common. The British people weren't all illiterate back then. Secondly, if Alfie went to a different family and not to Gwen Roberts, surely my grandma, Kathleen, would've been consulted about him returning to London without her. It's the argument my dad always raises, and it makes sense. If Kathleen had been kept informed, Gwen would've known, too, yet she's always denied knowing about Mum's brother, assuming she told the truth, of course. I mean, it isn't a big town. News and gossip would've spread like wildfire. Finally, he says he went back to a family in London, but Mum didn't have a family.'

Erin's shoulders droop. 'So what about Jerry?'

'Jerry's the right age, he arrived in Cirencester too, yet like Alfie, moved away, which begs the same questions. Why didn't my grandma and Gwen know? And there's nothing to explain why he ended up in Reading. My geography's not the best, but it's a fair distance, isn't it?'

'Give me a sec.' She opens an app on her phone, finds directions between the two points on a map, with a mileage calculation. 'Reading's approximately sixty miles, south-east.'

'Exactly my point. So, did Bernard and Alice have a house in Cirencester first, before moving away? Why would Jerry go with them? Would Kathleen have let him go?'

'It's possible, if he'd grown attached to them.'

'True but, again, why didn't Gwen know? How could two women living in the same house not talk to each other?' I run my fingers through my hair. 'And his name's completely different. That's not a clerical error.'

'So what now?'

'Nothing, because nothing fits, does it?

'Can you follow up on anything? Put their names into other searches?'

'There are a few places I can go to for more information, but I'm not holding out much hope. I certainly can't take this to Mum. Sometimes, I wonder if we're barking up the wrong tree.'

'All those surnames ... Barker, Baker, Parker, Miller? They're all occupations, aren't they? We talked about it in Social Studies.'

We fall into silence, deflated.

With one task falling flat, I turn to a mission carrying a greater chance of success. Encouraging Erin to leave, I'm keen to call Thomas before the working day ends. I can't afford to put him offside by catching him peeling potatoes for his dinner.

Erin takes her time closing down her computer. It's a warm evening and she throws her denim jacket over her arm. We say goodbye, and she's gone. I find Thomas's number and dial, worrying at a chipped nail while I wait. When a man answers, I launch in with a formal, polite introduction.

'You do realise this is the third time I've been contacted, and the last call was very upsetting. I'm not sure I've anything else to say,' he begins.

'I understand, Mr Barker. A dreadful mistake was made. But I'd like to talk to you, if it's convenient.'

I tell him my story, the search for my uncle, and the unfortunate path taken by Erin on my behalf but without either my knowledge or any encouragement.

'It was a nasty shock, Mrs Williams. I was furious at the time.'

'I completely understand. She's sorry, I'm sorry. We all wish it hadn't happened. Being pushed to talk about the fate of your siblings must have been very distressing.'

'It was. I never normally speak of it.' Silence. I wait. 'I suppose you want to know whether I'm going to complain?'

'I hope it won't be necessary.'

'The other one seemed less sure.'

My teeth clench. 'Our manager is a strong believer in rules. For her, Erin crossed a line.'

'Didn't take any interest in Michael and me ... your boss, not the girl.'

'Tell me, instead. I've read your letter, but I'd like to hear more about the people you stayed with. They treated you well, didn't they? It'd be lovely to hear about hosts who really tried.'

'Yes, the Beaumont sisters had good intentions. Gave me food, clothes and my own room with a feather bed and as many blankets as I needed. Trust me, it was a far cry from my childhood in London. Wasn't so bad when it was just me and Michael, but once Gerald came along, we were squashed on the one hard mattress like sardines. But the Beaumonts had a huge house with a big garden. Carpet, thick curtains, staff! I caught a few clips round the ears from them, calling me the little prince, but most of the time, they were good to me. On top of which, they sent me to a first-rate school where I won a scholarship to Winchester College, which set up my future. I was in my last year when the war ended, so I was an educated young man when I returned to London. My family hardly recognised me.'

I hear the same mix of Cockney and Belgravia noted by my colleague. 'Erin said something about your situation having downsides. Is that what you meant?'

'Yes, mixed blessing. I'm not ungrateful, but I never fitted back in. I don't think my parents ever recovered from what the evacuation program did to our family. They lost us all, one way or another.'

'Did you make friends in Cirencester?'

'Oh, yes. Funnily enough, one was the boy a few doors away, at least, until I got the measure of him. We were thick as thieves during the holidays. In all honesty, I spent most of my time in the other house and garden because there was so much more going on. The Babbington-Careys had three children—'

I repeat the surname in a strangled, high-pitched voice.

'Yes, why?' he asks.

'My mum, the little girl I spoke about, she was there, too, and played with their daughter, Lucy.'

'I remember the two of them! Goodness, she was your mother? What a turn up for the books. Ralph and I were older, so we didn't involve ourselves with the younger ones. Now I understand why this is so personal for you.'

'Thank you, yes, it is. So, are you Tommy? Sorry, I'll explain. Mum visited the house, years later, and met Aubrey, the dad, and Ralph. Aubrey referred to you by that name.'

'Yes, it's me. I dropped the shortened version as soon as I went to Winchester. Sounds odd to me these days. I wonder how Ralph felt being reminded of the past? We didn't stay in touch.'

'Can I ask ... does this mean anything? Aubrey told her you ate them out of house and home.'

'I doubt it. I was well fed by the Beaumonts. It was probably their own evacuee, Jerry, I think his name was. Stringy thing.'

'Jerry Miller?'

'I don't recall the surname, sorry. He ran away, you know, like Michael.'

'Did he end up in Reading?'

'I've no idea, but it caused quite a fuss.'

'Sorry, I'm getting distracted again. This should be about you, not my family mystery.' There's a gap. I suspect he's tiring of my company. 'It's a pity you didn't go to the service at St Paul's. Mum was there.'

'A lost opportunity. Far too old for another major event. We'll all be gone soon. How incredible we were in the same town and could've ended up at the same service. Will you tell her about me, please? Ask if she remembers me?' He pauses. 'Thank you for your call and for letting me chat. I find it hard to believe I'm talking to the daughter of a child I met all those years ago. It doesn't make up for not finding Michael, but it's something. I hope you have better luck with your search. At least we're clear she can't be my sister. Putting the accident to one side, if she travelled with her mother, she can't be the same girl. Mine stayed in London and somehow dodged the Blitz. Lived to a ripe old age.'

'I should be thanking you. You've given me a valuable suggestion about Jerry. Thank you very much.'

'You know, if that information leads anywhere, I won't mind you contacting me again.'

'Thank you, I will.'

'And I won't complain about your colleague. Let's leave it there, shall we?'

'Thanks again. Erin will be so relieved. She's a good girl underneath.'

'Goodbye and good luck. Oh dear, can't get away from the war time references, can we?'

'Vera Lynne?'

'It never goes away.'

The line goes dead.

I tap my fingernails, aware I'll be late home. Rick will worry, but I can't leave. I retrieve the scanned copy of Jerry Miller's correspondence, hands trembling.

When he answers, I choose my words carefully. 'Mr Miller, hi, it's Megan Williams from the Society for Evacuees. Do you have a minute?'

I use an excuse about entries for the database. Despite my good manners, his responses are brusque. I finish by asking him about his change of location from Cirencester to Reading.

'No great mystery,' he replied. 'I was moved the same day. Too many of us for that town, so they shipped me off to the couple who adopted me, the Thompsons. I said as much in my letter.'

He appears so sure. Who am I to question him? 'You did. So, no host family in Cirencester at all? You didn't stay with a family called the Babbington-Careys?'

'No. No. I've never heard of them.' His patience is waning.

'As we're trying to organise our materials, I might highlight the change of location to Reading.'

'Suit yourself.'

I pull up the digital copy of the cathedral guest list. Locating his name, I aim to end on a positive note. 'I see you attended the Seventieth Anniversary celebration in 2009. I hope it was beneficial, catching up with others who had the same experience.'

'Didn't know a soul but, yes, it was a lovely day. Gave us all the chance to chat and share our stories.'

'Good, I'm glad. Thanks, Mr Miller. You've been very helpful.'

'What was your name again?'

'Megan Williams.'

'Goodbye and good luck.'

The call ends. The Jerry who lived with and ran away from the Babbington-Careys, is another Jerry, and not the Jerry Miller who wrote to the charity and attended the cathedral service. I've exhausted every avenue. Dad and I have done our best. Betty Bloch, Erin, even Thomas gave a final promising lead which crashed on further investigation. Weary, I pack up my workstation, pick up my keys and stride out of the door.

I can set things straight with Lesley to save Erin, but, surely, this is it for Mum—her life search is over.

Thirty-four

Rick and I have brought coffee and rolls to Port Sunlight River Park. Neutral ground. To break the sizzling friction between us, I insisted we call a truce and discuss our relationship. He's hardly been home, working double shifts. Worst of all, he's still sleeping in the spare bed. I hear him toss and turn as I lie awake, exhausted.

Does Rick, like me, hold hopes relating to the name of the park? If sunshine, like Mum's catchphrase, fails to assist us, I have a block of Belgian chocolate to lift my mood.

We drive in silence, unpack the car and trudge between the industrial buildings. They house the filters dealing with the waste from this one-time landfill site. Once through the gate, the regenerated park and wetlands open out. The Mersey River and Liverpool on the opposite bank shimmer in the morning sunshine.

We continue down a gravel path to the lake, searching for a private place to set up our picnic. If anyone in authority asks, we're here to exercise, though the chairs will be difficult to explain.

'Will this do?' he asks.

'Yes, super.' A Red Admiral butterfly hovers and dips on a nearby buddleia. Ducks squabble on the far shoreline.

'Coffee? Sandwich?' I hold up the thermos.

'No, not yet. I want this sorted.'

'Me too.'

The silence returns.

When the awkwardness becomes too much, I say, 'I'm sorrier than I can ever express. I'm also sorry I mentioned our arguments. There's no excuse. It was wrong and didn't help.'

'No, it didn't.'

'What can I do? Tell me,' I beg.

'Phillip Harris, wasn't it?'

My breath stops. 'How? How did you...?'

'Taste of your own medicine. What's it like to have someone go behind your back?'

'Brenda.'

'God, no! It was Bob, chatting over the soccer about elderly parents. Didn't take long for him to mention Tina and Phillip, the solicitor, leaving his job in Kent to come back to Liverpool. I can use the internet, too, you know. Didn't take long to find him.'

'Did he suspect anything?' I visualise Bob recounting the conversation to his wife, her antennae quivering like a praying mantis.

'Don't worry. I was subtle. Couldn't get rid of those pictures of you with some stranger, so now I know. Tall blond hunk of a man, probably suave and gobby. He had to be blond, didn't he? Oh, and not a lorry driver. Classy.'

I bristle. 'None of it counted for anything. I was ... God, I said I wouldn't bring it up again, but I was in a bad spot. I couldn't have cared less about his job.'

'Then, why? It all comes back to that.'

'I'm in a complete bind here, can't you see? If I say I was unhappy and took the first—and only—opportunity to cheat on you, you'll be devastated. I would be too if you'd done the same to me.'

'But that's it, isn't it, when it all boils down to it?'

'Jesus, yes. He showed me a bit of attention and I...' Tears form. 'I'm so ashamed. So ashamed.'

Minutes pass. A warm hand covers mine. I sit upright, slowly, black spots swirling in front of me.

'When Lara was little, people used to comment on her hair. It never bothered me, but I often saw you cringe. That was why, wasn't it?'

I nod.

'And the two of them not being alike. I overheard Caryl saying it once.' He inhales sharply. 'But she has my blue eyes.'

The mental list I'd formulated over the past months slips off my tongue. 'And your asthma, and the funny bend in her little toe, and the way she waves her hands around when she talks, and the "tutting" sound she makes when she thinks someone's being stupid. There's a hundred ways she's like you.'

'Is it the only lie in our marriage?'

My mouth twitches. 'Except for the little things. The things everyone covers up. Like whether we like Mum's custard tart.'

A grin begins to form before he catches himself. 'Slippery slope, mind.'

'There's nothing, honestly. The worst is probably spending too much money on the girls and fudging the true costs. Oh, and I never liked the bracelet you bought me for our tenth. There, honest enough?'

'And I never wanted a new camera.'

'Even Stephens.'

'Talking of which, your dad's politics drive me up the wall.'

'Fair enough. He deserves that. In which case, you've bitten your tongue for a very long time.'

'This isn't a competition.'

I startle. 'No, of course not. Sorry, I thought...'

We fall into silence again.

Rick shifts on the uncomfortable chair. 'I get the white lie thing. But trust? I'm so angry with you. We were rock solid, Megan. Rock solid.'

'I know, and there's nothing I can do to change it.'

'What do we do?' He looks away. 'Do you love me?' he whispers.

'Oh, Rick. I've always loved you. You must know.'

'Everything's on thin ice, like I'm going to fall through any second.'

'Did you ever feel like this before? Did you worry about trusting me before you found out? Nearly thirty years we've been together.'

'No, I didn't but ... the doubts are there, if I'm honest.'

'Not if you take my word, like all the others you've believed and relied on. I didn't actually lie.'

'Including about what happened?'

Blood seeps into the vessels on my cheeks.

'I thought so.'

I grab his arms. 'For you, for you. I can't go over it again or describe it anymore. It's horrible, ghastly. I once heard about putting things in an imaginary box and locking it in the attic. It's what I've done with this.'

'Is it why you suddenly started to pull away when I nuzzle your neck?'

'Rick, stop. Please, stop.'

'There's another lovely image.' His face contorts as if listening to a dentist's drill.

I raise two palms in a gesture of defeat. 'I need a drink. You?'

He shrugs.

Thermos shaking, I dribble liquid into two plastic beakers, jolted by the thought that coffee precipitated my undoing. Handing over the cup, a question sticks in my throat. 'Do you love me?'

His prolonged hesitation guts me. 'Yes. No. I guess there are worse things.' He lets out a long sigh. 'I can't not love you.'

I stifle a moan. 'Can we try again? Please? There are so many good things, good times. You were my first love, so handsome with your lovely sing-song turn of phrase. I couldn't wait for the holidays, pestered and nagged Mum and Dad to go back to Conwy every time. It was like a second home, which became my reality when we married. I was so happy there until... And once Lara came along, we were complete, a little family, and you made me so proud the way you threw yourself into their hobbies and ever-changing likes and dislikes. I used to stand back and think, wow, what a great Dad, mine, ours. Always considering me and the two of them, loving us, caring for us. I've never had second thoughts, never.'

'Me, neither.'

'I'll be forever sorry I did this to you. I can't take it away, but I'll spend the rest of my life making it up to you.'

'Yeah, I believe you will.'

I sink back. So many words to choose from, swirling, twisting, as I search for ways to adequately articulate my remorse. 'Every day, I'm going to write a note and tell you what you mean to me. Big things, little things, all the ways you make my life worthwhile.'

His voice cracks. 'Sounds tidy.'

'And I'm going to start with this because we have to deal with it ... the wedding. Whatever happens, I know you won't want our problems to spoil Lara's day so, here it is. I've loved your excitement about walking her down the aisle. Loved seeing you hug yourself silly.'

'Add being a grandad.'

'And the news about the baby.'

'A little baby again. I've forgotten what to do with them.'

'You haven't, you certainly have not. There, that's tomorrow's note too. The way you held them both when they wouldn't settle and I was at the end of my tether. I couldn't have done it without you.'

Tears stream down my cheeks. His too.

'We'll be alright, won't we?' I whisper.

'I want it to be alright between us, I do, it's just ... today's been good, mind. Getting away. Talking. I can see how sorry you are, how much you want things to go back to where they were. And it was a long time ago, I agree, and I never knew or suspected, which suggests you're being truthful that it didn't mean anything. But...'

I sit, mute.

'You've made a hole in my heart which will take time to heal. I can't say fairer than that.'

'But we'll try? Please say you'll give it a chance.'

He heaves a sigh. 'I have to, even if it's hard. I mean, what's the alternative?'

'I don't want to think about it.'

'Exactly.'

Smothering a sob, I wait for his forgiveness, but it doesn't come. 'Can we cwtch up, at least.'

'I'm not ready for a cuddle, not yet, sorry.'

My stomach cramps, icy cold.

Thirty-five

Pulling into the car park at the back of the Victorian villa, I put aside memories of the fragile reconciliation with my husband. My work at the charity is complete, the materials organised, categorised and digitised. I'm proud but sad to leave. Reuniting Mum with her brother would have been the icing on the cake, even so, I've enjoyed my contract here.

I'm taking my time, tidying my desk, separating paper clips from thumb tacks, placing sharpened pencils in my plastic stationery tray. From there, I approach the bookshelves, casting my eye along the spines of archive boxes, ensuring the dates are all present and ordered. Taking down several, at random, I examine the contents, making certain they're accurately labelled and stored. The database is less worrisome. Being pragmatic and assuming new programs come along as computers morph and develop, the code is in a form which will be updated with every other twenty-first century digital footprint. Barring some kind of cataclysmic technological meltdown, it is preserved.

I'm going to miss my colleagues. Erin peeks at me, her face melancholy. Lesley hides behind her monitor, her mood unknown. I keep working, delaying the moment when we have to say our goodbyes, anxious Erin might cry or Lesley will drop a verbal clanger, something gauche and annoying.

I beckon Erin into the kitchen for a morning coffee, keen for a private chat.

'Cheer up,' I say. 'There's good news. I'm donating the coffee plunger. Can't deprive you of "almost as good as café coffee".'

'Thank God. I thought I'd have to scour the antique shops for one.' Erin smirks but I can see she's upset.

'Oy, missy.'

'I wish you didn't have to go. I've loved working with you.'

'Me, too.' There's more I'd like to say, but I'm struggling to find the words.

'And, thanks again for getting me off the hook with Lesley.'

'It was the only thing to do. Besides, Thomas got the whole picture when I spoke to him about Mum. It made your involvement completely understandable.'

'I'm grateful.' She stops for a beat. 'Sorry we didn't find your uncle. Would've been amazing, wouldn't it?'

'Came close. I honestly believed we'd cracked it when your phone call to Thomas led to Jerry. And remember, I didn't imagine we'd find anything at all. My whole life, I've relied on facts and figures instead of allowing myself to daydream, a little. You've helped me.'

'Right back at you, with your Mum's story. I spent months avoiding Jason, wishing he'd change, fantasising about having a different family. Turns out, it was up to me to find some common ground.'

'What was that?'

'D and D.'

I frown.

'Dungeons and Dragons. We build games where characters interact in a made-up world. It helps that I read fantasy books when I was younger. My job is to draw the scenes. We make up an imaginary city, island, or someplace else, and I try to get it down on paper.'

'Wow! Has it been a thing for long? The girls talked about it years ago.'

'Yeah, since way back in the seventies. Virtually prehistoric. It's never lost its popularity, though. And perfect for lockdown.'

'Steady on. I was a teenager in the seventies. But, good for you. And ... Luke? No reunion?'

'No. I've thought about him a lot, but he didn't deserve me. I can do better.'

'Good decision. There's someone worthy out there. Be patient.'

She grins. 'I can be now I don't hate the sight of my bro! And Lara? How's she?'

I drift back to the momentous Zoom call we held recently when Lara's news was shared with the rest of the family. She received the reactions we'd both predicted. Chloe was furious about not being told earlier and launched into a full-scale Q&A session about her care, progress, weight, eating habits and would have gone on and on if we hadn't stopped her. Darren merely offered a quick word of congratulation, which evened up the time score. Mum and Dad were visibly shocked, especially Dad, but soon came around when they could see Rick and I were happy. My insides flip as I recall the warmth of Rick's hand as it covered mine and squeezed gently.

Once the family was informed, I told my colleagues. Erin was delighted, whereas Lesley was slow to respond. I expected another barb about Lara's age; instead she offered congratulations tinged with sadness. In that moment, I knew I'd leave this place having only scratched the surface of her character.

I'm returned to the present by Erin's voice. 'Earth to Megan. Lara? How is she?'

'Sorry. Great. Glowing. If you have to marry while you're expecting, this is the best time. She isn't even showing, but she's bought a different dress. Online! Hope it fits.'

I check my watch. 'Sorry, Lesley wants to see me at eleven, but, before you go ... I meant what I said before. I know we didn't succeed, but we wouldn't have achieved half as much without your persistence and belief. And clever detective work. You've a good brain, Erin, learning to do the data entry so quickly. You should go back to college, train up for something new, find out what else you're capable of.'

'I've been thinking about stuff, too. As much as I love receptionist work, I'd like some new challenges.'

'Stay in touch. Let me know if I can help. You've got my number.'

'I was hoping you'd say that.'

'Done.'

'Good luck with Lesley.'

'Thanks. And one more thing. If I ever find my uncle, I'll let you know.'

She beams. 'Thanks. I'd love you to.'

~ * ~

On the dot of eleven, I'm called into Lesley's office.

She closes the door and says, 'I'm not good at making speeches, and I wanted to speak to you alone. Firstly, thank you for the great job you've done. The archive is safe. I've spoken to the board, and they're delighted. They want me to pass on their thanks.'

'Thank you. Much appreciated. Can you let them know for me, please?'

'I will. They're also excited about the potential for some positive publicity from the database launch. Are you happy to write a story for the website? If you send it to me, I'll pass it to our website contractor.'

'Of course. May take a few weeks.'

'As quickly as you can, please. And something else. As you know, my mother hasn't been well, so I've decided I need to be closer to her. It's taken me a while to come to a decision, so the timing's not perfect but ... I've spoken to the board about my replacement, adding administration of the website to the role. It will save the charity money and might be of interest to someone with computer skills. Someone who's already invested time in the database.'

I gulp. 'Are you offering me your job?'

'I'm suggesting you apply. The board would make the appointment.'

'Sorry, yes, of course. You think I might be suitable?'

'I'd go as far as to say I'm recommending you for the position.'

'I don't know what to say. This is most unexpected.'

'You're welcome. Would you want it?'

'Want it? I'd love it!'

'And the gap? I'm not sure how quickly the board will move, but if they know you're interested, I'm sure they'd speed things along.'

'I could get some temp work, I suppose?' Rick's face appears in front of me, deep frown lines furrowing his brow.

'What about polishing up your website skills? The organisation downstairs needs someone for two months to update their platform. It's not the best pay, but it might be useful to have some recent work on your CV.'

I stifle a sigh as my eyes drift to the staircase, and the office on the ground floor. I've not had the opportunity to make friends with the staff because of the virus, but they've always appeared welcoming. 'I'm definitely open to suggestions if it means having a shot at your job.' I shuffle my feet. 'Can I ask why you're doing this? Not that I'm ungrateful.'

'Life. It's a two-way street. I've learnt things from you, useful things. For one, I've seen the change in Erin. It was you, not me.

The other day, I caught her taking a personal call, and she panicked, assuming she'd get into trouble.' She smooths her hair, turning her head, to scrutinise the reflection of herself that bounces off the glass wall. 'It's my reputation, I know. But she blurted out the whole story about how you'd brought her and her brother together. It was Jason on the phone, wanting to know what she'd like for her birthday.'

'I'm glad it helped. And I'm glad you kept her on.'

Her nose twitches. 'I'm not sure I'd have approved of another phone call to Mr Barker but you smoothed the problem away for us all, including Erin.'

'I had to try. It was my responsibility.'

She nods briskly. 'And this situation with the virus. Everyone's at risk, you were ill, Mum's so poorly, yet I didn't have to worry about leaving because I knew you'd do a good job, which meant a lot when I was dashing to the other end of the country.'

'It was no problem.'

'Even so, this is my thank you to you. If you want me to let the board know you're interested in the role, I'll phone the chair today.'

'Yes, please. I'm more than happy to see where this goes, including anything on offer from the business downstairs.'

'I'll ring Patrick, the boss, and see if he can fit you in for a chat before you go.' She taps on a key to bring her monitor to life, no doubt searching for the contact details. 'Fortunately, there isn't as much red tape with temporary positions.' She realigns her mouse pad, then looks up. 'Those enquiries into your Mum's evacuation? I presume there was no further progress.'

'No. A series of dead ends. Again.'

'I'm sorry. Truly.'

'Thanks. I did my best, with Erin's help. By the way, does she know you're leaving?'

'Not yet. We can give her the short version at lunchtime. Don't let her hug you because I know she'll try. We need to keep our distance.'

With Lesley's directives for ultra-safe social interactions ringing in my ears, I return to my desk, smothering a grin, hardly able to take in her proposition. Manager, continuing overseer of the database, website administrator, supervisor and colleague to Erin, my adoptive daughter. I can send her on a business administration course, coach her, act as a mentor. If only I didn't have to take our bank balance into consideration. No, I'd make this work even if we lived on baked beans for the next six months. There was no way I was going to pass on this dream opportunity.

Towards the end of the morning, there's a flurry of activity behind me I'm pretty sure I should ignore. I purposefully turn away from the kitchen.

The moment arrives. I'm invited in, the table transformed by a white cloth, a cake sitting high off the table with glittery letters spelling 'Good Luck.' A lump forms in my throat.

'Couldn't let you leave without a bit of a do,' Erin says. 'Even if it's only the three of us.'

'It's the quality that counts,' I reply.

'Coffee everyone?' Lesley asks.

We take our seats while she boils the kettle and measures out the grounds.

'Megan's leaving the plunger for us, thank goodness. Couldn't go back to instant,' Erin says.

'I agree. A big improvement.' Lesley passes round the drinks and hands me a knife.

I stand, reach across and cut three big slices. Lesley blinks, a picture of calorie-conscious alarm.

'So, what's next?' Erin shovels the rich sponge and cream cake into her mouth.

'A few days off for the wedding. Then, who knows?'

Lesley eats a tiny forkful before pushing the plate away. 'You know "Good Luck" was an appropriate choice of greeting if Megan gets to stay.'

Erin's eyebrows knit together. 'What do you mean?'

Lesley signals her permission for me to break the news.

After explaining the changes, as predicted, Erin stands up, ready to launch at me. Lesley and I drop our forks and raise 'Stop' hands.

'Spoil sports.'

When she's safely back in her chair, I continue. 'We have to follow due process. It's not a done deal. The only certainty is we'll have to repeat this farewell soon, for Lesley.'

'Good. More cake! Oh, sorry. This means you're leaving, doesn't it? I got so caught up in Megan's news...' Erin blusters through an apology and words about congratulations and new horizons.

Lesley accepts them with good grace.

'What will you do for work?' I ask.

'I'll probably take a few weeks off then look around. Hopefully, there'll be something as pleasant as this.'

There's an awkward silence.

'Right, I'll go back to my pod and ring Patrick. And when you're finished, Megan, the board will approve if I let you go home a few minutes early.' She rises, rinses her cup and plate and leaves the room.

Erin and I shake our heads.

~ * ~

Patrick is delighted to offer me six weeks work. It involves updating the organisation's website—a mental health not-for-profit—which, fortunately, is modern and intuitive, built on a ready-made platform for small businesses that lack the finances for an expensive corporate version. It lacks zing, something I'm sure I can improve. The money is adequate enough, allowing me to make a strong case to Rick. The prospect of remaining physically close—on-call, virtually—for a position I covet, is a price I'm prepared to pay and I'm sure I can convince him of the same. I say 'yes' without consulting my husband, something I wouldn't have questioned a few weeks ago, but which niggles my conscience coming so soon after our lovely ceasefire. Heat floods my body as I reminisce over the make-up sex, slow at the beginning, intensely powerful, climbing the peak to blissful release as one, his eyes locked onto mine.

I hang back at the doorway to fan my face before striding forward and giving my colleagues the thumbs up. I need only move my personal belongings and emergency jumper to a new part of the building. Which, given I'll be using the downstairs kitchen, leaves the awkward business of the coffee plunger. Erin might need to visit a few antique shops, after all. A note in Lesley's handwriting is stuck to the edge of my monitor. I place it inside the box, next to my mug, an energy bar, a half full packet of cuppa soups, a scarf, toiletries and photo frame of my family.

The note reads, 'Phone Jerry Miller. Urgent.'

Part Three

Caryl
2020

Thirty-six

With the shielding rules relaxed, Megan has persuaded Stephen to let me accompany her on a car trip. We had hoped to visit Chester to buy our dresses for Felix and Lara's wedding, but both my husband and granddaughter were horrified by the suggestion, mask or no mask. Instead, I've dug out a simple outfit I bought for a charity event two years ago and Megan has taken her chances online.

Putting the disappointment aside, a day trip is a brilliant tonic after months in lockdown.

'Dad said we're not to rush,' she informs me.

'Are we going far?'

'You'll see.'

An hour later, we're on the M56, travelling north, then east. 'Are we calling in at Lara's?'

'No, not Manchester, Buxton.'

'Buxton? Whoever lives there? Though it's said to be a pretty little place.' She glances at me, her expression an odd mix of excitement and fear. 'What's the story?'

'I'm meeting someone.'

'Oh, you didn't say. I'll wait in the car.'

The road glides under us. Green fields flash by. Once past Stockport, the landscape becomes hillier, like North Wales. Dry stone walls surround fields, the same material used for farmhouses and cottages. I'm happy to sit and watch new scenery after months staring at four walls.

Megan had entered an address into her new-fangled navigation program back in Chester, the robotic voice speaking more regularly as we reach a little chequered flag. We pull up outside a long, single-storey building, a barn conversion, I'd guess, built of the same local stone and divided into four homes. Two baskets of brightly coloured flowers hang on either side of each jade green front door, with a wooden bench seat for every dwelling. We park in a large courtyard off a quiet lane.

'Don't worry about me, love. I might stretch my legs. It's safe enough out here.'

'No, come with me. Here, put this on. Dad's orders.'

She passes me a mask which I pull across my face and over my ears. Megan does the same with hers. 'Who is it?'

She doesn't reply, but scoots round to my door, opens it and offers her arm as I lever my arthritic hips into a standing position.

'I wish you'd tell me,' I grumble.

The door opens. An elderly man stands in the opening, his wavy hair gunmetal grey, exactly like mine. Another old coot, vulnerable, face covered.

'Mum, meet Jerry.'

I step forward, putting out my hand before Megan gently pats it away with a warning glare. 'I'm embarrassed, sorry. Megan hasn't explained who you are. I hope you don't mind.'

'Carol, how could I? I'm your brother.'

'What?' I turn to Megan, eyes wide.

'It's true, Mum.'

A gush of warmth swells inside. I blink back tears.

The little boy in the photograph finally turns and transforms into the man before me.

~ * ~

Once my shock has subsided, we sit in Jerry's garden, chairs appropriately distanced, sipping glasses of iced tea. I've yearned to hug them both and shower Megan with thanks and kisses. It's excruciating to be so close and unable to make any kind of physical contact. I remind myself of those less fortunate—this is a beginning, not an ending, like the tragedies that have befallen so many families.

My smile muscles haven't worked this hard in years, my shoulders sore from hunching them upwards and clasping my hands, an almost childlike gesture of delight. I don't care. I've waited eighty-one years for this moment. For once, I'm glad to be forgiven for acting silly and breaking social norms. I sense Jerry's indulgence, bringing more tears and a tantalising sense of the relationship we once had before we were ripped away from each other.

Megan glances between the two of us, mostly at me, her happiness paired with a worried brow. Her anxiety is justified. My heart is pounding, yet somehow, I'm not frightened. My body appears perfectly capable of managing this welcome, wild charge. Focusing on Jerry, I marvel at the name which slips so easily from my tongue now it's known to me. Had I considered it before? I can't truly say, but it must have been on the numerous lists of boys' Christian names I've read and studied, trying out the sounds and syllables for recognition. Tiny bubbles of elation tingle up my spine. We've found each other. More remarkably, we've found each other whilst both still alive. A miracle!

Megan leans forward. 'Are you sure you're alright?'

'Never felt better in my whole life. So, please, tell me more about yourself, Jerry. Wife? Family? Career? We've a lot to catch up on.'

Jerry summarises. He trained to be a teacher and ended his working life in charge of a school in Worcester. We exchange delighted comments about our parallel paths, which brings me close to him and lessens my ties with Gwen. He married a woman called Ruth, who died four years ago. He struggles to talk about her, continuing to suffer her loss. Describing his children and grandchildren transforms his demeanour, brightening his face and releasing the deep lines of grief. Two sons and a daughter, all married, with seven grandchildren among them. I get the impression their family is close, which pleases me no end.

I continue, indicating my daughter. 'I guess you know about me through Megan?'

Megan jumps in. 'Only the basics. I glossed over your evacuation story because I assumed you'd want to go over it together.'

'Good, but first ... I have to know. Did you write to the charity, Jerry, or see my notice in the newsletter? Is that how Megan found you?'

'Yes, I responded to a call-out for stories around the time of the cathedral service in 2009, but I didn't see your notice, sorry. Megan phoned me out of the blue because of a conversation with someone called Thomas Barker. It was her detective work. Just brilliant.'

My daughter catches my eye, her lips pressed into an apology. 'A little, towards the end, with my colleague Erin's help, but Mum's looked for you from when she was old enough to get out from under Gwen's thumb. Even when the rest of us doubted.'

'It's true. I've always felt you were missing. Like a lost limb. I've tried so hard, Jerry. All my life.'

His eyes find mine. 'Sorry, of course I know, Carol. We wouldn't be here without your determination as well.'

'This other chap, Thomas Barker. How does he fit in?' I ask.

Jerry tips his head towards my daughter. 'Megan?'

'He turned up on a list of boys who went to Cirencester at the same time as you. It was the name, Barker, Baker. We wondered if there'd been a spelling mistake and he was related to your brother. Anyway, he was billeted with two elderly sisters who also lived on Marsh Lane and became friends with Ralph Babbington-Carey. He remembered you and Lucy playing in the garden.'

'No! How amazing. So, hang on. Thomas, Tommy, must have been Ralph's friend.' I turn to my brother. 'Did you know I went back in 1995? It was the first time anyone confirmed I'd lived in Gloucestershire.'

'Yes, Megan told me.'

My daughter continues. 'And confirmed a boy called Jerry was there, too.'

I clasp my hands. 'So, let me get this straight—what you're saying is ... we were together in Cirencester! We did leave London at the same time. I've never known where I lost you.' I reach towards him, a gesture without risk. 'I was always so worried you'd been separated from us, because you were part of a school group. I found out about the policy when I went looking for you. Plus, you had a label on your jumper, and I didn't. So many clues but nothing ever led anywhere.'

'We should go back and start with London,' Megan suggests.

'Yes, with the photograph. Tell us what happened,' I say, leaning forward to hear every one of my brother's words, hoping an image or incident will spark my long-dormant memories.

Jerry takes a breath. 'I'll never forget that day. Mum took us to meet up with my friends and teacher. So, you're partly correct, but we were listed as family and kept together. I asked, over and over, what was happening. Why were we there? Why were there so many people? Mum said something about a trip to the seaside, which is where some kids ended up, I guess. The platforms were packed, and men in uniform buzzed about, rounding up groups, pushing them onto trains. We looked for ages before noticing a huge cardboard sign with the name of my school written on it. After the photo was taken, I was called over to one side and made to line up behind it, me clinging onto your hand for grim death. In no time, we were in a carriage and on the move. You fell asleep quickly, which I was glad about because I was frightened you'd disappear. You were naughty at home. Always slipping away from Mum and making a run for it. I worried you'd do the same and I'd get into trouble.' His lips press together.

'I'm sorry I scared you, but it's so good to hear we were together. So, what happened next? Did you go somewhere different from Mum and me?'

'No, we were taken to the Babbington-Careys' house to live with Aubrey and Julia, and their children Ralph, Oliver and Lucy.'

I burst into life. 'No, that can't be true. We went to "The Willows" to stay with Gwen! Please don't tell me she lied about her lie.' I whip round towards Megan, my fists bunching in my lap. 'Bad enough, for fifty-six years, I believed I'd gone straight to North Wales before being told I'd had a home in Cirencester. Now you're telling me we didn't stay with her? I mean, never? Are you sure, Jerry? I'm so confused. Besides, when I met Ralph, he didn't say a word. Why? Why didn't Ralph say?'

Jerry's head lowers. 'Because he was a bully, and I ran away, which had consequences for everyone. He probably didn't want to dredge it all up.'

'Ran away? Oh, poor you. Poor Mum. So was that the moment when...'

Jerry studies his shoes, fingers knotting.

Megan swallows loudly.

I choose my words carefully. 'You were a child, Jerry. You mustn't feel guilty for the things you did. Ralph being a bully doesn't surprise me. Even Gwen said the same thing. Said he'd cause trouble and put the blame elsewhere. She meant onto you, didn't she?'

He nods slowly.

'Did Ralph ever tease the dogs into snapping at me?'

'Yes, once. I was pulling them away from you when I got the blame, as usual. Gwen only saw the last few seconds and took a stick to me, thinking it was my fault.'

'Oh, Jerry. I'm so sorry.'

'She'd come through a gate in the hedge to tutor Oliver. That's when she saw you crying and jumped to the wrong conclusion. It wasn't long after you went to her place, and I ran away.'

'I recall Gwen saying Aubrey's wife, Julia, wasn't the best of parents, so maybe Mum felt we'd be better off at "The Willows" away from the family, especially Ralph. I guess if Gwen was willing, neither Julia nor the authorities would have cared.'

Megan and Jerry exchange glances.

'Carol, there's something else. Something big. I'm not sure how to tell you, actually.' He wrings his hands.

'Spit it out. Come on. Haven't I dealt with everything else?' My heartrate has picked up enough for me to mentally check where my tablets are located.

'So ... Mum didn't come with us. She had to stay back in London. We went to Cirencester on our own.'

I rock back in my chair, fists pressing against my chin.

'Mum wasn't with us?' I think back over Jerry's story so far and realise he's never mentioned her. She's been my assumption, put there by ... I glare at Megan who looks ready to receive a physical blow, though she's not the cause of the fury which rises and spews out of me. 'The bitch! The evil bitch.' I clap a hand to my mouth.

'Mum, we're so sorry. Do you need to take a break?'

'No! No. I can't stop. Why didn't she come?'

Jerry's face is a picture of concern. 'Are you sure? I'm with Megan ... I think we should stop. Have another drink or something.'

'Not until you tell me why.'

'It was her job. I found out years ago she had a role considered essential by the War Office. She'd worked in a clothing factory for years, but when the war started, the building was taken over to make uniforms. Because of the long hours, we had to be found a new home through the evacuation program.'

I jar on his words, the unfamiliarity of the story, yet somehow, I know it's true. Gripping the armrest for comfort, a tightness develops in my chest. 'But I was only three! How was I allowed to go when I was only three?'

'Little ones were sent away if they had an older brother or sister,' Megan says.

I turn to my brother. 'And you were expected to look after me? At, what, seven?'

Jerry bows his head.

'Because there was no dad look after us, was there?'

We fall into an uneasy silence.

I notice I'm grinding my teeth and ease them apart. Standing, I say, 'Do you mind if I have five minutes to myself? And a glass of water, please?'

Before either has time to object, I walk to the end of the garden.

Thirty-seven

I slow my breathing and racing pulse, determined to stay well enough to hear every last word of my story. Questions buzz through my head. Gwen's obscene, wilful deceit bubbles like lava. I didn't think it could get any worse, but I'm wrong. The implications arising from Mum's inability to travel with us to Cirencester jostle for priority—my life, my world, sucked into a black hole. Yet, like a photographic negative, I have the means, in Jerry, to develop a final and true picture—black returning to white, Gwen's counterfeit light condemned to the dark.

I turn when I hear Megan's voice calling me, her face anguished. She hands me a glass of water.

'Can you come back and sit down? Do you need your tablets?'

I return, retrieve the pills and gulp them down.

Deep grooves etch her forehead. 'I don't know what to do for the best. I know you want the full story but if it makes you ill...'

'I'll be better in a minute. Give me a moment, please?'

Jerry sits forward, his hands trembling. 'I wish it wasn't so hard. Gwen's lies are making it much worse. I didn't have those problems, you see. I was old enough to know what happened. But you? I can't imagine.'

Megan rubs at her temple. 'We should've given you more warning about Gwen, Mum.'

'And don't think I come out of this covered in glory, either,' Jerry says.

'Look, stop fussing, please, both of you, and keep going because what I must know is ... why didn't we go back to Mum in London? Not immediately, but at some point? Although, I've a horrible feeling I know.'

'Perhaps it's best if we go back to the Babbington-Careys, with you and me living there. Gwen lived next door but came into the house to tutor Oliver. You knew that, didn't you?'

'Aubrey told me first, then Gwen. Only when she had to, mind.'

'So, Gwen took a shine to you but assumed I was a troublemaker because of Ralph. Everything started to snowball when you caught scarlet fever.'

'So, my illness is true.' I snort, softly.

'Julia was beside herself and wanted us both gone, immediately, saying nasty things about the people living in the slums of East London and bringing their dirt and diseases with them. The thing is, we'd been living with her for nearly a year, so if we were dirty or ill, it was down to her and had nothing to do with where we came from. She wasn't nice to us, at all, Carol. These days, the social services would be involved, for her neglect.'

He pauses, angry. I think back to Aubrey's outburst and realise the words he threw at me were Julia's.

Jerry continues. 'Fortunately, Lucy enjoyed your company, so Julia was kinder to you because you kept one of her children happy and occupied. But me? I was always the last for anything, including food. Half-starved, I was, unless Aubrey was home. Anyway, that's beside the point. She wanted us gone so you didn't pass on the fever. As I said, Gwen was very fond of you. Whenever she came over to give Oliver his lessons, she'd spend time with you, cuddling you and giving you treats. I have to admit I was jealous. So when she heard you were ill, she offered to nurse you at "The Willows." Julia jumped at the opportunity, of course. That's when you moved in with her.'

'And you? Surely she took you in, too?'

'No. She hated me, remember. I begged her to, but she refused.'

'This is atrocious. On top of finding out you were mistreated by Julia and Gwen, it means Gwen knew perfectly well I had a brother, yet she swore she'd never even met you. Honestly, if she weren't already dead, I'd strangle her. Is that why you left? Because I moved next door?'

'No, there's more. While you were ill, we had a visit from the authorities. It wasn't good news, I'm afraid.' He held my gaze. 'Shall I go on?'

'As I said, I think I know, deep down.'

'It was about Mum. I shouldn't have been eavesdropping, but they told Julia she'd died in a bombing raid on her way home from work. I found out later that her part of London was a target and lots of people lost their lives to the Luftwaffe.'

Tears silently leak down my cheeks. 'When?'

'Summer of 1940.'

Megan hands me a tissue. Other facts, Gwen's letters to Morwen, click into place.

'She was never anywhere near Bryn-y-Maen, was she? My illness wasn't hers. No wonder we never found her grave. What a terrible way to go.' My head lolls, weighed down by sadness. 'But I suppose if we were orphans ... is that the truth, at least? No next of kin?'

'No, there was no-one.'

'And, if you ran away ... are you telling me Gwen did a good thing, after all? I presume Julia shared the news about Mum with her?'

'You'll have to be the judge, I guess. Julia did tell Gwen, including the fact the billeting officers were looking for traces of a family back in London. Although Julia didn't want to be saddled with either of us, it was a different story for Gwen. They took themselves off into Aubrey's study and closed the door. Try as I might, I could only grab snatches of their conversation, but I was sure Gwen was concocting a plan to keep you. My future was much less clear.'

'Oh, Jerry. How awful. Making you feel so unwanted.'

He pulls back his shoulders, bracing. 'Later that day, I went round to "The Willows" to see you. I'm not sure what I thought I'd achieve, but like you said, whatever happened next, I wanted us to be together. It was the last thing Mum said to me. "Look after Carol. Don't let them separate you."'

My throat tightens, recalling the stories Megan told me about her work with the charity. The letters from adults still reeling from the task they were given as children, some succeeding, many more failing. I catch Megan's eye and see her blinking fast. Jerry stops abruptly. I wave him on, dabbing at the tears that haven't already soaked my mask.

'Gwen only allowed me to look at you through a gap in the door. Worse, I felt sure you were going to die. I don't know what she said, or why I had that impression, but I went back to the Babbington-Careys thinking I'd lost you both. That night, I packed my belongings in a sheet and bolted, stowing away on a troop train. Managed to get as far as Reading before I was found. I stayed there for the rest of the war, with a couple called the Thompsons, who were wonderful to me, I might add.'

'Thank goodness. Some care and attention, at last. But .. don't get me wrong, I'm glad you were put with good people, but didn't the authorities, those billeting officers in Cirencester come looking for you? How come you weren't found and brought back to me? And if Gwen refused to take you in, we should've been adopted by someone who wanted us both.'

Megan takes up the thread. 'Do you remember Thomas? When I found Uncle Jerry, I contacted him again to help fill in the gaps. He was around during the summer holidays and knows what happened after Jerry ran away. He told me the billeting officers came back a few days later to say they'd found no trace of him. They'd also not found any family back in London. Thomas knew you were next door, but when the officers asked after you, Julia told them you'd disappeared, too, that you and Jerry had gone together. By the time they left, they were convinced two children had run away, not one. Presumably, this was when Gwen spirited you away to Conwy.'

'If Thomas knew I was next door, why didn't he say anything?'

'I didn't like to ask, straight out. But he did say he was confused. He was only twelve, Mum, and away from home, like you and Uncle Jerry, relying on the goodness of strangers. Maybe he thought he'd cause trouble, including to himself. I don't think we can blame him, and, in the end, he was very helpful, the key to the mystery.'

'Yes, alright, I can see that. So Gwen whisks me away—steals me—to be blunt. But ... what if you'd told the authorities about me? Wouldn't your account have been a risk for her?'

'It would all have hinged on whether they believed the story about you both running away. That must have been hers and Julia's plan,' Megan says.

Jerry's jaw juts, his back ramrod straight. 'And there's me, my sin. Gwen wouldn't have known I'd help her, but I did, unwittingly. This is hard, Carol, because, it wasn't only Gwen and Julia who lied. I lied too. I've lived with the shame every day of my life. The shame causing me to mislead Megan as well.'

I catch his eye, silently begging him to continue.

His words tumble out. 'When I arrived in Reading, I wouldn't talk to anyone. Became sort of mute. Not a single word for six months.'

'Self-preservation,' Megan blurts. 'Wasn't it, Mum? Traumatised, no doubt, after all the neglect and grief.'

I take up the charge. 'Precisely. Of course, you had to save your own skin. Come on, Jerry, we've seen it in our pupils, haven't we? You mustn't blame yourself.' He sits, brooding. 'Jerry, please! I'm really glad you were put with a good family and, presumably, they're the ones who adopted you?'

'I never told them anything about my past. I was a blank page. It meant they had to give me a new name, their name.'

'Thompson. No wonder I never found you.'

Jerry and Megan exchange glances a second time.

'What?' He doesn't respond. I'm pressing on an open wound and need to stop. I change tack. 'Good, so your adoption was above board. Gwen couldn't do the same for me, so she took me all the way to North Wales, to a tiny village in the hillside. But why lie so much about Mum? I mean, Julia was the only one who knew, and she wouldn't have blabbed. Why'd she do that?'

Megan continues. 'My job helps. When I realised three-year-olds were evacuated without a parent if they had older brothers and sisters, I did some research. Gwen must have done the same. People wouldn't have expected you to be on your own. It might have looked suspicious with neither a mother nor siblings because very young children, with no family to accompany them, went to local County Council homes dotted around London. There are photos of them—big houses, nurses cuddling babies, either orphans or the children of essential workers. Gwen wouldn't have wanted any awkward questions, so I think she invented a mum who died unexpectedly to explain why you were with her and not at one of those homes. Your bout of scarlet fever was probably the inspiration for Grandma's illness and death.'

'Unbelievable! It's only beginning to sink in, to tell the truth, but I am a stolen baby, aren't I? And she always knew about you, Jerry. She'd met you, beaten you and was the reason you ran away to God-knows-where. How could she do something like that? She couldn't have known you'd end up with a decent family. How utterly unforgivable!'

'If it's any consolation, she might have had second thoughts,' Megan says. 'Thomas told me once Jerry left, Ralph tried to play the same tricks on him, but Gwen caught him. He says she shook Ralph and slapped him, not only because of what he tried to do to Thomas, but demanded to know whether he'd set up Jerry, too. Ralph didn't answer, but Thomas is pretty sure the penny dropped.'

'And my searches for a boy called Baker never went anywhere because you ended up being adopted and were given a new name.'

Jerry breaks in, his tone low, cracked. 'There's more. It wasn't only my name.' He hesitates, head down. 'I'll be forever sorry about this, but, as well as keeping stum about my details, I didn't tell them I had a little sister, either. I believed you were dead, truly I did, but I can't forgive myself for not speaking up. I'm so, so sorry.'

I want to grab his hand and squeeze tight, seeing his anguish. The need for caution is killing me. 'No, I won't have you apologise. You were frightened, hurt. I don't blame you, not one bit. She's at the bottom of this, along with Julia. Two women who allowed orphaned siblings to be separated to satisfy their own needs.' I take a deep breath. 'So there we have it. Everything out in the open. And I'm glad, Jerry. The truth can never hurt as much as the uncertainty and lies.' I pat my palms on my knees.

'Well...' Jerry whispers, his voice rasping. 'As you said, Gwen wouldn't have known I'd refuse to talk, but there is one more thing. And it's the last, thank goodness. Carol, our birth name, my real surname, the one I didn't tell anyone in Reading, is

Miller, not Baker. You arrived in Cirencester with that name, too. Carol Miller. Carol, spelt the English way. Do you see? Baker, Miller, they're names for people in the breadmaking trade, occupational names. Megan says her colleague gave her this clue, but she missed it.'

My eyes bulge. 'Are you saying Gwen changed my surname! Stephen always questioned the Welsh spelling of Caryl, but the surname? Oh, God! What chance did I ever have of finding you?'

'None. Even if you'd known my first name and I wasn't a Thompson, it wouldn't have helped. I was at the Seventieth Anniversary celebration listed as a guest, but neither of us recognised each other's names. I was checking the guest list for Carol Miller, not Caryl Baker.'

'Oh, God. We were both there? All those years ago, what, eleven? We could've met, phoned each other. It's appalling to have lost so much time.' I put my face in my hands. 'You said that's everything. Tell me it's true. I don't think I can bear any more.'

Megan pushes forward, hesitates, then closes the gap between us and throws her arms around me.

Thirty-eight

Megan and I cry and hug, taking several minutes to regain our composure. Jerry watches, pained, before stirring.

'Excuse me a moment.' He stands and walks through the back door.

My daughter disengages, a question of concern hanging in the air.

'I'm fine,' I say, painting on a smile. 'Wherever did she get my birth certificate? Has it crossed your mind? If I'm a Miller, it must be a forgery, mustn't it?'

She returns to her chair. 'I guess so.'

'Where would she get one of those in 1940? Although, I've heard it was the perfect time. Forged documents were two a penny during the war years.'

'Possibly.'

'Can you imagine Gwen in some dodgy, backstreet office, talking to a scoundrel wearing one of those special lenses, one eye all magnified and huge.' A bubble of laughter bursts upwards, followed by a howl, making me sound demented. I snap shut my mouth. 'I can't believe she'd take such a risk. I mean, Gwen!'

'I've been thinking of nothing else since I phoned Jerry. Remember what he said about her cuddling you, giving you treats? I'm not for one minute defending her, but I think she loved you. You were worth breaking the law, risking everything so she could keep you. Cutting Jerry out of the picture was ... I can't find the words, but I think she adored you.'

I huff and cross my arms.

'You never had a bad word to say about her until you found the teddy bear and the photograph. Nothing I was aware of, anyway.'

'Yes and no. We never saw eye to eye about a brother. And, as you know, Dad didn't help there, either. She must have loved his support, casting me as a fantasist. Crikey, what will he say when I tell him what's happened today?'

'Go easy on him, please? Gwen covered her tracks, remember. And he'll be delighted, guaranteed.'

Jerry returns with an envelope, handing it over as he retakes his seat.

Megan shifts, looking uncomfortable. 'If Jerry doesn't mind, I'm going to sit inside. Let you two carry on.' She bolts for the door and disappears.

I'm gripped by curiosity and trepidation. 'What is it? My real birth certificate?'

'You'll see,' my brother says.

I untuck the flap and slide out a six-by-four black and white photograph. Three familiar people stare out at me. I suck in air. 'Is this mine? Did Megan give you a copy?'

'No, I've had it for over eighty years. It's been hidden away for most of that time.'

'But ... how?'

'Mum sent two copies to the Babbington-Careys. I kept one and tucked the other inside your teddy bear.'

'So, it was you! You should have seen Gwen's reaction when I first found it. Plus, another lie. She said she recognised Mum, but how could she, if they never met?'

'It might not be. The letter arrived on a day when she was teaching Oliver. Ralph grabbed it from me and held it up, out of my reach. She came out to tell us to pipe down because I was hollering about a photo of us and our mum.'

'Anyway, it's the last piece of the puzzle Megan and I could never work out. The piece which set this whole thing in motion.' I hold the image near Jerry's face, tilting it in a vain attempt to prove a likeness was—is—there. 'It's nearly driven me mad, you know. Not merely the photograph, but everything.'

'I know. Megan told me.'

'I mean, even this.' I point to the bear in the photograph. 'I only had the faintest twinge of recognition when I found it.'

'You didn't get chance to play with it much, which was my doing, I suppose. Ralph snatched it from you when we arrived and began pulling off its arms and legs. When I wrestled it back, I put it in this huge blanket box in our bedroom to keep it safe. I gave it back when I came to visit you when you were sick.'

'I can't believe we went to that family first. A moment ago, I dredged up something else about their house. When I visited Aubrey and Ralph and was shown through the hallway, I was struck by a little cupboard under the stairs. It was the perfect size for a child, with a sloping door. I convinced myself Lucy had brought me inside to play, but if we lived there for nearly a whole year, is it any wonder I remembered it?'

Jerry blinks, his words slow, haunted. 'It was my bolt hole. You showed it to me one day and I began hiding there. Until Ralph found out. As a result, Julia found a key and locked it. Lucy was cross, too. The two of you used it as a sort of doll's house.'

'Oh, God. It gets worse. Sorry to bring up more horrible memories.' I hand back the precious image. 'Here. Keep it safe.'

'Don't worry. It's a copy. When Mum and Dad died, I finally told Ruth the truth about my past and had the original restored. She helped me choose a fancy silver frame and it has pride of place on the mantlepiece.'

'Me, too. Silver, as well.' I pause. 'Was telling her difficult?'

'Apart from you and Megan, she's the only one who's ever known my guilt.'

'Jerry! Stop, please. How did she take it?'

'Shocked. Forgiving. Exactly like you.'

'I'm glad.' We sit in companiable silence. 'Tell me ... what was Mum like?'

He shakes his head. 'She looks prim, doesn't she? Dressed herself up to take us to Waterloo, I reckon. Looking back, as an adult, she wasn't what you'd call a reliable mother. Heart of gold, though. She loved us to bits but was always busy, stressed, trying to look after us and earn a living. Meals arrived at all hours, assuming she'd had time to get to the shops. Or bargaining with the milkman when she didn't have change. She'd be in and out, taking us down to the neighbour when she had to work. I guess they were different times, with people willing to help out. When she was at home, she'd sing and dance. Waltzing me round the room or throwing you about in her arms. You'd squeal and shriek with delight.'

'I love dancing, always have. It's one of the few pastimes Stephen and I really enjoy, apart from gardening.'

'Some days we'd go down to the river and scavenge on the mud flats, filthy as coal miners, we were. If we found anything, she'd be so happy, grinning from ear to ear. I dug up a silver cigarette case once. God, was she excited? Pawned it, most probably, to get some extra cash. One day we took a bus to the beach. Southend, I think. I'd never seen the sea, only the dirty river. It was a big deal to go so far, but when we arrived, the weather was terrible. But she had this saying—'

'"The sun shines on the brave".'

We turn to each other, Jerry's face pale.

'How do you know that?' he asks.

'Why, it's not the same, is it?'

'Exactly the same. I can't believe it.'

My eyes prickle again. 'Did I learn it from her? Oh, Jerry. Wouldn't it be wonderful to have something of hers? I always supposed I'd made it up, changing the other phrase about fortune favouring the brave. I used it to get James and Megan out into the fresh air on gloomy days. Just like her.'

'I bet there's more hidden away in the memory vaults now you know the truth.'

'Plus, I have you. Come on, what else?'

'She'd tell me stories from her work at the clothing factory. Some were quite blue, but I loved them. Made me feel like a proper grown up. Trouble was, she expected a lot of me. When she was home, everything was rosy, but there were nights when we were left on our own. I remember lying in bed, not being able to sleep until I heard her key in the door. And her laugh. She brought men home sometimes, too...'

Jerry's correct. I'm struggling to fit the image I know so well to this three-dimensional woman, warts and all. 'You said there was a neighbour downstairs? Where did we live?'

'In an upstairs flat, if you could call it that, on Albany Road, Southwark. She rented it from the women who owned the whole terrace and lived on the bottom two floors. It was all she could afford, I suppose. Didn't have a proper kitchen, so she cooked in the communal kitchens nearby. Took us there a few times when there was no-one to keep an eye on us.'

'Never heard of such a thing!'

'Oh yes. Lots of families used them. Carried the roasting dish home with a towel draped over the top.'

'She sounds like such a character. Full of life. I wish I'd known her.'

'She'd be proud of us both, you know. Two Cockney kids growing up to be teachers with families of our own.'

'I hope so.'

'And I'd love to know more about your family.'

'Can it wait? I've so many questions. For instance, do you know where she's buried?'

'She's in the New Cemetery in Camberwell. Her name's in the burial register.'

'And a grave? I'd like to see her real one. Did Megan tell you that story?'

'Something about it being unmarked?'

'I'm such a fool believing it, but when you're young, you accept things. Anyway, yes, Gwen told me Mum was buried in a local churchyard and, I suppose, she did allow me to grieve her when we visited and took flowers. But was it because she cared for me, or was it to shore up her story?' I flick my hand to banish another bitter thought. 'What's it like, the cemetery?'

His eyes slide away. 'It's just a field, I'm afraid. So many war dead. They call them general gravesites. I went there in summer, so there were plenty of wildflowers, which was lovely. But no headstones. There's a wall of remembrance for four hundred civilians who died in the Blitz, but her name's not among them, only in the register.'

'It could be another good thing from the bad. The churchyard I mentioned, Bryn y Maen, the locals refer to it as the Cathedral of the Hills, which sums it up perfectly. Very beautiful and, perhaps, better to have sat there.' I pause. 'I'd like to visit her grave sometime.'

'Perhaps we can go together when this damn virus is under control.'

'I'd love to. And our dad? You were inside a moment ago when Megan and I realised my birth certificate was most probably a forgery. It says, "unknown," but I'm wondering if it's true.'

'I don't rightly know, except Mum had a soft spot for one chap called Bert. When he came to the flat, he was always friendly towards us, bringing us sweets and toys. My prized possession from him was a model airplane. Thinking about it, he might have bought you the teddy bear, because I can't imagine Mum having the money for it. I asked her once if he was our dad, but she looked sad and said he was married.' He shrugs. 'Who knows?'

'I wonder what happened to him?'

'He talked differently to us. Posh. Before we were sent away, he came round in uniform. Blue. Royal Air Force. Proud as punch, he was. Said he was going to be a pilot.'

I swallow. It was all guesswork, but … what if this man was our real dad, the real war hero? Somehow, I couldn't share the incredible, farfetched speculation that it was our mother who had a war hero as her partner. It only reminded me of Gwen.

'Right,' I blurt, slapping my knees. 'Enough sadness. I won't be gloomy on a day like today.'

'I took the liberty of buying some champagne. I never drink it, normally, but my daughter Sue brings it out often enough. What d'you say? Shall we go back inside and find Megan?'

'I'd love one,' I reply.

We find my daughter in the lounge reading a magazine and put forward our proposal.

'I'll be under the limit with one, won't I?' Megan says.

When the bottle has popped and fizzed, we raise three glasses, masks lowered at last. Jerry leads the toast. 'To never forgotten family and making up for lost time.' I gaze at my brother's full face, as he does mine.

'Perfect,' I say, clinking his glass, then Megan's.

'I know family comes first,' she says to Jerry, 'but would you like to meet Erin, my colleague? I'm not sure we'd all be here celebrating, if it weren't for her.'

'Of course,' he replies.

'Prepare to be pounced on. She's like an excitable puppy!' Megan says.

'I don't mind at all, and I'd like to thank her.'

'Count me in, too!' I say.

'And something else.' Her eyes twinkle. 'Can I ask him?'

'About what?' I reply

'Lara and Felix's big day.'

'Oh, yes. Yes, please.'

'Uncle Jerry, would you like to come to your great niece's wedding?'

Thirty-nine

Standing in the ladies' bathroom of the Sale Town Hall in Manchester, examining myself in the mirror, I am as content with the image thrown back at me as I ever am these days. I pat down my dress and apply a last puff of powder. The outfit I found in my wardrobe is perfectly appropriate for a civil ceremony, an occasion which necessitates forced enthusiasm from me. I know it's legally binding and marks a milestone, yet I can't help viewing it as a practice run, a prelude to the real event with all the usual rituals.

So many traditions have gone by the wayside. Lara couldn't go to her mum's house, a source of great disappointment for them both, so there was no fun morning with the bride and bridesmaids having their hair and make-up done, drinking champagne. No candid photographs of the preparations. If they'd wanted to arrive in one of those tacky stretch limousines, they wouldn't have been allowed. According to Megan, each set of guests must travel alone with no opportunity to meet up for lunch or a drink before the start. I'm ashamed to feel slightly dismal and make a promise not to let on to Megan or the bride and groom. Grabbing my mask from my handbag, I walk back outside.

I rejoin Stephen in the lobby of the registry office. He's smart but dated in a double-breasted pinstripe suit which he last wore many years ago. I wish we had more occasions to dress up like we used to, events having dried up since we dropped out of work-related circles. Mask wearing has compelled us to find new ways to communicate what our full faces used to show. A flare here, a flutter there for Stephen to show his approval of me and for me to signal my appreciation in return. Whilst currently flawless on the outside, I know the inside of my mask will be a mess of pink and red smudges when I finally take it off.

Megan and Rick arrive, happy but stiff, taking a position the required distance from us. We wave and wrinkle our eyebrows, the only way to show our excitement. The dress she chose is a great fit on her slim body. Rick, dashing but awkward in his suit, a buttonhole teetering dangerously from a badly placed pin. I want to fix it but know I probably shouldn't. They exchange glances, the practised moves of a close, happy couple. I envy their understated romance, the small gestures which whisper—rather than shout—enduring love and respect. Thinking back, there were cross words between them when they lived in Conwy, before Lara was born, but never since, as far as I'm aware. A good example to Lara and Felix of an unbreakable, committed relationship. Stephen and I are far more scratchy, though it's most probably our age.

Chloe and Darren skip up the stairs in lockstep. They might not be married, but we all know their relationship has as much chance of success as any, ring or no ring. She looks fabulous in a ruffled number which makes me want to say "Tea Dress" but for the short length and clumpy high-heeled shoes. Darren fiddles with his tie. Apparently, he too has abandoned business attire whilst working from home. I know because Megan passed on

Chloe's complaints about t-shirts and jogging pants, or worse, on days when he has a video call, the newsreader look—shirt and jacket on top, boxers below the waist. It makes an old lady blush! Even without lockdown, I've noticed few men wear formal attire these days. Today, uncomfortable with the restriction, they tug at their necklines.

The officials begin to fidget, recognising the start of an extremely unwelcome "gathering." They make their move, determined to intercede and stop us mingling. We are ushered into the room allocated for the service with signals to sit on perfectly distanced chairs. Risk avoidance is so strict there isn't an exemption for couples, which so far, includes every set of arrivals. I see one pair indicate their status, their gestures to move furniture firmly rejected. With Stephen's sister unwell with the virus, Rick's parents unwilling to travel, and my son James and wife Elle preferring to wait for the later celebration, it's a sad irony we won't exceed the strict guest allocation.

The chamber is bright with soaring ceilings, waist-high wood panelling and large windows with heavy velvet curtains. There are flowers on a table and on several windowsills closest to the place where the service will, presumably, take place. I'm surprised by how imposing and decorative it is, which quells some of my disappointment. As I take in the surroundings, new people arrive, strangers, from Felix's side of the family, I presume. I nod and flick my eyes, hoping my greeting is clear. It's the best any of us can do.

I take my seat before remembering Jerry. He only knows me and Megan, and she's far too busy. Rising, Stephen reaches up and pulls on my arm, eyebrows forming a question. Shaking him free, I turn back towards the lobby only to have my exit barred by one of the officials. I calculate a plea for a bathroom break will work more efficiently than a long explanation about a single, almost unknown, member of the family arriving alone and hope he didn't see me disappear inside the ladies' lavatories earlier on. He gives me a swift nod.

The lobby is empty. Rather than wait, I move outside, down the steps and away from the watchful officials. The building is in a suburb of the city which is normally busy, and I'm struck by the silence, the ability to hear birdsong. Swivelling, I take in the bright, blue skies, thankful for a beautiful day, hoping the same weather patterns prevail on a date yet to be determined. Lara's pregnancy has helped ease the disappointment of a long-standing delay for a "proper wedding." She and Felix are resigned to waiting until the new baby is here and old enough to manage a full and busy day. When Megan told me, she admitted not daring to mention sleep deprivation, breastfeeding, never mind a saggy stomach!

I turn back towards the road. Jerry hovers at the edge of the opposite pavement, upright, distinguished. Sun rays bounce off his highly polished shoes. He crosses over to join me.

'Jerry! Thank goodness. I didn't want you arriving without a welcome party.'

'Let me look at you, again,' he says. 'That first visit ... all the emotion ... I couldn't take you all in. But you've kept the waves in your hair, like Mum. And her eyes, too. If only I could see more behind these damn things.' He snaps at the elastic of his mask.

He tilts his head, drawn by footsteps behind me. My husband has arrived.

'And this is Stephen. Stephen, meet Jerry, my brother.' I hold his gaze. I can't help myself, reminded of all the years he's refused to believe my story.

'Very pleased to meet you, Jerry. Sorry we can't shake hands. Will an elbow do?'

He's making light of the moment, but I know, deep down, he regrets his behaviour. I make a silent promise my comment will be the last, especially today.

Movement catches my eye. It's Felix, running at a clip, hair wild and floppy, his suit jacket flapping. 'Is she here? Please say she's not here, yet. Bloody car wouldn't start. She'll kill me if I'm late.'

'You're fine. Slow down,' I say, the last few strained moments happily broken. 'We don't want you falling flat on your face.'

He smooths his shirt, rakes fingers through his tousled locks and pats his pockets, clearly satisfied. 'Thank Christ! Oops, sorry. Better get in, I suppose.' He disappears with a wave.

'We'd better go in too,' Stephen says.

A car pulls up and a lone passenger steps onto the pavement, dressed elegantly in a white, sixties-style, satin knee-length dress and pillbox hat, clutching a small posy, for all the world like a blond Jackie-O or Grace Kelly. A tiny expansion to her usual, nipped waistline is the only sign of her condition.

I gasp. 'That's definitely our cue.'

Rick jogs towards us. 'Sorry, sorry, can I catch up with you later? There's something important for me to do.' Glancing at Jerry as he passes, he whispers, 'Can't wait to meet you properly, mind. If I'm honest, I never believed this day would come for Caryl.'

We all watch as Rick turns his head left and right to check for the officials before kissing Lara on her hairline, the only piece of exposed skin. He isn't allowed to walk with her, but he's there to give her words of comfort, a dad's love.

I step forward, rebelliously linking arms with my brother's, a sign the contrary little girl captured on the platform at Waterloo station hasn't entirely disappeared. Stephen's look of horror brings me to my senses. With a sigh, I unlink them and take a sensible, socially distanced step sideways.

'Come on, Jerry, come and meet the rest of your family.'

Acknowledgements

'*You need that one person.*' Huge thanks to Jeanne Smith, Executive Editor, Wings ePress Inc, and Michael Cybulski, agent, New Authors Collective, who believed in my work and gave me this opportunity.

'*Make sure you like your book because you'll read it a hundred times.*' As did my brilliant editor, Andrea Barton, whose knowledge, skill and generosity went above and beyond my expectations. Thanks also to Lauren Elise Daniels, Lisa Darcy, Carindale Writers' Group and the New Authors Collective beta reader group who all contributed to the final version.

'*The writer's journey is lonely ...*' and so it is. Thank you to the people who have taken an interest in my writing career; listened endlessly to plots, characters and led me out of the blind alleys I've written myself into; dragged me out of despair with heartwarming words or told me to pull up my big girl's pants. Tom and Doug, you have cheered from the sidelines, adding your own perspectives about the highs and lows of the creative process; my extended family especially my sister, Pat; Claire Harrison, my running/walking partner (so all of the above plus puffing); my overseas email warriors – Sally Parkin, Scilla Purington, Debby Grace, Jo Kimberley and the late Jan Scott; and local friends Regina Mullins, Mike Levy, Cynthia Wardle, Debbie Terranova and Madeleine Basquiat Green.

'Why is it doing that? I didn't ask it to do that! That's yesterday's work gone, GONE!' To my technical saviours, Nick and Tom, honestly, I'd have lost everything without you!

'It takes a village ...' To the wonderful local organisations and their members, who have welcomed, educated and supported me – Brisbane Book Authors, Sisters in Crime Qld and the Queensland Writers Centre.

'A picture tells a thousand words'. To Lee Avison who interpreted my ideas and turned them into the gorgeous artwork for my book cover. To Trisha Fitzgerald-Jung at Wings ePress, Inc. for her invaluable support.

Finally, to my husband, Nick, my greatest supporter, who has multi-tasked across categories. Thank you for the countless cups of tea that have mysteriously appeared on my desk, the hours spent brainstorming with me or taking on the role of unpaid copy editor, apostrophe fixer and technical saviour. You have championed my efforts, encouraged me when I needed a lift and been the voice of calm in a crisis. If it weren't for you, the need for acknowledgements would be utterly redundant.

Author's Note

My story was inspired by the extraordinary event that took place on 1st September 1939. Fearing for the safety of children living in London and other strategic cities around the country, the British Government commenced Operation Pied Piper. On that day, 1.5 million school-age children, mothers and their pre-school children, and pregnant women were evacuated to the safety of the countryside. Over the course of the war, it is estimated that 3.5 million people were displaced.

Many photos were taken on that first day. Unlike my book cover – simplified for artistic reasons - station platforms were crammed with children, parents, teachers and other volunteers. With only a label pinned to their clothing, children were escorted to country towns and villages and into the homes of complete strangers.

My story involves one family caught up in this chaotic and frightening time. Whilst the movement of so many people was complex and filled with risk, I want to reassure readers that children did not go missing. I have only come across one personal story where the author mentions never seeing a sibling again. If you would like to read more about Operation Pied Piper, please go to The Imperial War Museum: www.iwm.org.uk and The National Archives: www.nationalarchives.gov.uk. Personal stories can be found at The British WWII Evacuees Discussion Group: https://members.tripod.com/~Gerry_Wiseman/feature_article.htm

My main character's daughter takes a job at the Society for Evacuees. This is a fictional organisation based on The British Evacuees Association who champion the 'forgotten' casualties of war, ensuring the experiences of former evacuees are properly recognised. The Association's work has resulted in an evocative sculpture of children, situated in the National Arboretum, Staffordshire; a hugely successful memorial service held at St Paul's Cathedral, London, in September 2009, to commemorate the 70th anniversary of the start of the Pied Piper program; and the inclusion of former evacuees in the annual Remembrance Day parade in Whitehall, London. Sadly, the Association is struggling to survive. At the time of this writing, their website is: http://www.evacuees.org.uk/

The 2020 Covid-19 pandemic is used as a backdrop to the contemporary timeline. Though living in Australia during that period, I took a keen interest in the UK response because family and friends lived there. I have made every effort to reference events accurately, however, there may be some elements of the story which are not exact, to fulfill important plot lines. I take full responsibility for any inaccuracies.

Much of my story is set in North Wales, in the Conwy, Llandudno and Colwyn Bay area. Any errors in locations or descriptions are mine. The village of Bryn-y-Maen exists, as does the churchyard referred to as the 'Cathedral of the Hills'. It is a truly beautiful part of the world and the perfect setting for the mystery at the heart of my story.

Meet Diane Clarke

Before completing her debut novel, *The Photograph*, Diane's writing journey began with short stories. Her writing credits include flash fiction and short stories published in several anthologies, including success in the Sydney Hammond Memorial Short Story Competition—*A Life Lesson*, 2nd place (2019) and *Courting Danger*, Longlisted (2020).

Though happily settled in Brisbane, Australia since 1996, much of her inspiration comes from the UK. Using stunning locations as the backdrop, her novels feature restless women craving truth, identity and love. She propels her female protagonists into complex family predicaments where they must deal with the agony of missing siblings, absent fathers or ethical dilemmas. When not writing, she takes long walks in the Australian bush, upcycles vintage furniture, spends time with family and friends and spoils her cavoodle puppy.

Dear reader,

I hope you've enjoyed reading this tale drawn from the
pages of world history.

Your opinion is valuable to other
readers like you,
who may be looking for books like mine.

Please consider taking a few minutes to post a review,
however brief,
on the site where you purchased this book
or on the Wings ePress web page.

You may also want to visit my author page
at the Wings' website.

Thank you!

Diane Clarke

Visit Our Website

For The Full Inventory
Of Quality Books:

Wings ePress, Inc

Quality trade paperbacks and downloads
in multiple formats,
in genres ranging from light romantic comedy to general
fiction and horror.
Wings has something for every reader's taste.
Visit the website, then bookmark it.
We add new titles each month!

Wings ePress, Inc.
3000 N. Rock Road
Newton, KS 67114

Printed in Great Britain
by Amazon